THE BODY
in the BELFRY

THE BEELER LARGE PRINT MYSTERY SERIES

Edited by Audrey A. Lesko

Also available in Large Print by Katherine Hall Page
The Body in the Basement
The Body in the Bog
The Body in the Cast
The Body in the Kelp

THE BODY
in the BELFRY

Katherine Hall Page

BEELER LARGE PRINT
Hampton Falls, New Hampshire, 2000

Library of Congress Cataloging-in-Publication Data

Page, Katherine Hall
  The body in the belfry.
    p.   cm.—(The Beeler Large Print mystery series)
    ISBN 1-57490-277-6 (acid-free paper)
    1 Fairchild, Faith Sibley (Fictious character)—Fiction. 2.
Caterers and catering—Fiction. 3. Women detectives——.
Fiction. 4. Massachusetts—Fiction. 5. Cookery–Fiction.
6. Large type books. I. Title II. Series.

PS3556.A334 B64 2000
  813'.54—dc21   00-023733

Published in Large Print by arrangement with
St. Martin's Press

BEELER LARGE PRINT
is published by
Thomas T. Beeler, *Publisher*
Post Office Box 659
Hampton Falls, New Hampshire 03844

Typeset in 16 point Adobe Garmond type.
Printed on acid-free paper, sewn and bound by
Sheridan Books in Chelsea, Michigan.

For Alan

"Love must not be, but take a body too. . ."

—*John Donne*

ONE

FAITH FAIRCHILD, RECENTLY OF NEW YORK CITY, paused to catch her breath. Benjamin, her five-month-old son, was sound asleep, securely strapped to her chest in his Snugli. Her aching shoulder blades and the fact that she had been focusing on the worn path beneath her feet instead of the autumnal splendor to either side reminded Faith that Benjamin was definitely getting a bit too chunky for this mode of transportation. She straightened up and looked around.

It was New England with a vengeance: riotous orange and scarlet leaves beneath enormous, puffy white clouds suspended in a Kodacolor blue sky. A calendar maker's dream. And of course brisk, clean air as crisp as a bite of a McIntosh apple just off the tree.

Faith hated McIntosh apples.

She walked up the Belfry Hill path a bit farther to a small clearing, which gave her an unobstructed view of the Aleford village green far below. She sat down and sighed heavily.

Her life was becoming terribly quaint, Faith thought. Time was when "village" meant "the Village" and "town" was up or down. And when did she start using phrases like "time was"? She let another sigh escape into the pollution-free landscape and longed for a whiff of that heady combination of roasted chestnuts and exhaust fumes that meant autumn to her.

There wasn't even any litter in Aleford, she mused wistfully as she hummed a few bars of "Autumn in New

1

York" softly to herself so as not to awaken Benjamin. Memories of the angry looks she used to hurl at offenders tossing candy bar wrappers on the sidewalk were conveniently pushed to a far corner of her mind, a corner somewhere near Lexington and 59th Street.

She stared fixedly at the green—so very green and like a tablecloth spread out for a tidy picnic. She blinked and wondered, not by any means for the first time, how Fate could have plucked her from her native shores and placed her in this strange, wholesome land.

But then Fate had nothing to do with it. It was plain old love and not a little of plain old sex. All in the seductive shape of Thomas Fairchild, a New Englander born and bred, and, to make matters worse, a minister.

For Faith, the daughter and grandaughter of men of the cloth, who had sworn all her life to avoid that particular fabric, was the village parson's wife. It had been and was a terrific surprise. Not at all what she had had in mind for her life.

Benjamin gave a tiny burp and Faith welcomed the slightly sour, milky baby smell that, delighted as she was with her infant, she knew only a mother could love. She stroked his soft cheek and cooed, "You sweet boy, you."

Hitching him up farther on her chest to a possibly more comfortable position she added, "My darling benign little, growth. " Faith was fond of outrageous endearments and the Snugli always reminded her of those trees with the bulges growing to one side, so obviously not a part of the original trunk.

A trunk in Faith's case more like a sapling's. Faith was as slender now as she had always been, despite a pregnancy punctuated by voracious cravings for H&H bagels with

Zabar's herring salad, which her mother kindly supplied. Her mother had also supplied Faith's big blue eyes. Her father's family was responsible for the blond hair, which she wore in a blunt cut that just touched her shoulders. She was neither tall nor short. In fact she looked like a lot of other women, and people had a tendency to greet her warmly in the street, only realizing that she wasn't "Nancy" or "Jill" when they were actually face to face. But when they were, they always looked twice—an act that had never displeased Faith. Just now the despised New England air had given her complexion a rosy glow, which matched Benjamin's, and she looked beautiful.

Faith frowned and resumed her climb. She was annoyed with herself, all these Victorian sighs. But it was hard not to think about what was wrong, and she was drawn to her misgivings just as one's tongue irresistibly searches out the sore place in one's mouth to see whether it still hurts and of course it always does.

I have everything anyone could possibly want, she told herself sternly. A darling baby who sleeps through the night; a wonderful husband who fortunately doesn't. Good food, good health, and a pretty little house; maybe a mite too much like an illustration for *Mosses from an Old Manse,* but as parsonages go, a jewel. No damp and plenty of working appliances.

This wasn't a question of physical well-being. She had never felt better in her life. This was a mental sore spot. And the worst possible kind. She was bored. And not only bored, but homesick.

The parish, as well as the whole town, had welcomed her warmly, but there were few women her age who weren't working and those were busy with hearth and home. Faith was pretty busy with these things herself. Benjamin took up more time than she would have believed possible for one small infant. She didn't begrudge it, but at the same time he wasn't exactly a scintillating conversationalist. Tom was around more than many other husbands—the parish office was in the church, which was in turn a mere stone's throw away from the parsonage, if one had been inclined to throw stones at the church, that is, and Faith had not reached that point.

She wasn't actually unhappy, she told herself. Yet there was an insistent, insidious whisper murmuring in the porches of her ears that nothing had ever happened in Aleford, at least not since 1775, and that nothing ever would. Especially to Faith.

She stood up and shook a mental finger at her pathetic weaker self. The whole thing was absurd. Things didn't just happen, one made them happen. Sure, it was easier in New York, but she had to start looking at Aleford as a challenge.

Her steps assumed a firmer character and she realized she was almost at her destination, the top of Belfry Hill and the reconstruction of the original belfry erected for the Bicentennial. Inside the wooden structure, which looked like the top of an old schoolhouse without the bottom, was the reconstructed original bell. The bell that had sounded the call to arms on that momentous April morning. Now it was solemnly tolled for only three occasions: the death of a president; the death of a descendent of one of the original Aleford settlers; and the alarum for the Patriot's Day reenactment of the skirmish. A very serious bell.

While all of this was of mild, and possibly even mildly

increasing, interest to her the longer she lived in Aleford, Faith was not on a historical pilgrimage. She was headed for one of the benches inside the belfry that the town fathers and mothers had thoughtfully provided for weary tourists. The benches were solid and had supported the Bicentennial hordes without a crack. Now they were used by occasional visitors, but more frequently by the inhabitants of Aleford. Faith liked to sit and eat her lunch here while gazing out the doorway to the town below. From the hilltop, the church, with its tall white steeple surrounded by prim clapboard houses and brick sidewalks, reminded her of those tiny wooden villages in gold mesh bags she and her sister, Hope, used to get in their Christmas stockings.

Today she had one of her favorite sandwiches tucked in the pocket of her Girbaud jeans—a *pan bagna* with ripe tomatoes, hard-boiled egg, tuna, and a little olive oil on her own homemade bread. She felt more cheerful just thinking about it and as for the sighs—the ennui, the restlessness, the lack of someone to give her a really good haircut—well, she would just have to cope.

Besides, there simply wasn't any choice. Some people wore their hearts on their sleeves. Tom Fairchild wore his on his face and Faith had only to picture this charming visage with the slightly off-center nose to know that there was no place he might go to which she wouldn't happily go along. She might be homesick, but there wasn't a blessed thing she could do about it.

Blessed? When had she stopped swearing? She sighed before she could help herself and continued up the steep path.

Faith Fairchild, née Sibley, had not only been bred in

Manhattan, but born there. Faith's mother, a capable and beautiful woman with the deceptively simple name of Jane, was descended from several of New York's old families, the branches of the tree heavily weighted with Stuyvesants and Van Rensselaers. She had married an impoverished divinity school student on a sudden uncharacteristic romantic impulse and accepted the role of minister's wife, but gently and firmly refused to leave the city. It would have been impossible to consider giving up its many amenities—Carnegie Hall, the MOMA, the Metropolitan, Bergdorf's and Balducci's—even for God's work. Jane was sure there was plenty for God, through Lawrence Sibley, to do in New York and no doubt she was right.

Jane Sibley was a real estate lawyer specializing in litigation involving new construction, of which there seemed to be ever increasing amounts in the city.

When Faith, and then Hope, one year younger, were born, Jane had stopped working briefly before firmly putting her little Frizon-clad feet back into place. There were no more babies after Hope, which Faith attributed in part to her mother's understandable aversion to the name "Charity," "Chat" for short. The first three girls in generations of Sibley families were always named "Faith," "Hope," and "Charity," after a pious ancestral trio. Boys were named "Lawrence" or "Theodore," nothing for short, after equally distant kinsmen.

Faith's father, a Lawrence, grew up in New Jersey, virtually another country for Jane, who was raised in solitary splendor, or rather "comfort," high above Fifth Avenue. She still felt more wary about crossing the Hudson than the Atlantic.

Lawrence settled into life in New York City, his adaptation perhaps hastened by the winds of change that swept away the old farms surrounding his father's church. The rolling meadows and gentle-faced cows, which had been his boyhood neighbors, were replaced by shopping malls and parking lots. In New York, he told himself, you knew where you were and no one, not even Donald Trump, would ever think of blacktopping Central Park.

As Faith and Hope grew older they were allowed to roam around the city on their own—a very carefully circumscribed part of the city, that is. They walked from their apartment to school—Dalton, and to various lessons at which they did not show any genius, but did not disgrace themselves either.

College followed Dalton as night the day. Both Faith and Hope returned to the city immediately afterward, but there the resemblance stopped.

Hope, when her turn came, burst meteorically upon the skyline and landed a terrific job at Citibank, began to dress for success, and bought a Bottega Veneta briefcase. Faith was still busy wondering what to do.

But when Faith finally hit upon her life's work, it satisfied her every requirement. No one at home would like it much and no one at home could do it. She was amazed that it hadn't occurred to her before.

Faith had always loved to cook, and from the time she was a little girl would happily mess about the kitchen inventing surprisingly good things to eat whenever her mother would let her. Now she started quietly taking advanced culinary courses, coming home a bit befloured and flushed from the hot kitchens. As no one asked where she was spending her days, she didn't say.

Later she went to work for one of the city's top caterers at a ridiculously low salary and started to dream of Japanese vegetable flowers and salmon coulibiac. At this point the family knew she was doing something with food, but assumed it was a hobby.

When Faith announced she was dipping into the small but adequate trust fund set up by her grandfather, "and mine own" she reminded them, to start a catering business, they were amazed. However, nothing daunted, she went forward and *Have Faith* was born. The rest is history, culinary and cultural. As soon as the initial confusion over the name was straightened out—people thought she was a new cult, an escort service for the guilt ridden, or, worst of all, a food service specializing in lenten fare—New Yorkers were vying for her services and she was a year ahead in her bookings. The fact that she had been at their parties as a guest added to the image. Now she supplied not only her beautiful self, but her beautiful food.

By the time Faith met Tom at a wedding she was catering, she had been featured in *Gourmet, New York Magazine,* and the *Times.*

Thomas Fairchild was in town to perform the ceremony for his college roommate. Tom had grown up in Massachusetts on the South Shore. His family was not particularly religious. They went to church every Sunday and the four little Fairchilds regarded it in much the same light as the invariable Sunday dinner that followed, or as playing baseball in the town league or doing well in school. This is what the Fairchilds did. Not with a lot of show, but solid and steady. This was what life was all about. The family had lived in the area for generations and Tom's father's business, Fairchild's Real Estate, had several counterparts: Fairchild's Ford in nearby Duxbury (Tom's uncle) and Fairchild's Market in town (Tom's grandfather and another uncle).

The wedding was a small one in an apartment overlooking Central Park, and if Faith had divined the past and present of the man hovering over the buffet when she went to check on the supply of *saucisson en brioche,* she might have approached with a little trepidation. As it was, all she saw was a terribly attractive, tall, handsome stranger. Always good qualifications. She liked his reddish-brown hair and figured she could get rid of the straggly mustache once she got to know him better. Nobody told her he was the minister and nobody told him she was the caterer. They started to talk.

They were still talking several hours later, huddled under blankets against the February cold, riding in one of those tacky, impossibly romantic horse-drawn carriages around Central Park. If Faith gave an embarrassed thought to what her friends would say if they could see her in one of these, it quickly vanished in the moonlight.

And there was a lot of moonlight.

The mustache came off the next day.

Tom gave Faith the Fairchild engagement ring, a tiny little diamond, when she came to visit him two weeks later. It was so sweet Faith thought she would cry. She made a mental note not to wear the more noticeable stone her grandparents had given her for her twenty-first birthday until they had been married a couple of months.

Then as he slipped the ring on her finger she realized with a start that she was not going to have her cake and eat it too. The cake being Tom and it, New York City.

9

Not just *Have Faith,* but her cozy little apartment on the West Side, the first place all her own, and a social life that could be as dazzling as she chose. She also knew from experience that parish life was a goldfish bowl, however holy the water. Tom had told her the ministry wasn't like this anymore and she could behave as she wished.

He was a dear, of course, but Faith knew better.

Then in church the next morning she had subtly scrutinized the congregation and come to the conclusion that they looked like ordinary God-fearing souls who would mind their own business and let her mind hers. She wanted to believe. Later Faith and Tom, recalling this optimistic moment, had dissolved in tears of laughter, and other things too.

After the quick study of her fellow worshippers, she had turned her attention to Tom, who was stepping into the pulpit. His sermon was filled with common sense and occasional poetry. She got a lump in her throat and her heart was filled with nonsinful pride. She felt devoutly thankful. Thankful for Tom and thankful she had managed to find him.

She knew, she told herself that night in her bed back in New York, if it hadn't been Aleford, it would have been someplace very like it. Tom found it puzzling that she could even consider living in New York City. Nor would he raise a family there. Faith had often found this true of people who didn't live in the city. Very intelligent people, too. Surely they knew when one told them one had been born and raised in New York that that meant one had spent one's childhood there, and lived to tell the tale; but they continued to speak as though Manhattan and the five boroughs were inhabited only by adults.

In Tom's view, Faith and Hope were somehow exceptions. No other children had ever been raised there.

Another thing Tom was firm about was not using any of Faith's trust fund. He considered that it was for Faith's future (read lonely old age, widowed at ninety) and the children's. It wasn't that Tom didn't like money and what it could buy. He was as pleasantly hedonistic as the next parson—or lawyer or firefighter or anyone else. And he was happy for Faith to work and bring home "beaucoup de bacon." A sophomore year in France had left him fluent, permanently in love with the country, and prone to such expressions.

Faith agreed with him about the money—up to a point. She had replaced what she had initially withdrawn with *Have Faith's* profits and was happy to have the fund merrily accumulating "beaucoup de interest."

As for the trust, she decided to let the matter lie for the time being. Certainly they would educate their children well and then the darlings were on their own.

She had no intention of a frugal old age trying to make ends meet on a parish pension when her arms were no longer capable of beating egg whites in her copper bowl. The trust fund could make those golden years a little more golden, preferably somewhere sunny like Provence. But it was not something that concerned her now. She figured she had years ahead to convince Tom.

Meanwhile the only exception she was quite firm about was clothes. Faith could not see herself in Filene's Basement beating other women over the heads for a skirt from Saks that no one had wanted to buy in the first place; nor was she about to plug in a Singer and start

11

running up tea gowns. No, she would pay for her own clothes and Tom, blissfully ignorant of what a little black dress cost these days, gracefully acceded. She would also be allowed to give him an occasional present, and it was her fervent hope to wean him away from Brooks and a little closer to Armani. Tom was heir to the Yankee pride in the longevity of one's wardrobe. He would gleefully point out articles of clothing from days gone by that Faith would have donated to charity years ago.

Now more than a year and a half later as the Tavern on the Green faded into the grass of the village green, she had Tom. And she had a baby.

Said baby wriggled against her and she felt inexplicably happy. So I'll get the business going again and meanwhile what better way to spend one's time than sitting with this lovely little brown-eyed bundle, she told herself.

Faith had reached the end of her journey and turned to enter the belfry. The doorway was low and she had to duck slightly. Sitting down, she reached into her pocket for the sandwich and put it on the bench beside her, while she started to unloosen the straps of the Snugli.

That was when she realized she wasn't alone.

In the dim light inside, she had not noticed that the bench against the other wall was occupied. Whoever it was was awkwardly slumped over in sleep. Faith stood up to leave. She would eat outside. Benjamin could be waking up any moment and would no doubt disturb him or her. Benj was not an easy waker and protested the abruptness of the transition from sweet dreams to rude awakenings with a particularly lusty cry. She took a step closer to the other bench as she went out and all at once several things became abundantly clear.

First, it wasn't a stranger. It was Cindy Shepherd, a member of the parish and in fact, President of the Young People's Club.

Second, Benjamin wouldn't disturb her. She was not sleeping. She was dead.

At least Faith assumed she was, since there was a kitchen knife sticking out of her motionless rib cage.

A kitchen knife that also impaled a single pink rose.

Having taken in all these details with the precision of a slow-motion camera, Faith suddenly covered Benjamin's already closed eyes with her hand while she moved quickly to the center of the belfry.

A murder had occurred and that meant a murderer. There was only one thing to do.

Faith grabbed the bell rope, pulled with all her might, and sounded the alarum.

TWO

IN THE DAYS THAT FOLLOWED, THE ACTUAL MURDER itself was almost eclipsed by the debate that raged within the town over whether Faith should have rung the bell or not. Leading the group that opposed the action was Millicent Revere McKinley, great-great-great-granddaughter of a distant cousin of Paul Revere. It was this progenitor, Ezekiel Revere, who had cast the original bell.

"I don't know what Grandfather would have said," Millicent remarked in a slightly sad but firm tone that went straight to the hearts of many of her listeners—in the post office, the library, the checkout line at the Shop and Save. Wherever she could gather a crowd. Faith grew accustomed to dead silence and slightly guilty smiles when she entered these places.

Millicent wasn't smiling, though. It was her belief that Faith could have run down the hill as quickly as possible and then screamed loudly. Millicent did grudgingly admit that screaming from the top of the hill, however therapeutic, would have been useless.

After the grandfather line, she would generally add, "It's just not going to be the same on Patriot's Day when we sound the *real* alarm," and drift out of whatever public site she happened to be in toward home.

Best actress in a supporting role, Faith thought bitterly.

This was not Millicent's first foray into local controversy. She was also the main and most impassioned supporter of a proposal, which surfaced at Town Meeting every year, to change the name of Aleford to Haleford. She averred that the *H* had been inexcusably obliterated by the mists of time and the town was actually named for a family with the illustrious name of Hale. The fact that she was not in the least related to them gave her campaign a disinterested sincerity—as she was quick to point out.

Opponents logically argued that the very earliest town documents recorded the name as Aleford and there was no question in this case of *s*'s that looked like *f*'s to confuse the issue. The town was probably called Aleford because of a well-known and well-frequented tavern conveniently close to the best ford of a branch of the Concord River that ran through the town. Ezekiel himself may have hoisted a few at said hostelry.

Any suggestion of this was enough to make Millicent see red, white, and blue. A member of the cold water army from birth, she scorned the base suggestion that either grandfather or the town had anything to do with ale. And so the battle raged.

Tom and Faith privately sided with the Aleford contingent as opposed to the Halefordians, and wished that the tavern hadn't burned down one particularly boisterous night. Millicent and friends had managed to prevent the licensing of any others. There was no Ye Olde Groggery in town. If you wanted a drink, you had to go to Byford, the next town. So called because it was near yet another ford, not as Millicent might have contended because of an ancient family named By. More familiarly it was known to some Aleford inhabitants as the Packy Run.

The question of the bell promised to be as engrossing as the Haleford/Aleford issue, and Millicent, or "Thoroughly Militant Millie" as she had been irreverently tagged, certainly must have felt just a tiny bit grateful to Faith in an unexplored corner of her heart.

For the bell had certainly been rung—furiously, conclusively, and with all the strength Faith could muster from arms that felt like limp strands of pasta. This done, she had raced down the path, literally colliding with the town police chief, Charley MacIsaac, several of his men, and almost everyone else within hearing distance. It was pretty hard to stop on Belfry Hill's sharp incline once you got going.

They were quite surprised to see Faith, having expected to catch some wayward juveniles (not from Aleford, of course) fooling around with the bell. And they were flabbergasted when she blurted out, "Cindy Shepherd's been murdered and the body's in the belfry."

The crowd immediately rushed off, leaving Faith and Benjamin in the dust. No one wanted to be left behind.

Murder victims were about as rare in Aleford as Tories.

Faith took one look at the solid phalanx of retreating hacks and decided that the safest place for a mother and child was home.

It had apparently not occurred to MacIsaac and his troops that the murderer could still be lurking about concealed in the underbrush, ready to strike again. It did occur to Faith, however, and this is why she left the scene of the crime; to answer the questions of all those who have audibly wondered why she didn't stick around and own up to *A*: ringing the bell and/or *B*: murdering Cindy, or even *C*: discovering a body in a town monument. Not a few held this to be the most heinous crime of all.

When the chief got to the belfry, saw Cindy's very obviously dead body, and turned to ask Mrs. Fairchild a question, he realized she wasn't there. He quickly sent Patrolman Dale Warren, new to the job and pleased as punch at the turn it was taking, outside to find her. Dale never thought that she would simply go home. This explains the brief APB which went out all over the state for Faith and Benjamin after Patrolman Warren made a thorough search of the hill. Rather than being annoyed when she finally heard about it, Faith was terribly pleased that he had subtracted several years from her age—he made her twenty-four.

In any case, everything was straightened out that afternoon. Or, rather, nothing was straightened out about Cindy, but everything was straightened out about Faith.

Except she never did correct Dale. Young people today had few enough illusions to hold on to now that Martha Stewart was doing commercials for K mart.

Tom, meanwhile, had been running errands as a break

from pastoral duties, and after leaving the bank was waiting on line in the post office when the person in front of him turned around and seemed mildly interested to see him there.

"Don't suppose you know that your wife found Cindy Shepherd's dead body up in the old belfry?" he remarked.

Tom had heard the bell pealing earlier and wondered what was going on, but to say the idea that Faith was ringing it after finding the corpse of the president of his Young People's Club was the farthest thought front his mind would be to place that thought somewhere on Venus. He rushed home, correctly divining Faith's natural instincts. She had locked all the doors and was in the bedroom, shivering, with her down quilt pulled tightly around Benjamin and herself. Benjamin was smiling in cozy comfort and blowing little drooly bubbles.

She sobbed, "Where have you been, Tom? I've been calling the office for hours!"

Then she burst into tears. It was not unknown for Faith to cry, in anger, sadness, and especially at the movies; but there was a qualitative difference to these sobs and it took Tom a long time to calm her down. Finally all three of them were bundled under the quilt and Faith started to talk.

"You can't imagine how terrified I was, Tom. I kept expecting some maniac with a meat cleaver to come after us. And the body! I've never seen a dead person not in a coffin !"

Tom was holding her close and making comforting noises.

"All I was going to do was have a picnic," Faith wailed, "and there she was! Of course it was lucky it wasn't

17

somebody I liked."

Tom looked as though he were going to say something and changed his mind.

"You were going to say I shouldn't be speaking ill of the dead."

"Maybe something like that, but two things stopped me in time. It sounded inappropriately pontifical and besides I agree with you."

Faith nestled closer to him. Tom might be a little too pious on occasion, but he was no hypocrite.

She was feeling very drowsy and now that she was safe she found her mind wandering to all kinds of interesting questions, such as who killed Cindy? And given her personality, why had he or she waited so long?

Faith started to tell Tom, but when their two heads bent as one toward Benjamin, they both drew back quickly and she spoke first. "My turn or yours?"

By the time Tom had changed Benjamin, wondering as he often did how one tiny infant could produce such a volume of odiferous *merde*, the police had arrived, having eventually figured out Faith's whereabouts.

She gave Charley an account of what she had seen or rather hadn't seen. There had been nothing to note that she could think of. They left, then returned an hour later. They had forgotten to fingerprint her and the CPAC unit from the DA's office was screaming for her prints so they could eliminate her. Faith noticed MacIsaac's fingers were inky; it looked as if his had had to be eliminated, too.

It was close to nine that night when the phone finally stopped ringing with calls from assorted well-wishers and gossip mongers. Even the most desperately curious would never break that New England taboo and call after nine o'clock.

Faith was curled up in the blue wing chair next to the fireplace, which she had filled with pots of fiery gold and russet chrysanthemums until the weather called for logs. She was beginning to shake off the feeling of being terribly cold and terribly nauseated at the same time.

Tom walked into the room and threw himself down on the couch.

"These calls are beginning to drive me crazy, Faith. They start out sympathetically, but somehow everyone manages to work in the bell. I really think they would rather you had put it to a vote at Town Meeting before you rang it."

Faith had her legs draped gracefully over the arm of the chair. She had poured two glasses of Armagnac while he had been on the phone the last time and she held one in her outstretched hand now. She had been thinking about the murder and was starting to enjoy herself.

"I'm sorry you have to deal with all this, Tom, but think how much worse they'd be to me. Has anybody said anything about suspects? Other than Ben and I?"

"No, a few have mentioned feeling sorry for the Moores, but mostly they ask kindly if you and the baby are all right, then go straight to the bell. Oh, Mrs. Keller did offer the opinion that it was probably a tramp—not Cindy, you understand, but the murderer."

"Tramps don't usually carry around roses, Tom. That's the part I don't get," Faith said speculatively. "Who does something like that—a disappointed lover? A mad botanist? Somebody who's read one too many Georgette Heyers?"

She took a sip of brandy, savored it, and continued.

"And why kill Cindy in the first place? I mean, sure, there were any number of reasons to kill her. Even you, Tom, could have done the deed after a particularly heated Young People's meeting. But why kill her now when she was about to leave town, presumably for good?"

"Just to set the record straight, I was talking to Mrs. Norris at the register of the Shop and Save. I was in fact returning a quarter I had found on the floor."

"Are you sure you're still not an Eagle Scout or something? I hope you do have to go to court and establish an alibi. There haven't been too many trials with such exciting testimony lately."

Tom grinned.

"Well, she did see me pick it up, Faith. I suppose I could have said I would put it in the plate. Anyway I didn't kill Cindy, despite the number of times I've said to you I'd really like to kill that girl."

Cindy Shepherd had arrived in Aleford at age five, when her parents were killed in an automobile accident, to live with her aunt and uncle, Patricia and Robert Moore. Since that time, she had managed to antagonize the majority of the town's inhabitants by ferreting out the one weakness an individual most wished to hide and relentlessly bringing it forth into the light of day with her treacherously sharp tongue. Kids were easy prey and she honed her skills on them. Although she did have friends—anyone who preferred to be in the quiver rather than impaled on the target. These friends also helped in the information-gathering process and loyally elected her to anything she wanted to be—president, director, whatever was in charge.

Adults were not safe; in fact, she enjoyed the challenge.

When she was younger she would adopt an air of youthful ingenuousness to deliver her remarks: "Oh, Mrs. Martin, did I see you in town last week? Wasn't it on Tremont Street? Near that cute shop where they sell the wigs?" When she got older, she didn't bother with subtlety and adopted the simpler method of pretending not to see that the person was standing nearby before she aimed.

Her behavior was a terrific embarrassment to her aunt, who was acutely aware that, although her female friends pitied her, they were also extremely angry. Women tended to come in for more scorn than men, since as Cindy matured she began to like men very much and women not at all.

Patricia Moore had spent countless hours talking to Cindy about hurting people's feelings, hours that could more productively have been spent filling holes in a dike with sand. After one particularly trying day when Cindy, aged fourteen, referred to the Whipple sisters as "dried-up old maids who needed to get some," Patricia burst into tears while she was telling Robert.

"I know everyone blames me, but short of preventing the accident, I don't know what I could have done differently."

"Nothing, my dear, you have done more than enough. The only thing that could have happened that didn't was Cindy's presence in the car with them," he said, sighing.

Faith had heard all these stories and new ones continued to circulate. They were all coming back to her now.

"Think, Tom. Even after eliminating one of the town's most respected members of the clergy who clearly harbored ill will toward her, we can certainly list countless others. It's not hard to come up with suspects, however unlikely. What keeps puzzling me is the timing. That's a bigger mystery."

"You're right," he agreed. "Who didn't want her to leave, absurd as that seems? Or had she done something recently to someone that was so monstrous he or she had to kill her and the fact that she was leaving is coincidental?"

Tom was an inveterate mystery reader and he was beginning to enjoy himself too, especially as Faith, slightly flushed from the brandy, was obviously more than all right.

"This is good, Tom; let's try to think of all the possible connections. How about someone who didn't want her to get married—an old flame, her future in-laws, or maybe some secret girlfriend of Dave's?"

Cindy was engaged to Dave Svenson, much to the town's surprise, although they had gone out together for years. The only logical explanation anyone had been able to come up with was that she had cast a spell on him.

It wasn't a wedding Faith looked forward to. She had already attended one function catered by the firm hired for Cindy's reception and the pathetic attempt at "continental cuisine" in the form of Chicken Kiev with what Faith detected as Cheese Whiz in the center had convinced her that it wasn't a moment too soon for *Have Faith,* Benjamin permitting. She was continually astounded at what her neighbors ate. Locating her business in Aleford would amount to an act of mercy. She herself drew the line at boiled dinners. Furthermore, if they were going to want beans it would have to be *cassoulet.*

"I've never heard of any other girlfriend. It's been my impression that Cindy and Dave have been going steady for a long time," Tom mused.

Faith had been delighted to discover that Tom was quite interested in gossip, unusual for a minister. Her own father could never get even the most straightforward scandals right and was apt to let his mind wander, presumably to a higher plane, whenever she tried to impart or extract any information. Tom spent a great deal of time with the kids in the parish. He was worried about the kinds of choices they faced, and was also aware that a congregation needed young people to keep going. If Dave Svenson had had another girlfriend, particularly one passionate enough to wield a kitchen knife, Tom surely would have known about it.

"It's more the kind of thing Cindy would have done rather than have done unto," he remarked.

"I'm not sure of the grammar, but that's what I've been thinking. If anyone was going to commit a murder in this town, it would have been Cindy, and I'm sure she would have thought she had a pardonable reason for it. That leaves us with an old boyfriend of Cindy's—of which there are legion—or a new boyfriend?"

Cindy was notorious for regularly staging scenes with Dave that, Faith correctly assumed, then gave her the excuse to go off with someone else for a while. Often she didn't even bother with the scene.

"Let's see, it's hard to keep track, but it was about a month ago that she told me for the thousandth time that Dave took her for granted and needed to be taught a lesson. I believe that coincided with the Calthorpes' nephew's visit," Tom recalled wryly.

23

"So maybe he fell desperately in love with her and decided if he couldn't have her, nobody would."

"That would solve things nicely, Faith, but he is presumably in West Germany for the semester. At least the Calthorpes drove him to Logan and put him on a plane for there. Still I know you won't rule it out."

"If it's not sex, then it's money," she said, ignoring this last. "It has to be one or the other."

"Why? There must be plenty of other reasons people kill other people. Anyway I thought that was why people got divorced."

"Virtually the same thing. Murder, divorce. Gone is gone." Faith waved one hand summarily in the air. "Now the money. Cindy was going to be rich, we know that."

If Cindy Shepherd had lived to turn twenty-one, she would have come into a very tidy little fortune from her parents. Nobody had mentioned the exact figure, as Faith had discovered when once she had asked Tom just how tidy it was. She was always surprised how seldom anyone in New England ever mentioned actual dollar amounts and how much they appeared to think about them.

"She must have made a will. Maybe Pix knows." Faith furrowed her brow. Their neighbor Pix's husband, Sam Miller, was a lawyer and had been known to let harmless but tasty tidbits of information fall from the table.

"Please, Faith," Tom protested, "After all this mess with my mother's family I don't even want to hear the word *will*."

"I'm sorry, sweetheart, just thinking out loud."

Tom's grandmother had died the previous spring and Marian, his mother, fully expected to claim the garnet brooch, wedding pearls, cameo, diamond lavaliere, and other mementos, which her mother had indicated were her birthright since she was a little girl. It had been a shock to discover that her mother had left her house and its contents to Marian's brother, who had moved in with his wife to take care of her seven years earlier. Even then Marian had assumed they would share and share alike as was the right thing to do. Months of wrangling and eventually a hefty lawyer's fee trying to prove undue influence had left her without so much as a jet hat pin.

Faith shook her head.

"No, I don't think it was money. If she had already inherited, then it would make sense. And anyway, given Cindy, sex is a more logical motive." She held out her empty glass. "Un peu more brandy, s'il vous plait," she said, slipping into Tom's eccentric French. (She had noticed that married people seemed to pick up each other's habits, although so far she didn't see Tom adopting any of hers.) "It helps one think so much more clearly. Except that we should be drinking Scotch and calling for Asta."

Tom took her glass and looked down at her reprovingly, "Have your fun tonight, Nora Charles. I'll talk with you about all this until the cows come home, but if you have any idea of doing some sleuthing, with or without your Nick, forget it. I like you without roses stuck in your side."

"Don't be silly, Tom. What can I do, after all? Maybe ask a few questions here and there. Do admit, this is pretty exciting. When is the last time they had a murder in Aleford anyway?"

"I have no idea. Although I did hear something about one of the Hales running amok in the thirties and killing his wife's dog, then being prevented just in time by a neighbor from giving its mistress forty whacks as well."

"So mine could be Aleford's first real murder!"

"I doubt it, Faith, and in any case it's not yours."

"Ours then."

"No, absolutely not."

"You're just being cranky because you're hungry and so am I. Did we have any supper? I can't remember. Anyway, I'm starving."

Faith was always starving, Tom thought happily. What a good idea it had been to marry someone who shared and satisfied his hungers so well.

He followed her into the large kitchen and sat at the big round table while she split some bread in half and liberally covered it with *chèvre* and toasted walnuts before running it under the broiler for a moment. The kitchen bore little resemblance to the room Tom had used infrequently during his brief bachelor days in the parsonage. Faith had kept the old glass-fronted cabinets, but everything else had been torn out. She had actually shuddered when she saw the electric stove, vintage to be sure, and the single sink next to a small drainboard, the only counter in the room. Now with her gleaming, glassfronted refrigerator, Garland stove, rows of hanging pots and pans, miles of white formica counters with a marble insert for pastry making, and a black and white tile floor, Faith felt at home. The table stood by a bow window overlooking the garden. As a concession to the setting, Faith had covered the window seats and chair cushions with Souleiado Provençal fabric. "But no country, Tom, nothing with cows on it and not even one dried flower wreath, please," she had stated emphatically.

In between crusty bites, Faith kept talking about Cindy.

"It has to be a disappointed lover because of the rose."

A poetic gesture, the final symbol of their blighted romance."

"If any romance was blighted, it was Cindy and Dave's. You know, Faith, I never could understand why those two were getting married."

"Elementary, my dear Thomas. Because Cindy wanted it and Dave wanted her. Think about it, or rather, imagine yourself at twenty—not that long ago to be sure—and all those hormones and Cindy walks into your life. Those proverbial curves in the correct places, that long black hair with the blue highlights just like Wonder Woman's in the cartoons. It was sex. Frequent, prolonged, and poor Dave got hooked."

"Keep talking, Faith. I find this not only mesmerizing but kind of a turn-on."

"I'm not sure why Cindy wanted poor Dave, though. Maybe she wanted to get marriage out of the way and go on to bigger and better things, like affairs." She saw Tom's look. "Bigger and better for Cindy that is, silly. And Dave is a good catch. Steady, dependable, bright, and handsome. You know, I wouldn't put it past her to have chosen him because she wanted a blond to contrast with her looks."

"'Poor Dave' does sum it up. I tried to talk to him about Cindy several times, but he never seemed to want to. We were due to start the prenuptial pastoral counseling soon and I thought I might understand the whole relationship better then."

"Yes, and probably you would have given Dave the courage to back out. Although short of having his parents fill his ears with wax at birth and tie him to the liberty pole in the middle of the common, I don't see how he was going to resist her call. But if you did, then Cindy would have killed you and Dave both. The invitations have gone out, and she was not a girl to be spurned lightly."

Tom finished the last morsel on his plate and stood up and stretched.

"It is pretty horrible, Faith. I've been thinking about her wedding service and now I have to write a funeral oration instead."

"These theological dilemmas are bound to come up, Tom, but I have no doubt that you will rise to the occasion." Faith smiled primly, secure in the knowledge that rising to that sort of occasion was something she would never have to do.

"It's certainly not one of the topics we wrestled with in Divinity School. Now what do you say to some sleep? Frequent and prolonged or whatever."

"Good idea. I am exhausted. This has been a very busy day, if I may be permitted the greatest understatement of my life, so far anyway."

"You may and it is," Tom agreed.

Faith followed him upstairs and wondered briefly if he had found Cindy attractive. She had worn sex the way other girls wore makeup. Depending on the circumstances, it could be the full treatment or a hint of lipstick and powder. Whatever it was, though, it was always there, unsettling and devastatingly provocative. Faith started to ask, then changed her mind. It was one of those questions, like whether there really is life after death, that she didn't want answered for sure.

They looked in at Ben, marveled at that splendid

accomplishment babies perform—breathing—and went to bed.

They were not prepared for an insistent ringing at six o'clock the next morning. Faith woke up and wondered groggily why Benjamin was making such an odd noise. She was at the side of his crib looking down at a peacefully sleeping child before she realized it was the doorbell.

She ran back into their bedroom, fully awake.

"Tom!" she cried, "wake up! Somebody's at the door!"

Tom was a very sound sleeper. She shook him.

"Tom! Somebody's ringing the bell!"

"What? Not again?" he mumbled.

"The doorbell! Someone is ringing our doorbell!"

"All right, all right." He roused himself, got out of bed, and struggled into his robe. Faith followed him downstairs, hovering anxiously.

"Be sure to ask who it is, Tom," she cautioned as she moved toward the poker by the fireplace.

"Faith, murderers usually don't ring the doorbell," Tom said. Like Benjamin, he was a slow waker and apt to sound snappish. "But if you like, I'll ask." Feeling slightly foolish, he addressed the solid oak door. "Who is it?"

"It's me, Dave. Dave Svenson." Tom quickly opened the door. "I hope I didn't wake you folks, but I thought with the baby, you'd probably be up by now and anyway I was getting tired of waiting."

It turned out that Dave had spent most of the night crouched under the large willows in the backyard, and he looked it. There were deep circles under his eyes and his normally ruddy Nordic complexion was pale and wan. Tom led him straight into the kitchen for some sustenance, wondering what was going on besides what was going on.

"Dave," he said soberly and with as much dignity as an old plaid Pendleton bathrobe could lend, "I know how you must be grieving. It is difficult to lose someone you love whatever the circumstances, but to have it happen in this cruel and senseless way tests all our belief. It is not much comfort now, but time will help and I hope you will come and talk with me whenever you feel like it."

Dave was looking at him in some bewilderment and Tom wondered if he was in shock or if the bathrobe was simply too incongruous.

"That's very kind of you, sir," he said as Faith entered the kitchen. She had hastily thrown on a pair of jeans and a shirt and grabbed Benjamin, hoping not to miss anything. She hadn't.

Dave opened his mouth and a garbled bunch of words came tumbling out.

"The cops are looking for me everywhere and they may be here soon. They think I did it and they're right. I mean," he amended hastily after seeing the looks of horror and disbelief on Faith and Tom's faces, horror for Tom, disbelief for Faith, "they're right that I *wanted* to kill her. I didn't actually do it, but I could have. I really think I would have done it if somebody hadn't beaten me to it."

"But Dave, if you didn't do it, why are you avoiding the police" Tom asked.

"It's a long story," he answered, looking out the window anxiously as if he expected MacIsaac to be peering in.

Faith took his arm and led him to the table.

"Sit down. I'll get us something to eat and you can tell us about it," she offered.

She put Ben in his playpen and stuck some plastic keys in his hand. He smiled benevolently at her. She was not deceived. She just hoped his fascination with the toy lasted long enough for Dave to tell his story.

She took some of her sour cream waffles from the freezer, put them in the microwave, and started the coffee. A lot of coffee. She had visited the Svensons and the house always smelled like freshly baked bread and Maxwell House. It was unusual to see one of the Svenson family without a mug in hand. Dave had started to talk again; he grasped the cup she put in front of him as it was a lifeline.

"Wednesday night Cindy and I had a wicked big fight. I had finally told her I couldn't marry her. I know I shouldn't have waited this long, but every time I tried I just couldn't tell her. We'd been together so many years and—well, she could be very nice at times."

Faith had a pretty good idea of what being nice meant and gave a small knowing nod toward Tom.

"I came home and told my parents and I planned to tell the Moores on Thursday, but I didn't want to see Cindy. I knew if I stayed away from her for a while I could stick to it. We've broken up before, but I always went back when she called. You don't know how much I've hated myself this past year. And hated her."

Faith pried the empty mug from his grasp and gave him a refill along with a stack of waffles.

"I'm sorry, Dave," Tom said, "I wish I could have helped you. I must confess I didn't think the marriage was a good idea, but I thought you wanted it."

"So didn't everybody. Even my parents. I guess a lot of people thought I was marrying her for the money. And she did give me a lot of expensive things, like this watch."

He looked at the Rolex on his wrist in horror as if it had suddenly started to ooze slime. He quickly took it off and dropped it on the floor. Faith retrieved it and put it on the counter. A Rolex was a Rolex, after all.

"The truth is, I was marrying her because I didn't have the guts not to. She's had her whole life planned since she was eight years old. She picked me then and in her mind there was no backing out. But I did."

"Dave, just because you fought doesn't mean the police suspect you," Tom said firmly.

"Maybe not, but the fact that the person she was waiting for in the belfry was me does."

"What !" Faith exclaimed.

Dave nodded his head. The circles under his eyes made him look like an underripe jack o'lantern. One of the sad ones.

"She called my house all day Thursday and I wouldn't talk to her, then Friday she called at the crack of dawn and told my mother her parents wanted an explanation, which was a lie, I'm pretty sure. She never told them anything. But my mother was getting upset, so I told Mom to tell her I'd see her and she said she'd be waiting in the belfry at noon. We used to go up there a lot."

"S-E-X," Faith mouthed over his head. Tom pretended not to see.

"She called back later to make sure I'd gotten the message and Mrs. McKinley was there drinking coffee with Mom and heard the whole thing. So you know there wasn't a person in Aleford who didn't know I was meeting Cindy in the belfry."

"But Dave," Faith said, "I started walking up the hill around noon and I didn't see you and I would have. It's not that big and the top is flat."

"That's because I didn't go. I didn't like going against my mother, but she didn't know Cindy the way I did. I guess I didn't trust myself and maybe I hoped I'd make her so mad, she would agree to break up. I started going in that direction, then turned and went for a walk in the woods by the railroad tracks instead. The later it got, the freer I felt. Then I went home, got my car, and drove into town to do some studying at the library. I didn't even hear she was dead until I got home last night."

"And of course nobody saw you down at the tracks," Tom said.

"That's the problem. Some guy on a dirt bike buzzed by, but I have no idea who it was or what time he was there," Dave answered morosely.

"I know they're looking for me" he went on, "be- cause they've been to the house twice. My parents were worried sick and when I walked in they both started talking at once."

Which must have been an event tantamount to sunshine in Stockholm in January for the taciturn Svenson household, Faith reflected.

"They hadn't told the police anything except that I was at school and things were fine between Cindy and me."

Dave was a senior at BU and had applied to law school for the following year. He had wanted to get a degree in agriculture at U Mass, but Cindy did not fancy herself a farmer's wife, even the kind of farmer Dave had wanted to be, a researcher in alternative food sources. "It's all cow cakes, Dave, no matter how you slice it," she had said, laughing at him.

"When the police get me, they don't have to look any

33

further. I wanted to do it and so far as anybody knows I was there. Even my parents thought I might have done it. I've been pretty crazy lately. All I know is I'm not going to be locked up."

"Dave, believe me we'll straighten this out. It looks bad, but we'll do everything in our power to help you. You must remember, God protects the innocent. Hold on to that," Tom consoled.

"Thank you. I guess that's why I came. I need your help, though unless you find out who the real murderer is, I'm not sure what you can do."

"Then that's what we'll have to do," Faith said briskly, suddenly seeing Dave twenty years ago, a replica of her own darling babe. The thought stabbed her, but it was nothing compared to the hardball of a baleful glance that Tom threw across the table. She took it bravely full in the face and got some more waffles. Benjamin was still contentedly in training for a lock-picking career.

After Faith had spoken Dave looked a lot better, eating waffles steadily and to all appearances without a care in the world save whether State would take the pennant this year or not. It amazed Faith that even someone as relatively grown up as Dave still invested real adults with so much power. Faith considered herself to be one of the real adults since starting her business and even more since Benjamin was born. Unreal adults were all those yuppies somewhere in their twenties for decades who appeared intent only on making a fortune, brushing their teeth, and having an inordinate amount of fun. They weathered market fluctuations and favorite restaurant closings with equal aplomb. The wages of sin weren't what they used to be.

Tom continued to look at her, cartoonlike balloons coming out of his mouth: "Don't make promises you can't keep." "This could be dangerous." "Stay out of it."

"I don't see why I can't devote a little time to thinking about all this," Faith muttered to herself. "It's not as if I'm going to get myself killed."

She had leaned over to pick up Benjamin, who had started to demand a new diversion, when they heard a car pull into the drive. Dave was out the back way before the engine stopped.

Faith thrust his dishes into the dishwasher.

"Now, Faith," warned Tom. She motioned for him to be quiet, scooped up the Rolex, and put it in her pocket.

"Now, Faith," he said with greater determination.

"Let's just see who it is and what they want. Don't worry, Tom, I'll be good."

"That's what I'm afraid of."

The bell rang.

THREE

TOM OPENED THE DOOR. IT WAS CHIEF MACISAAC, ALL right, and he was not alone.

Charley MacIsaac was a large man—stacks of oatcakes in his youth in Nova Scotia—but he was completely dwarfed by the man at his side. Clad in what Faith noted with surprise to be a rather modish Burberry raincoat, the giant was about six-foot-seven and hefty. His dark hair, streaked with gray, was curly like a perm, but Faith, a specialist in snap judgments, immediately concluded that this wasn't the sort of man who went in for perms. A mother, most likely his, would have described his face as having character; others equally charitable would call it homely. When he greeted them with a thin-lipped regulation smile, uncharitable Faith barely repressed a shudder.

"This is Detective Lieutenant John Dunne from the State Police," Charley said, "They've been kind enough to give us a hand in this unfortunate business."

Dunne looked at Charley with tolerance bordering on annoyance. The case would have been a whole lot easier if MacIsaac had never had his hand anywhere near it. In their initial excitement, the Aleford Police had trampled Belfry Hill like a pack of puppies not yet housebroken, destroying evidence that might have been there and leaving their tracks all over the place. These small town guys might be likable as hell, but they were a pain in the ass to work with.

Dunne moved into the room, quietly for a man his size.

"I hope you don't mind going over this again, Mrs. Fairchild," he said in a tone of voice that left no alternative. And a tone of voice that revealed other than Yankee roots.

"Not at all," Faith replied politely as she steered him toward the wing chair, the only one in the room she trusted to hold him safely. There was a superabundance of spindly New England furniture in the parsonage and one of those chairs would fall apart like balsa wood if he sat in it.

Where did they find this guy? she wondered. He sounds like he comes from the Bronx. And what kind of a name was John Dunne for this decidedly unpoetical creature?

She was terrifically disconcerted to hear her unspoken

thoughts answered.

"I understand we are fellow New Yorkers, Mrs. Fairchild. I grew up in the Bronx."

This was probably supposed to make her feel at ease Faith reflected, if such a presence could. Why was it that the police had this effect on her? She hadn't murdered Cindy, but she felt as wary as an about-to-be-uncovered serial killer.

"Yes, I'm from Manhattan." That sounded like one upmanship. She hastily added, "Though of course I know the Bronx—the Zoo, the Botanical Gardens, but I must confess I mostly go there for egg creams."

It was Dunne's turn to be wary. He looked at her hard. Egg creams were nothing to joke about.

He stood up and took off his tan raincoat. It reminded Faith, as Tom jumped up to take it, of a frost heave—huge boulders suddenly emerging from the earth. Dunne sat down and the terrain settled.

Faith put Ben in the playpen again, showering him with all his favorite toys, Happy Apple and a stuffed clown that never failed to send Ben into gales of laughter. It was doing so now and Charley shot an avuncular smile at the baby, but Dunne never gave him a tumble. This wasn't going to be easy.

Tom tried to catch Faith's eye. She deliberately ignored his rather impassioned glance. Subtlety had never been Tom's strong point.

"Would anyone like some coffee? It's already made," Faith offered.

"I never say no," Charley answered. He could usually be found having a cup at the Minutemancaféevery morning at eight and every afternoon at four. When Faith used to roam the town restlessly before Benjamin's arrival, she would see him there and would join him for the Minuteman's surprisingly good muffins. The café had replaced the old country store as gathering place and information center, not that she had ever seen anyone there engaged in idle chatter or gossip. But somehow they managed to keep on top of things by nods over their coffee mugs and monosyllabic hints.

She looked over at Detective Lieutenant Dunne.

"Thank you, no," John Dunne replied as he took out his Filofax.

Faith was startled. She hadn't seen a Filofax since she'd left the city; her own was gathering dust in a drawer upstairs. She knew it was simply a matter of time before Dunne would get her to confess the infractions of a lifetime, starting with stealing a bottle of red nail polish from Woolworth's on a dare in sixth grade up to the present suppression of the whereabouts of a key suspect in a murder investigation. She would have found whips and chains easier to resist than calculated organization.

She left, quickly returned with coffee for the rest of them, and sat down next to Tom on the couch.

"Now, Mrs. Fairchild, could you tell me what happened yesterday? I've read the reports, but it would help to hear it in your own words."

This was something she could do. Faith sat up straight and patiently went through what was beginning to seem like something she had dreamed.

"I started up Belfry Hill just before noon with Benjamin."

"Excuse me, but how did you know what time it was?" Dunne was looking at her watchless wrist.

"No, I didn't have a watch on," she answered, correctly interpreting his gaze, "I don't wear one unless I need to. I knew it was near noon, because when I was halfway up the hill, I heard the bells ring at the Congregational church."

Dunne nodded, "Okay, so it was slightly past noon when you reached the belfry."

"Probably about five after," Faith corrected, recalling her self-pity stop. "I was walking rather slowly. I got to the top, went inside and sat down. I took my sandwich out and put it on the bench and started to loosen the Snugli straps."

Charley interrupted this time, "Sandwich, Faith?"

You didn't mention a sandwich before." He appeared hurt.

"I'm sorry, Charley. It was tuna, tomato, and egg."

"And I thought we had something there," he said glumly. "We're having it analyzed."

"Just plain tomato and egg," said Faith, "But the tuna is from Dean and DeLuca in New York. It's imported from Italy."

MacIsaac had been eyeing her hopefully as if perhaps she would remember that she had left her particular sandwich on the kitchen counter yesterday, but this last piece of precise information squashed that.

"You still have the rose," said Faith gently. "And the knife."

Charley paused and cleared his throat, "Yes, we still have the rose and the knife. A rose that grows in pretty near every garden in town and the kind of knife that is used in every kitchen, including mine. And whoever used it was damn lucky or knew a lot about surgery."

Faith hoped he was not going to turn cynical over this

business.

"It looked like a good sandwich. Too bad we didn't know sooner."

Faith was relieved. Chief MacIsaac was on the job, but he was not off his feed. At least not yet.

John Dunne had clearly had enough of this meandering. It was often helpful to let a witness go off on tangents, but this was getting ridiculous. Imported tuna fish and Snuglis, whatever they were.

"When you entered the belfry, Mrs. Fairchild, can you describe exactly what you saw? Sometimes it helps if you close your eyes."

Faith obediently shut her eyes, looked at the mental picture, and carefully began to put it into words.

"It was very bright out, so it was a few seconds before I saw that somebody else was there on the other bench. I thought she was asleep because her head was on the bench. It looked like a very awkward way to sleep. Not very comfortable, tumbled over to one side. I stood up to leave, because I thought Benjamin might start to cry and disturb whomever it was. That was when I realized it was Cindy and that she had a knife with a pink rose twisted around it sticking out of her side.

"I tried to think what to do. She wasn't breathing and I knew she was dead. I remember thinking it wasn't any use to try to resuscitate her."

Faith's big blue eyes flew open, filled with some of the fear of the day before. "My next thought was that the murderer must be close by."

"Why did you think that?" Dunne queried.

"Because the body was warm. Oh, that's right. I put my hand in front of her mouth to see if I could feel any breath and I touched her neck to find a pulse. There wasn't any, but the skin was still warm." Faith shivered. "I knew she couldn't have been dead long. So I rang the bell."

"And a good thing too," MacIsaac noted. He was solidly in Faith's camp on the bell controversy and was contemplating nominating her for the Bronze Musket, a plaque awarded on Patriot's Day to a citizen who has contributed above and beyond the call of duty to the town. Had it not been for Faith's quick thinking, they would have wasted valuable time apprehending the perpetrator. Of course they hadn't apprehended anyone yet, but they would. Towns like Aleford had few secrets for long. His thirty-year sojourn had taught him that.

Dunne nodded in agreement. "Now one or two other points, Mrs. Fairchild."

Faith stiffened slightly. What on earth was she going to say about Dave? Just then Benjamin began to scream angrily from his cage. Her relief was enormous. She started to get up, then changed her mind. Who knew what Tom would say if she left him alone? By their very nature, most ministers are notoriously poor liars. His innate goodness, something she cherished, had the effect of both buoying her up and weighing her down. This was one of the times when she could feel the water level rising. She put her hand on his shoulder.

"Tom, dear, would you see what Ben needs and I'll come help as soon as we're finished here?" Faith hoped the emphasis she put on "finished" wasn't too obvious, but obvious enough to get them out of her living room.

Tom took Benjamin upstairs grudgingly, well aware that his wife was about to tell any number of, to her, perfectly justifiable falsehoods.

Dunne turned back to Faith and asked, "How did you know so quickly that it was Cindy Shepherd?"

She was surprised and momentarily relieved. So he didn't want to know about Dave. Not yet anyway.

"It wasn't hard. I recognized her hair first of all and she had on a nice turquoise and black Benetton sweater that she'd worn to the last Young People's dance at the church."

She was also wearing those black stirrup pants, tacky and already passé, and turquoise ballerina flats, Faith recalled to herself. It was definitely an outfit and she was pretty sure what Cindy was wearing underneath was black lace or nothing at all. Not a class act, but proven effective. She wondered if Charley would tell her about the underwear if she got him alone some time.

Tom was back with a fussy Benjamin in his arms.

"I'm afraid he needs your particular talents, darling," he said with a touch of smugness as he handed Ben over.

"We're just leaving," Dunne said and stood up, occupying most of the airspace in the room. He walked over to Faith with MacIsaac at his heels. She noticed Dunne had on a well-cut Harris tweed sports jacket. She felt a little sorry for Charley, whose plain clothes usually took the form of an ancient Celtics jacket or shapeless brown overcoat. He'd been widowed a long time and his wardrobe had definitely remained in mourning.

Faith faced the two of them squarely. This is it, she thought.

Dunne spoke sternly, "What we are investigating here is a murder. And the murderer is still at large. We don't want to alarm you or your husband, but you must exercise simple caution until this is all wrapped up."

"You can't mean that you think somebody wants to kill me?" Faith protested.

"Remember, the murderer may think you saw something you didn't."

Faith blanched.

"We don't want you to lock yourself in the house day and night, Mrs. Fairchild. Just report any odd behavior to Chief MacIsaac or to me. Here's my card with numbers where I can be reached day or night. For instance, let us know if someone asks you a lot of questions about what you saw."

"But that will be the whole town! You might as well arrest Millicent McKinley and be done with it. Sorry, no pun intended."

Dunne smiled, or grimaced, it was hard to tell. "None taken. Believe me, I'm used to it. My mother was a poetry lover," he added.

Charley spoke up, "She does have a point, John. Just about the entire town will have an unhealthy interest in all this. Maybe it would be better to focus on the folks who don't talk about it."

Detective Dunne looked at him with something like respect, "Please be careful, Mrs. Fairchild, and keep in touch. Above all, don't play amateur detective." He turned to Tom, including him in his remarks, "You'd be amazed at how many people who are involved in crimes like this think they can do better than the police."

Tom was standing near the fireplace. "You don't, say?" His deliberately neutral tone was belied by a sudden flush on his face that could scarcely have been caused by the flamelike chrysanthemums.

"I blame TV," Dunne said, moving across the room to

43

the door with the others in his wake. He stopped just before opening it.

"By the way, we haven't been able to locate Cindy's boyfriend, Dave Svenson. Do you happen to know where he is? We'd like to ask him some questions."

Before Tom could speak, Faith stepped in front of him.

"No," she said firmly, "We don't know where he is, but if we see him, we'll give him your message."

All of which was perfectly true, she told herself, crossing her fingers behind her back to be on the safe side.

Since Dunne didn't say anything further, she added, "Is he a suspect then?" There was no harm in asking.

Dunne looked at her intently. "Everybody's a suspect until we have a suspect." It was a good exit line and had never failed him yet.

MacIsaac was listening to a different drummer. A beat that kept you lingering on the doorstep.

"Oh, Tom, we'd like a list of the members of your Young People's group and anything else you think might pertain," he said.

"No problem. I'll get everything together for you and call the station. I would also appreciate it if you could let us know when the funeral can take place. I'll be seeing the Moores this afternoon."

Charley looked at Dunne, who obviously wanted to be in the car backing out of the driveway by now, for an answer.

"They're doing the postmortem this morning, so I'd say Monday or Tuesday. Tuesday to be on the safe side." He strode off purposefully.

Tom shut the door.

"Faith, what can you be thinking of? And crossing your

44

fingers behind your back does not make a lie any less of a lie, as I believe I have told you God knows how many times before!"

"Hold on a minute, Thomas! First of all, God does know what I mean and even so I know very well what makes a lie and what doesn't. And next, I didn't see you blurting out that Dave had been here for breakfast!"

Tom looked uncomfortable.

"All right, all right. I just can't believe he had anything to do with it and it may be wrong—no, I know it's wrong—but I couldn't turn him in."

"Besides," Faith consoled him, "we honestly don't know where he is."

Tom smiled. "Besides, we don't know where he is." The smile disappeared. "What I'd like to do after I get the stuff for MacIsaac together is try to find him and get him to go to the police with me. The longer he stays away the worse it's going to look."

"That's a great idea, Tom. I'll help you find him. He must be with one of his friends. That's where kids always go when they run away. Not that this is your typical kid running away because he doesn't like the curfew his parents slapped on him."

"That's exactly what I don't want you to do. Help, that is. I want you to stay as close to home as possible until they find out who did it. 'They' being the police. Honey, don't you see? I don't want anything to happen to you!"

"I don't want anything to happen to me either. And nothing will. Anyway, what can I do! Get a plaid cape and a magnifying glass? I'm simply going to keep my eyes and ears open, that's all. But first, if I don't feed this baby, we're both going to explode."

Dunne and Charley had come to the same conclusion that Tom and Faith had and they were on their way to the Svensons to get a list of the names of Dave's friends.

"If they don't give us much, which will probably be the case, there are a bunch of other people we can ask," Charley told Dunne.

"Well, the kid's all we have so far, so we'd better concentrate on finding him. Now how much of a problem is this Mrs. Fairchild going to be? I know the type—couldn't wait for us to leave so she could sit down with her husband and solve the case."

MacIsaac laughed. "She's an intelligent woman. I don't think she's going to put herself in any danger. I doubt she'll interfere and Tom's as sensible as they come."

"If she's so smart, too bad we can't recruit her to fill out all the damned reports and let us get away from the desk long enough to get a handle on things."

The paperwork was Dunne's least favorite part of the job. He wasn't sure he had a favorite part, but he knew what he hated. His father had been a cop. He'd died of a massive coronary while chasing a suspect. Dunne was three years old and too young to hear the pros and cons of the business. His mother wanted him to go to college and he'd ended up at Columbia on a Regent's scholarship. He stayed for two years, developed a taste for elegant clothes and New Orleans jazz, then enlisted in the army. He knew he'd be going to Vietnam, and he wanted to do it on his own terms. When he returned from the war, he became a cop, just as he had always assumed he would. Anything else would have been boring. All the paperwork in the world could be balanced by ten minutes of action. He married and moved to Massachusetts, the midway point between his family and his wife's in Maine—a bitch of a drive either way. That was ten years ago and he'd mellowed a little. This bothered him occasionally. Without the city to keep him perpetually in a state of alert, he worried he might be losing his edge, and this Aleford case didn't promise to be much of a sharpener. It was probably the boyfriend or someone like him. One look at the girl had told him that. Of course it was these easy assumptions that always turned out to be wrong. That was the fun of it.

"All right, Charley, we'll look for the kid, then I'll toss you for the reports."

Charley looked a little askance.

"Just kidding."

Tom called the Svensons as soon as the police left, but they either didn't know where Dave was or weren't saying anything. So he started going down the list of kids who he knew were friends of Dave in the parish. At noon, he called it quits.

"He does seem to have vanished into thin air, Faith. At any rate, if someone I spoke to does know where he is, he'll get the message that I'm looking for him and maybe he'll show up here again."

He went upstairs, donned his collar, and got ready to go to the Moores'. They had asked Faith to come, too. She wasn't sure whether it was because they wanted to talk to her about finding the body or because she, as the minister's wife, could offer support to them in their grief. She was still new at the support business and hoped it was the former. She was looking forward to some discreet inquiries into the life and death of Cindy Shepherd and it would be hard to direct the conversation that way if she was going to be limited to empathetic nods and gentle pats on the shoulder.

They left Benjamin at home with thirteen-year-old Samantha Miller from next door, whom Faith was grooming for a life of baby-sitting bondage. She fervently hoped Samantha's shyness lasted through high school. Not that she wanted her to be unpopular, but the baby-sitter wars in Aleford made the War for Independence look like a fistfight. And the parsonage didn't have Nintendo or big screen TV to lure anyone. Sure, the snacks were superior, but Samantha, like most teenagers, preferred Doritos and diet Coke to *tarte tatin* and Faith's secret recipe puff pastry cheese straws.

Faith had fallen in love with the Moores' house the first time Tom took her there, and further acquaintance had served to deepen the passion. It was the most beautiful house in Aleford, just on the other side of the river and a short drive or long walk from the center, depending on one's time and temperament. Cindy had never walked once she got her license; Patricia Moore only used the car for shopping.

Behind the house the garden sloped gently down to the water. When the river flooded, some of the flower beds were submerged and the old swing set that stood on the banks was an informal yardstick of the severity of the storm. One wet spring the swings had floated back and forth with the current for a week. No one had ever thought to move them or take them down now that the children were grown. They had always been there and so they stayed. Which was the case with most things in the house. Whatever found its way inside never left. The house was a fantastic, glorious muddle of the treasure and trivia of many generations.

Patricia Moore's great-great-grandfather, Jeremiah Cox, had been a ship captain and later owner of a fleet of vessels, which, from the look of things, had never unloaded cargo except at this landing. He built the original square clapboard house, but it was Patricia's great grandfather, Martin, who added a wing here and there as his family and fortunes increased. Now it was a rambling house, painted that buttery yellow so beloved of New Englanders, with black shutters and white trim. It looked like a smaller, slightly eccentric version of Longfellow's home in Cambridge. Patricia's grandparents had added a deep porch, which stretched across the back of the house so they could sit in their wicker rockers and watch the river go by. It wasn't screened in. Mosquitoes either never bit people in Aleford or were studiously ignored, which amounted to the same thing. Maybe everyone put repellent on behind closed doors. The first time Faith went to one of the church picnics and took out a container of Off!, the whole congregation looked as if she had whipped out a hip flask of hootch.

Tom and Faith climbed the front stairs. Patricia had seen them from the window and was opening the door. She had been born in the house and as she stepped forward to greet them, Faith suddenly imagined a whole line of Patricia's ancestors making the same gestures and smiling the same warm but not gushing smile. And Patricia's grandchildren and probably great-grandchildren, too, would watch her and inherit the legacy of this graciousness. Her two children, Rob and Jenny, had. Cindy hadn't.

Faith's small apartment in New York had been the last word in stripped-down High Tech. The only color had been the flowers delivered by Madderlake each week. Yet she coveted every square inch of Patricia's house, from the patchwork quilts on the spool and four-poster beds to the china closets crammed with export porcelain, and set after set of Limoges wedding china.

They sat down in the living room and Faith stopped her usual envious inventory to listen.

Patricia started right in with plans for the funeral.

"We would have wanted things to be simple in any case, Tom, and the fact that it was murder makes that seem all the more important somehow," she said.

"Not that it's something to be ashamed of, my dear," Robert interjected.

"Oh, no," Patricia responded, "It's just that there will probably be a lot of newspaper reporters and people who don't even know us. So we thought a brief service now and a memorial service sometime in the spring."

Patricia looked very tired and drawn. So did Robert. Faith was used to seeing them hale and hearty. The Moores looked remarkably alike. Or perhaps, Faith mused, it was true that married people grew to look like each other. She darted a quick glance at Tom and felt reassured.

Both Robert and Patricia were tall, fair-haired Yankees with slightly equine faces and well-shaped feet and hands. Capable hands.

Patricia was an avid and knowledgeable gardener, president of the local garden club, The Evergreens. Robert was some kind of lawyer. Faith never heard him talk about his work. Only sailing. The Moores had a summer house on the coast of New Hampshire and Robert sailed every chance he could get. They were still tan from all this outdoor activity, but the tan seemed to have faded overnight, like one of the countless watercolor landscapes done by Patricia's forebears that hung on the walls, bleached from years of sun.

Even Patricia's normally crisp white round-collared blouse looked wilted. Faith always wondered where on earth Patricia found her clothes and had decided that she must have a stockpile of vintage Villager shirtwaists in Liberty cottons, John Meyer A-line wool skirts, matching sweaters, and blouses. Patricia also wore those Pappagallo pumps that look like bedroom slippers and she had on the discreet diamond and sapphire circle pin Robert had given her when they got married. Aside from her gold wedding band and diamond solitaire from Shreve's, it was the only jewelry Faith had ever seen her wear. And the diamond was usually in a dish by the sink, since Patricia's hands were usually in the soil.

"Did Cindy have a favorite poet or piece of music that would be appropriate to the service?" Tom was asking.

Faith thought for a moment that a look of irritation crossed Robert's face before he replied, "None of which we are aware, Tom. Why don't you choose something?"

"Maybe Wordsworth? 'A slumber did my spirit seal'? Or part of 'Tintern Abbey'?" Patricia offered.

Patricia had been an English major at Wellesley, Faith recalled.

Reaching back to her own British Poets 101, she thought "I travell'd among unknown men" would have been more appropriate, but she kept her mouth shut.

"Wordsworth has always been a family favorite,"

51

Patricia said and stopped abruptly. She started again before Tom could say anything, "And to be perfectly honest, if Cindy had a favorite, it would undoubtedly be inappropriate if not blasphemous."

Faith decided it was time for someone to do something about the situation. These people were simply too good to be allowed to suffer like this.

"Patricia, Cindy was not Tom's favorite youth group member and although I am appalled and angry at what has happened, she was not someone I found easy to like either."

The Moores breathed a collective sigh of relief.

"That's it exactly, Faith. Thank you. We have to make the service a decent one, but not ludicrous. Cindy hurt a great many people in this town. It was our fault, really, for allowing her to get so out of hand, but we can't be hypocrites. The last few years with her have been very difficult ones and enough people, which is to say all of Aleford, know, so any pretentious show of mourning would be a lie," Robert spoke bitterly.

"We *are* to blame," said Patricia, "but I don't know what we could have done differently. The person I feel sorriest for is Dave. He's lost his fiancée and the police suspect him of murder, which is, of course, absurd. Apparently Cindy and Dave had a fight Thursday night and the police believe her murder was a crime of passion." She gave a somewhat crooked smile.

Tom spoke. "We can't believe it was Dave either, and I'm hoping he'll get in touch with me." Faith noticed he didn't say "again." He was learning, or maybe already knew. "I wouldn't be surprised if he came to you, Patricia, you've always been so close."

"Yes, I keep looking out at the garden, half expecting to see him there."

Dave had started helping Patricia in the garden when he was a little boy and it had grown into a labor of love for the two of them.

The door opened and thirteen-year-old Jenny Moore walked into the room. She looked a good deal worse than her parents, genuinely distraught. Either that or, Faith quickly conjectured, like a person with something to hide.

"Jenny, why don't you show Mrs. Fairchild the garden while we finish up in here?" her mother asked.

"Sure," muttered Jenny, a terse monosyllable from this normally bouncy kid.

Definitely hiding something, Faith concluded.

They walked out into the late afternoon sunshine. The garden was filled with mums—not stiffly in pots nor those funny football pompoms, but cascades of white, lavender, and gold—all sizes and shapes. Here and there a rosebush was still in bloom. Patricia was famous for her roses. Some were very old; varieties mostly vanished from the seed catalogs, with names like "Old Blush" and "Rosa Mundi." They filled the air with a sweet fragrance that mingled with the bitter smell of the mums. Someone was burning leaves. Maybe autumn in Aleford wasn't so bad.

Faith sat down on a bench under one of the rose trellises and stretched her legs out to the sun. Jenny sat next to her. Clearly the girl was miserable. Her eyes were filled with tears. Could Cindy and Jenny have been close? Somehow Faith automatically assumed that anyone she liked couldn't like Cindy, but Jenny was virtually her sister and she *had* lived with her all these years.

"Jenny, is there anything you want to talk about with

me? Anything you want to ask? I know this has been a terrible shock for you."

Faith put her arm around Jenny's shoulders and Jenny began to sob.

"It's Mom and Dad! This is so awful for them and it's just like Cindy to do it. She caused them so much trouble when she was alive and now she's dead and it's worse than ever! The phone rings all the time and all the newspapers have stories about us. It's even on TV! Robby called from college and some reporter had gotten into his dorm." She stopped a moment and grinned through her tears.

"His buddies helped him throw the guy out the window." She gave Faith a reassuring look. "Not a very high window."

So much for grief, Faith thought.

"Jenny, I know that at the moment things must be terrible for you and your parents, but they will calm down soon. The police will find the murderer and the public will find something else to talk about. You'll see."

Here was a chance to practice. Was this what a minister's wife would say? What would her mother say? Actually she found it impossible to imagine her mother in this situation. The idea of one of her father's parishioners getting murdered was just too crazy.

The idea of one of Tom's was as bizarre, but here they were.

Jenny had stopped crying and, impelled by her promise to Dave and by native curiosity, Faith started to probe.

"Jenny, this may sound strange, but do you think Cindy was seeing anyone else besides Dave?"

Faith was sure there was another man involved in this business somewhere. She was banking on sex. Tom thought it was money. They had bet each other a dinner at a restaurant of their own choosing once the mystery was solved. Faith had something like Le Cirque in mind and Tom, she was sure, would opt for Durgin Park. Remembering the giant slabs of beef hanging over thick china plates unceremoniously banged down on the table by a waitress whose surliness was supposed to be some kind of treasured Bostonian tradition, Faith felt she had to win. For Dave, for herself, and for *la qualité de vie.*

"One! Try twelve or thirteen," snorted Jenny. "Cindy thought she was Scarlett O'Hara or something."

The movie had been on TV recently. Faith nodded sagely.

"But was there someone particular?" she asked.

Jenny looked evasive and didn't answer right away.

"I think there might have been. But she didn't talk to me about that stuff much," she said finally.

I'll bet she didn't, Faith thought, conjuring up a distasteful image of Cindy boasting to little Jenny about her sexual conquests. But why was the girl lying?

"You know it's not all Cindys and Scarlett O'Haras,' Faith said.

"Oh, you mean sex, Mrs. Fairchild? I know that. Look at Mom and Dad," replied Jenny.

Faith was surprised. The Moores had always suggested cozy comfort rather than Alex Comfort, but then one never knew. In any case, Jenny was okay and apparently not soured on men, women, and relationships for life despite her close association with Cindy.

"So how did she look anyway ?"Jenny asked after a moment.

"You mean Cindy?"

"Yes. That is, if you don't mind talking about it."

Absolutely no need to worry about Jenny, Faith thought again, and proceeded to give her what she hoped was a satisfactory description of the scene in the belfry. Although Jenny did seem a bit disappointed that there hadn't been more blood.

As they strolled back toward the house, Jenny looked up with a bright face. "They're going to bury her in her wedding gown, just like in the books, only Cindy didn't go mad with unspeakable horror on her wedding night."

What kind of books was this child reading? Then Faith remembered the rows of turn-of-the-century ladies' novels that lined the Moores' bookshelves mixed in with first editions of T. S. Eliot and Henry James.

"You don't think that it's too weird, do you?" Jenny wanted to know. " The wedding dress?"

Faith did think it was a little weird. She supposed they had to bury her in something, but a Priscilla of Boston wedding gown did not seem much like a winding sheet, which was what Faith vaguely imagined most people were buried in.

"I haven't decided whether I want to be buried or cremated," continued Jenny, "How about you?"

Faith reached for Jenny's hand. She was reassured. Jenny was definitely fine. Whatever it was that Faith sensed was bothering her had not dulled her normal adolescent ghoulishness.

"Neither, dear," she answered her, "I plan to float gently into the sky at the moment of dissolution only to return to earth as an unforgetable meteor shower." Faith had read this in a novel recently and it sounded good to her.

Jenny giggled. "Does Reverend Fairchild know about this?"

"Absolutely," assured Faith, "But he doesn't like to talk about it, so don't mention it, please."

The girl giggled some more and they went into the house.

Jenny seemed okay, but Faith, returning to the living room, wasn't so sure about her parents. Maybe they were just tired. It was a strain, after all, and, as Jenny had pointed out, they were constantly being bombarded by the media, the police, and everybody else in Aleford with good and bad intentions.

But would that totally account for the deep circles under Patricia's eyes and the new furrows on Robert's forehead? Robert Moore had been brutally honest about his feelings for Cindy. But was there something he wasn't saying? Faith felt more puzzled than ever. Even if, by some stretch of the imagination unimaginable, the Moores had killed Cindy, why now? They were getting rid of her in December. Somehow Faith didn't see Cindy running home for marital advice or tips on how to make good pie crust. Once she was married, she would have been gone.

The arrangements for the funeral service were complete and the Fairchilds got ready to leave. Faith stood in the large hall looking at some ship paintings on the walls while Tom went with Robert to find their coats.

"Grandfather Martin's ships," Patricia said affectionately, "I've always loved these paintings. They were the last ships under sail that the family had. When we were children, we always called them the Nina, the Pinta, and the Santa Maria, much to my grandmother's annoyance. I'm afraid we have always been a bit too caught up in the past in this family—we were all raised with a heavy dose of quite sinful pride."

"I don't think it's a sin to be proud of the accomplishments and personalities of another generation. We are their inheritors, after all—and the fruit on my own family tree makes quite an assortment," Faith commented. She studied the ships again. "We had some seafarers, too, and I wish I had paintings of their vessels. These really are treasures."

"Oh, Faith, as you can see, this is an acquisitive family. Not much ever goes out of here." Patricia was smiling at her genetic foibles. A shadow crossed her face. "I had planned to give Cindy some family things as a wedding present. Now they won't be leaving."

And a good thing, too, thought Faith.

The next morning Faith sat in church with anticipation.

Tom had been up late the night before writing his sermon, having abandoned the one he had worked on all week. She liked Tom's sermons, and not just because he was her husband. They were a mixture of good sense, eloquence, devotion, and almost never were boring.

She looked about. Sunday had dawned fair and bright, but no one seemed to have skipped church to rake leaves or go for a drive to see the foliage. The sanctuary was full.

Tom had selected "A Mighty Fortress Is Our God" for the opening hymn, and the congregation did it full justice, then worked its way through the service to the responsive reading of Psalm 22. Faith began to have some idea of where Tom was heading when she heard him intone, "The Lord hear thee in the day of trouble; the name of the

58

God of Jacob defend thee"; and the congregation's response, "Some trust in chariots, and some in horses: but we will remember the name of the Lord our God."

It was a time of trouble. The worshipers had entered the church in relative silence, without the usual cheerful Sunday buzz of greetings. There had been a few uneasy glances toward the Moores as well as at other fellow parishioners. It was clear that nobody knew what to do.

The Old Testament lesson was from Job, chapter 24. Faith had predicted that book, and now she congratulated herself on how well she knew her husband.

The New Testament lesson was Matthew 12. "A house divided against itself shall not stand." Tom spoke the words slowly, with precision, and a note of warning in his voice.

At last it was the sermon. He climbed the stairs to the pulpit, which was raised above the congregation. All eyes were drawn upward. He didn't waste any time.

"Murder is an abomination against the Lord.

"The murder of one is a murder of all. We have lost a young person of this parish, slain before her maturity and we are slain with her. The task we face now is to comfort the grieving and look to this house. Not with suspicion, but with strength. Not with the gossip that inevitably accompanies such a tragedy and has been such an affliction for her family, but with words of care and concern.

"It is a time that bewilders us. Which, like Job, tests our faith and poses fundamental questions.

"But like Job we must arrive at the same answer. He cries out, 'And if it be not so now, who will make me a liar, and make my speech nothing worth?'

"Job knew the answer. We know the answer. It is here with us in this place and in all the other places we inhabit. It is God who makes Job a liar and liars of all of us who curse him for the random events of this earthly life.

"Fear walks among us. I can feel it coming from you today, but our fears must take us closer to God, not away. We must walk with our fears toward God the fortress and make our house endure in his love and justice.

"Now let us pray. For strength in God and each other and for Cynthia Shepherd."

Faith bowed her head. The sermon had been longer, but these were the phrases she turned over in her mind as she prayed. The silence before the service had not been as quiet as she thought. It was full of apprehension and unspoken fears. Tom had tried to dispel it, and when they stood up and shook hands with their neighbors at the close of the service, she knew he had been successful. Patricia and Robert went up to him and he embraced them warmly.

They walked home after retrieving Benjamin from the volunteers who ran the child care during the service. Faith took Tom's hand, "It couldn't have been easy, Tom. But somehow you managed to do it. All the awful things I've been thinking about Cindy dropped away and I felt terribly, terribly sad. She should be very grateful to you."

"Thank you. I think the congregation is going to be fine, but it's a tough time."

As they went through the back door into the kitchen, the phone rang.

"Probably more plaudits, darling. Why don't you get it?" Faith said, "I'll start lunch."

Tom picked up the phone, listened, and exclaimed, "

Oh, no! Of course, I'll be right there. Have you called the police?" He listened again briefly, said good-bye and hung up. Faith was by his side in a flash.

"What's happened?"

Tom looked grim. "Apparently while we were all in church taking in that uplifting sermon of mine, someone broke into the Moores' house and ransacked Cindy's bedroom. Patricia is very upset and Robert asked me to come."

Faith grabbed her coat. "I'm coming too!"

"I thought you might say that."

FOUR

THEY WERE AT THE MOORES' IN RECORD TIME. THEY managed to disengage the seat belt from Benjamin's infant seat without waking him. Unpredictable as he was in almost everything, he could always be counted on to fall into a deep sleep at one in the afternoon. Faith thought it was Nature's way of evening up the score.

Tom carried the baby bucket with Benjamin up the front stairs, where they were momentarily halted by Patrolman Warren. It was no surprise. There must have been five or six police cars in the drive. Faith put her finger to her lips and pointed to Ben. Whether it was the sleeping baby or the memory of his earlier mistakes in judgment, Dale hurriedly opened the door and ushered them in. Patricia was waiting in the hall.

"Put Ben in the study, Faith, there's too much commotion upstairs. We'll be in the living room," she said softly.

61

Faith walked into the living room just as Robert was finishing a sentence, ". . . never been broken into in its entire history. Such a violation!"

"Do you have any idea what they were looking for? Did Cindy keep cash or valuables around?" Tom asked.

"She had some good jewelry that belonged to her mother, but that's at the bank. I suppose there were some other things of value, but nothing much, and I doubt she had any money. She seemed to think credit cards had replaced currency," Robert answered.

"The police brought us her jewelry box a short while ago to see if anything was missing. It had been dumped out, but her pearls and a watch she wore when she dressed up were still there." Patricia stopped, then spoke again in an anguished tone. "Just think of all the other valuable things in the house, the silver, the rugs, the paintings . . ." Patricia's face tightened as she catalogued her beloved possessions. "Thank goodness we surprised them and they didn't get that far," she added.

"But why start in Cindy's room?" Faith asked.

"Exactly," concurred Robert, "We have to asume it's tied in with the murder, that there was something she had that would incriminate the murderer."

Faith wondered how she could get upstairs and take a look at Cindy's room. The police were obviously going over it with a fine-tooth comb for fingerpints, stray hairs, distinctive buttons, calling cards. She was pretty sure from the way the chandelier shook that Dunne was up there.

It was going to have to be the old bathroom trick. She stood up and excused herself demurely.

"Why don't you use the one upstairs, Faith?" Patricia never missed much.

The stairs and upper hall were carpeted with an oriental runner, so Faith was able to linger undetected for a moment outside Cindy's bedroom door. "Ransack" had been a mild description. Detective Dunne, his back to her, stood in the center of a room that looked as if the Vikings had joined Attila the Hun to pay a call on the Sabine women. All the drawers were pulled out, the bed torn apart and the pillows slashed. Enough shoes for an Imelda were flung about the room, and pictures had been ripped from their frames. Faith was fascinated. From what she could see, it seemed Cindy had an entire mirrored wall of closets. She glanced at the ceiling. No. Robert and Patricia must have drawn the line somewhere.

She was just about to take a step nearer when John Dunne glanced in one of the mirrors and their eyes met in mutual annoyance. He turned abruptly, strode to the door in one step, and shut it.

Faith continued down the hall to the bathroom. She might as well use it as long as she was there; it would give her time to think. It was possible that the Moores had interrupted the intruder before he or she had had a chance to find anything. This was certainly the thought behind Dunne's thorough search. Faith doubted she would be asked to join the team, so she had to think of something else. Or someplace else?

She went back downstairs and stopped in the study to check Benjamin. He was sound asleep and looked cherubic. These were moments to treasure and recall when you were wiping baby cereal off your clothing.

Jenny was outside the door. She looked a little lost and more than a little angry.

Faith said sympathetically, "I know. Cindy again. It is

dreadful and shouldn't be happening."

"She would have been very ticked off at the mess they made of her room, though," Jenny said with some satisfaction.

Faith looked at Jenny and the tiny thought that had sprouted upstairs burst into bloom.

"Jenny, maybe what they're looking for was never in Cindy's room. This house must have dozens of hiding places. If they bothered to rip open picture frames, it must have been small. Can you think of any place she might have hidden something that size?"

"Well, the maple secretary in the study has two secret drawers and so does a little lap desk that they used to take to sea long ago, but I doubt she would use these because we all knew about them. And besides Mom is always cleaning and she might find it."

Jenny paused. "If I were going to hide something, I think I'd put it in the playhouse, because no grown-ups ever go there and there are no little kids anymore."

"Where is the playhouse?"

"Down near the river. Do you want to go look?"

I thought you'd never ask, Faith thought as she replied, "That sounds like a good idea."

She ducked her head into the living room to tell Tom she was taking a walk with Jenny. He was discussing the funeral again with Patricia and Robert and she knew she wouldn't be missed.

It was beautiful outside and warm. They rustled along in the leaves down the long slope to the river. Nestled under the trees was a white playhouse, the kind every child dreams of having—a small porch in front and two child-sized rooms. There wasn't much in it—two chairs, a table, and a wooden play stove in one room; some doll beds and a brightly painted chest of drawers full of dress-up clothes in the other.

The house was big enough for Faith to stand up in. She and Jenny systematically went through everything. Nothing. Faith reached up to feel on top of the wide, exposed ceiling beams.

Just over the door she found it. A tin box. She grabbed it and it came tumbling down with a crash. It was an old Louis Sherry candy box that had probably once held someone's treasured mementos. Cindy's collection spilled onto the floor. Jenny rushed to her side.

"What is it? Do you think that's what they wanted?"

Faith looked down at a bunch of photographs, a couple of joints, some cash, a matchbook or two, and some cocktail napkins. There was also a roll of film.

"Yes, Jenny, I think we can safely say this is what everyone is looking for. Could you run back to the house and have your parents tell the police what we've found? I'll stay here. Tell them we haven't touched a thing."

Jenny sped up the hill.

But looking is not touching. Faith crouched down as close as she could get to the contents without disturbing anything. She was the one who had found it, after all. And John Dunne didn't seem the type to exchange boyish confidences.

Obviously it was the pictures. And they were hot enough to have melted the box. Cindy was evidently into porn—with herself as the star. The photos Faith could see completely featured Cindy in bed with different partners. It looked like Cindy had set the timer on the camera and raced back into position, unless there had been a third

65

party to the fun. In some shots, the man was asleep, or exhausted. In others, the man was awake. Faith didn't recognize them. Some of the shots were close-ups. Unusual to collect snapshots of male organs you have known, but everyone has to have a hobby of some sort, Faith supposed. She didn't recognize any of those either.

Another photo was partially covered, but she could make out a city sidewalk, a convenience store, and part of another building. What was it doing mixed in with Cindy's personal *Playgirl* gallery?

The backs of some of the photographs had initials and dates. One had the name of the Crowne Plaza—Holiday Inn's answer to the Ritz Carlton—printed below the date. An enchanted evening?

Then there was the money. Quite a bit of money if all the bills were Ben Franklins, as the top ones were. Was Cindy blackmailing someone? If she had been, why? Cindy had a lot of money of her own, and would have more. She probably demanded and got a generous allowance. Why would she have blackmailed people? Faith knew you were never supposed to be too rich or too thin, but it still didn't match her image of Cindy.

Then there were the joints, two small ones, the matches, and the napkins. The matchbook she could see was from a motel in Ogunquit. It didn't look like the sort of place the Moores would have stopped for a family vacation. It did look like Cindy's speed—the right cable channels and one of those beds that ate quarters. The other matchbooks and more photographs were under the napkins.

Faith was trying to decipher the letters and numbers written on a napkin when Dunne arrived. She stood up quickly. He was leaning over the porch and peering in the door. There wasn't a ghost of a chance that he could get in the tiny building.

"The next time you have a hunch, would you be so kind as to tell us, Mrs. Fairchild? This isn't one of your Upper East Side scavenger hunts," Dunne said in what Faith knew was a controlled voice. He obviously wanted to scream at her.

"West Side," she said, pushing it. She knew she should have told them, but how was she going to help Dave at all if she didn't find things out on her own?

"Did you touch anything?"

"Only when I reached for the box. It's open because it fell."

Dunne looked at her skeptically. She inched past him and started back to the house. He called after her, "Mrs. Fairchild."

"Yes?"

"Your baby's crying."

She didn't bother to thank him.

Tom was in the kitchen pacing up and down with Benjamin.

"I think he's hungry, Faith. But the Moores want to know what's going on, so I'll keep him out here while you tell them, then we'll go."

"Oh, Tom, this isn't going to be easy. How do you tell two people who've just had their home broken into that their recently murdered ward may have been, from the look of it, a blackmailer?"

Tom stopped, shook his head, and said, "I know this is happening, Faith, but tell me it's not."

"The Pandora's box Jenny and I found was full of

naughty pictures of Cindy and her conquests and a large amount of cash. Undoubtedly she kept the photos for her own entertainment, but it's possible that several of her beaux might not have wanted them for the family Christmas card. Some of the pictures seem to have been taken while her partner was asleep and unknowing."

Tom looked grim. "What else did you see?"

"Nothing else that made any sense to me, but I'll bet everything in there was something that could threaten somebody."

Faith told the Moores as gently as she could and was a bit startled at their reaction. They seemed relieved that the break-in had a specific object in mind, an object that was now found. It wasn't an attack on the house, or on them—just on Cindy.

Tom and Faith packed Benjamin back in his car seat and left, passing Eleanor Whipple, some sort of ultra-removed cousin of Patricia's, on the drive. She was carrying a pie and a shopping bag filled with what looked like all the produce she had put up the summer before. She continued swiftly up the walk with that purposeful Yankee stride that age seems not to diminish, but intensify. Oswald Pearson, editor of the town paper, notebook in hand and hot on the trail of another sensational story for *The Aleford Clarion,* was a few paces behind her. Obviously the word had gotten out.

On the way home in the car, Faith told Tom about the Moores' reaction to her news.

"Faith, at this point, I don't think anything Cindy did would surprise them. They're numb. Maybe when it's all over it will hit them, but right now I imagine they simply want to get the funeral over with, have the police find the killer, and go back to their lives."

Which was just about what Patricia said the next day at the monthly meeting of the Ladies' Alliance, now the Women's Alliance—but nobody ever remembered to call it anything but the Alliance.

When Faith arrived in Aleford as a new bride, she had no idea what to expect of the group, which she knew it was one of her duties to join.

"Only if you want to, Faith," said Tom. "Really, this is my job, not yours. What you do is totally up to you."

So sweet and so naive, thought Faith.

To her amazement, she enjoyed the meetings in the church social hall and discovered the group did an enormous amount of good in a characteristically unobtrusive manner. Originally founded as a sewing circle to make feather-stitched layettes for orphans, the women now raised money for some of the church's projects, but mainly for The Pine Street Inn in Boston, a shelter for the homeless; and a local drug and alcohol abuse program. Additionally most of the women worked as volunteers at one or the other place. The Alliance Christmas Bazaar was a blockbuster moneymaker, with people arriving from all over the Greater Boston area to snap up Mrs. Lewis's pinecone wreaths or an Attic Treasure from the table of the same name. Faith couldn't believe the amount of money they made each year, but seeing how industriously they stitched away at each meeting, it was perhaps inevitable. Idle hands and all that. She had had to start knitting again, something she loathed, but it was the only handwork she knew how to do other than the running stitch. She did not burden last year's fair with her lumpy muffler, but gave it to Tom for Christmas instead. The ladies were more than pleased to get jars of her *fraises des bois confiture* with cassis and dozens of melt-in-your-mouth hazelnut cookies, most of which never made it past the church parking lot.

Faith wasn't surprised to see Patricia. She was beginning to learn a lot about Aleford and one of the things she had learned was not to be surprised. Whatever might be going on at home—and in this case there was plenty—one still had one's obligations.

They listened to the minutes of the last meeting and had a formal discussion of bazaar plans before they turned to the real business, which was drinking coffee, sewing, and talking.

Patricia had turned to them and with her mouth set in a firm line told them, "I know what you're all thinking about, so let me just say Robert and I are fine. It's been a terrific shock, of course," her voice faltered a bit, then rallied, "and you've all been wonderful, sending food and calling. You know how much we have appreciated it. The funeral is tomorrow and after that we are going to try to get back to normal."

Eleanor Whipple gave Patricia's shoulder a reassuring little pat. So demonstrative.

"We'll all be there, Patricia, and you only have to ask if you need anything."

"Thank you, Cousin Eleanor. I know that. One realizes how much one depends on friends and family at these times."

They sewed for a while in companionable silence. There was a sense that Patricia hadn't quite finished and it was correct.

70

She blushed a little, looked around the group, and said, "When the funeral home asked for a dress, I sent over her wedding dress."

Did Faith imagine that an eyebrow or two went up? Maybe she wasn't the only one who thought it a bit odd.

"It was because the morning we bought it was one of the last times I remember having a happy day with Cindy."

Or one of the only times, was the thought in not a few heads.

Patricia spoke wistfully. "She was so excited and the dress was perfect, white velvet with tiny seed pearls. She looked like a Renaissance princess. The saleswomen were all oohing and aahing over her. Afterward we had lunch at the Copley to celebrate. I began to think marriage might change things."

The women listened as they stitched away. Over the years they had quietly heard so many revelations—breast cancer now thankfully in remission for one of them; problems with children; once even the possibility of an unfaithful spouse; though as a rule husbands, where they existed, were seldom mentioned. They seemed oddly out of place at an Alliance meeting. As if one of them had suddenly taken it into his head to join them and crochet.

Patricia sighed. "But of course it didn't. She was just the same at dinner that evening, making sly digs at Robert and leaving in the middle of the meal."

And probably without being excused, thought Faith, a sin in her own family not unrelated to ax murder, certainly considered in as bad taste.

"She seemed especially on edge lately," said Patricia, "I keep wondering if something was wrong that we didn't know about."

There wasn't much to say to that, or rather there was a lot to say that no one quite had the heart to bring up.

The group adjourned at five o'clock as usual and rushed off to the Shop and Save to pick up something for supper. Faith's beef carbonnade was all made, waiting to be reheated with some of her fresh egg noodles. She strolled leisurely along Church Street with her next door neighbor, Pix Miller, toward their respective houses. Pix always had pizza on Alliance nights. She had somehow managed to convince her family it was a special treat.

"Poor Patricia," Pix said to Faith, "As if Cindy wasn't enough of a pain in the neck when she was alive. Now they'll lose their deposit with the caterers and everything." Pix was eminently practical.

Faith was thinking of what Patricia had said about Cindy's digs at Robert and wasn't really listening. "What? Oh, the deposit. I can't imagine a caterer keeping it under these circumstances. I certainly wouldn't."

Pix laughed and said, "Well, with your food you wouldn't have to. These guys have to get whatever they can before you go back into business."

It was true that Faith had had a slightly nervous exploratory call from one of the local caterers about her future plans. She had been suitably evasive and quite flattered. New gun in town, or rather new whisk.

"It wouldn't have occurred to me," Pix said, "except I was with Patricia in Talbots the other day and she decided not to get a new coat. Something about it never hurt to watch one's pennies."

Which meant Robert could be making a killing—or be on skid row, in typical local parlance. New Englanders

72

seemed to watch their pennies most when the pennies were either pouring in or pouring out. Still it gave one pause. Which was it for the Moores?

She said good-bye to Pix and went into the house. Tom was in his study presumably working on the eulogy for Cindy. When Faith came in after tapping lightly on the door, he was staring at the wall.

This was one of the more difficult tasks he had faced so far in his ministry, and the full wastepaper basket by his side attested to the amount of luck he was having getting it done. Benjamin was lying in his playpen by the small bay window staring at a mobile with a slightly puzzled expression, obviously wondering what fish were doing flying around in the air instead of under water where they belonged.

"Tom," said Faith, "What do you know about Robert and Cindy's relationship?"

"Robert, you mean Robert Moore?"

"Yes. Patricia remarked that she used to make 'sly digs' at him at the dinner table."

"Faith, I imagine Cindy made 'sly digs' at anyone unfortunate enough to share a meal with her at one time or another. I never saw him, or Patricia either, treat her in anything but a reasonable way, which makes them both candidates for any kind of sainthood you could mention. What are you getting at? Still Sherlocking ?"

"I admit it's farfetched, but she could be so sarcastic and after years and years of it, you might explode."

"Yes, but on Belfry Hill—with a rose and a knife? Sorry, Faith. Try something else."

"All right. Have you heard anything about Robert being in financial difficulties? Pix says Patricia didn't buy a coat

73

last month because she was watching her pennies."

"Which probably meant that Patricia thought she had a perfectly good coat at home and didn't need a new one."

"Yes, probably one from college. One of those duffel coats."

Tom looked hurt. He had been very fond of his duffel coat in college and couldn't understand why Faith had been so firm against another one as a winter coat. "I have a rule, Tom, that my clothing should never weigh more than I do and I think you should adopt it," she had said.

Faith reluctantly abandoned her line of inquiry, "Okay, you're probably right. I may be grasping at straws—or toggles, as it were. Anyway the Alliance is going with the 'deranged tramp now someplace far away' theory." This was the going theory in town and a lot of people thought MacIsaac should buy it or pretend to and not waste his time and valuable town money on the case.

Tom looked at her in shared disbelief. They laughed and went over to Benjamin.

As he bent into the playpen to pick up his son, Tom said, "What did they say about Dave?" He never underestimated the Alliance as the prime news-gathering agency in town.

"He's still missing. His mother was at the meeting, so of course no one said anything, but Pix and I talked on the way home. She pointed out that Eva looked pretty terrible, but not out of her mind, so she must somehow know he's safe. Which makes sense."

"Yes, I'm sure he's in the area. I can't believe he would run away from all this."

"I wonder if he knew anything about Cindy's photographic interests? Maybe the two of them were

74

involved in some sort of blackmail scheme with Cindy as bait, but that doesn't go along with my impressions of Dave."

"Nor mine, but this whole town is beginning to resemble one of those tanks at the aquarium—a few sleepy frogs sitting on rocks at the top and underneath, tangled seaweed and fish frantically darting around. I could almost believe anything."

"I like the fish image. Maybe you could work it into a sermon."

They moved out of the study toward the kitchen. Tom turned to Faith, "I'm convinced the key to the whole thing is one of those pictures. You're sure you didn't recognize anyone ?"

"It was an odd context, but I'm sure." Faith had been mentally undressing Aleford's male population ever since her discovery.

"It's very puzzling. And what about the joints in the box? Although it wasn't enough to suggest an opium den. And then there's the money—it might not have been blackmail; she could have been selling pot."

Faith sighed. "I wish we'd hear from Dave, then maybe we could get somewhere."

But Dave didn't call and the next morning was the funeral.

Faith stood in the cemetery, shivering in the bright sunshine. Tuesday was as glorious a day for Cindy's funeral as Friday had been for her death. Yet Faith was cold despite the warmth of her Lauren suit. The shrill orange and red of the sugar maples and the black clothes of the mourners reminded her of Halloween. All Hallow's

Eve. The night when the dead rise from their graves.

There is nothing quite so silent as a burial.

All the birds must have already gone south, Faith thought.

Then Tom's solemn, measured voice cut through the air.

He was reading the Wordsworth and it was beautiful; Patricia had been right:

A slumber did my spirit seal;
And I had no human fears:
She seemed a thing that could not feel
The touch of earthly years.

Poor Cindy, thought Faith. So young. Death must have been the last thing on her mind. She was completely alive, grabbing at life with amoral abandon. She deserved something for the way she lived, but was it death ?

They were lowering the casket now. Faith pictured Cindy still beautiful, lying in its satin interior in her wedding gown. Somewhere her would-be groom, Dave Svenson, was at large. It was all quite impossibly morbid and melodramatic. Faith gave her arm a surreptitious pinch to remind herself she wasn't in some Victorian time warp.

Even the cemetery contributed to the illusion. It was an old one, of course. People were always coming to make rubbings of the headstones for notions of interior decoration, which Faith had never understood. Virtually every home in Aleford had one or two of the most lugubrious examples framed in the hallway—all those skulls with the wings of angels and drooping willows. The oldest section of the cemetery, by the river, blended well with the motifs of the headstones. Actual drooping willows grew so thick they blotted out the sky above. The lawn was mostly moss. In the summer the dark shade and damp, warm ground below gave it the lush sultry feeling of a bayou, quite alien to its Puritan roots. Despite the obvious romanticism, Faith preferred the newer section.

Here the trees had not yet reached the stage where they blocked the light, and the grass was green, very green. There were pretty white benches and plantings kept up by the Evergreens. Last year, shortly before Benjamin was born, she often used to stroll here, too unsteady for more ambitious walks. It was peaceful and suited her slightly philosophical musings on beginnings and endings. Unlike its murky neighbor, it was a cemetery in which one could believe life would go on forever. Today, at the end of Cindy's life, those spring thoughts seemed a long time ago.

Faith looked around at the people gathered at Cindy's grave: the Moores; youth group members, looking scared and awe-stricken; parishioners; friends of the Moores; just about everybody else in Aleford not in one of the other categories; and a few obvious reporters. Only the putative chief mourner was absent.

In fact he wasn't. As Tom moved onto Wordsworth's second stanza, Dave Svenson was gazing down on the assembled group through binoculars from a small hill north of the cemetery. Unlike Faith, he was not thinking about what Cindy was wearing. In fact, he found it hard to believe it was Cindy, but he knew that the lowering of the casket and those clods of earth that fell upon it were once and for all signaling an end to some part of his life—for better or worse.

Since leaving the Fairchilds on Saturday morning, he had been staying with various friends. He managed to call his parents, but did not tell them where he was so they wouldn't have to tell any lies to the police. His mother had cried, but she didn't advise him to turn himself in. He knew he had made the right choice.

All his friends were trying to piece together what they knew and what they heard that the police knew, but so far it was a total mystery. No one, least of all Dave, could figure out why Cindy had been killed. And especially why she had been killed in such a strange way. The Alliance might have been buying the tramp theory—or saying so—but none of Dave's friends were.

He had spent most of his time with Steve, who lived on the outskirts of town. Steve's parents had bought a farm in Aleford during the sixties, intending to live off the land. Now in the eighties, they found themselves making a small fortune selling *chèvre* and wild mushrooms to New York and Boston specialty stores. Dave had been living in their barn and eating whatever Steve could sneak out to him. He was heartily sick of goat cheese and hoped he would never have to eat it again. It was fine for his Swedish relatives, but he frankly preferred Velveeta (a fact that, had it come out at the time, might have taken the edge off Faith's partisanship).

So Dave stood under the gaily colored tent of leaves that in another time and setting might have been his bridal canopy.

He focused his binoculars on individual faces: his parents, dour and Ibsenesque; the Moores harder to read, a mixture of confusion and something that might have been sadness. Faith looked as if she was thinking of something else and Reverend Fairchild just perfect, serious, but not fake either.

Dave was so intent on the scene before him that he did not hear the branches snapping behind him. He was leaning against a tree trying to figure out what exactly he was feeling besides relief and fear when the biggest hand he had ever seen in his life came down hard on his shoulder. He froze.

"Dave Svenson?" the hand's voice asked quietly.

"Yes," said Dave, figuring it was pointless to argue or run.

"My name is Detective Lieutenant John Dunne. I've been looking for you."

Dunne was happy. He was seldom disappointed. They just couldn't stay away. You could count on it. They always turned up for the funeral.

Down in the cemetery, the group had dispersed. Many of the mourners, or more accurately, attendees, had returned to the Moores' house for the traditional funeral baked meats—in this case, thimbles of dry sherry and tea sandwiches. Faith eyed the sandwiches suspiciously. Anchovy paste on crustless triangles of white bread and maybe some egg salad spread a tenth of a millimeter thick. Still, people were managing to put away quite a lot of them. What would they do with real food? Faith asked herself. If ever a demand existed, it was here.

She took some sherry in a fragile glass and looked at it appreciatively. Sandwich glass, the exquisite blown-three-mold variety. Just what she would have expected at the Moores. It was lovely not to be disappointed. In a way, the sandwiches matched the setting and occasion, too, but there was such a thing as going too far. She walked over to the window seat, covered with chintz roses, and sat down to think a few wistful thoughts.

It was still a beautiful day and people were strolling in the garden. It was not really a mournful occasion, but there was an undercurrent of tension, not lessened by Charley MacIsaac's presence at the funeral and now back at the house. He joined Faith, balancing a tiny Spode plate heaped with sandwiches and something that was not dry sherry in a tumbler. Faith smiled up at him.

"Hi, Charley, where's your big friend?"

"He does give you a start at first, I'll say that," Charley replied, "but I don't know what he's up to today. Said he was coming to the funeral."

"Maybe he's busy tracking down a hot lead," Faith said. "In any case, what's the talk down at the station? Anything new?"

"Now, Faith, you know I can't discuss it with you."

"Charley! Is that fair? After all, if I hadn't found her, you wouldn't even have a case," Faith argued with perfect illogic, which nevertheless seemed to convince MacIsaac.

"Well, you know we're looking for a certain person to question and after that maybe we'll have something to say."

"Oh, that's as ridiculous as the tramp theory! You've known Dave all his life. You can't honestly believe he would kill anybody!"

Charley looked Faith straight in the eye and drained his tumbler. "Faith, anybody can be a killer given the right place and the right time. Even you would kill to protect that baby of yours, right? Or Tom?"

"Yes, of course, but it's not the same!"

"It's all the same in the end. And I'm not saying Dave did kill Cindy. We just want to know where he was and where he's been."

Faith had to be satisfied with that and, disgruntled, left MacIsaac. Of course he was keeping something from her. How was she ever going to help clear Dave if she couldn't find out what was going on? She felt it was rather mean of Charley not to share what he knew. It wasn't as if she would snitch to Detective Dunne.

She looked around the room for Tom. How long did they have to stay anyway? She had had enough of the mystery for one day, and the sherry on an empty stomach—no, she would not eat fish paste sandwiches—was making her slightly queasy. Or maybe it was MacIsaac.

Oswald Pearson was busily jotting down notes and Faith wondered what he could be writing. Descriptions of what everyone was wearing? She noted today he didn't seem the dandy he usually was. Oswald was a round little man in his early forties who had compensated for an early loss of hair by growing a precise Van Dyck beard. The few hairs left on his head were carefully drawn across his scalp and had a tendency to rise together in a solid phalanx whenever a breeze drifted by. Today his pink and white complexion looked gray and white. Faith couldn't imagine that he was upset at Cindy's death, especially since the headlines it was producing were increasing his circulation beyond the town limits. Maybe he was coming down with the flu. Where was Tom? When she was forced to medical speculation about the inhabitants of Aleford, she knew she had reached boredom's rock bottom.

Just then Robert Moore came into the living room with Charley MacIsaac and said something to the Svensons. They all went out into the hall and Faith saw Erik Svenson reach for the phone. Eva Svenson clutched his arm. As if a message had been delivered, those who had been outside in the garden came in and the talking stopped.

MacIsaac left the hall, went out to his car, switched on the radio, its blare jarring the silence unpleasantly. No one could make out what was being said. Abruptly, Charley drove off.

Erik put the phone down. With Eva quietly weeping at his side, he came into the room and told them, "Dave is at the police station. That was Detective Dunne. What he said exactly was they're holding him for questioning."

Eva stood absolutely still, with a bewildered expression on her face. Her eyes were locked on one of the portraits of Patricia's ancestors and she looked as though she wished her family had never heard of the Moores—or Aleford either. That they could all have stayed on the farm in Sweden and never come across the ocean at all.

Tom stepped forward. "I'll go down with you, Erik, let me get my coat." He came over to Faith, gave her a kiss, told her he would meet her at home, then left the room. The Svensons waited immobilized, until Tom came back with Robert. Robert took Eva's arm. "I've called another lawyer and he's meeting us there." That seemed to trigger something and Eva began to sob openly. They hurried out to the cars.

Those left looked stunned and then all began to talk at once. There was a lot of anger, but also a lot of fear. It had been hard to connect the day's events with the murder. It had been a funeral like every other funeral. There had been a sense of security in going through the established motions. Now they all remembered. It wasn't just any funeral. The dead woman was a murder victim. And someone, however unlikely, had been picked up by the police.

Faith went home soon after and sat in Tom's study nursing Benjamin in the big old rocking chair her Aunt Chat had given them when Benjamin was born.

"You'll use it more than any booties or sweater I could knit," she had said, and it had been true. It was comforting to sit and rock and Faith fell asleep with Benjamin nuzzled close to her breast. When she woke up, it was dark outside and cold. She felt stiff. Tom still wasn't home.

Faith realized she hadn't eaten anything all day and after she changed and bathed Benjamin, she went into the kitchen to make herself an omelet. She had just broken the first egg when Tom walked in. He looked horrible: His face was drawn and there were circles under his eyes that hadn't been there earlier. She broke some more eggs and got out the remnants of last night's *capelli d'angelo* and pesto to make a frittata.

"I can't believe they are putting this kid through all this. They've been at him all afternoon. About Cindy. About the damn photographs. Even the minuscule amount of marijuana they found."

Faith had never heard Tom sound so depressed and she quickly left the frittata to put her arms around him.

"This is too much, Tom. The funeral and now this."

She poured him a glass of Puligny-Montrachet.

"I'll admit I'm totally overwhelmed. They really think

he did it! MacIsaac and Atlas or whoever he is. Poetic mother, my foot, more likely straight from Barnum and Bailey's!"

"Now, Tom, he can't help his genes and he's really not so big, he simply looks it—big bones."

Tom eyed her in astonishment and began to laugh helplessly. "And what, pray, is the difference?"

"You know what I mean. He's not fat like those before-and-after ads where the man has his whole family standing in a pair of his old trousers. He's just big."

Faith was drying the lettuce, a thankless task. Tom walked over to the sink. His glass was empty and he was feeling slightly better. He planted several kisses on the back of her neck. She always smelled terrific—if it wasn't the kitchen, it was Guerlain's Mitsouko. He couldn't decide which excited him more. But the day's events crowded in again.

"Oh, Faith, I kept looking at the Svensons and thinking how we would feel if anything like this happened to Benjamin. I felt so useless. At least Robert had the sense to get on to his law firm and they sent their top criminal lawyer. Fortunately Dave had refused to say anything until his parents got there and by that time, the lawyer was on the way, so he didn't incriminate himself. The way he was going on to us—about being guilty in thought. That's all the police had to hear."

"What did he know about what was in the box?"

"Nothing. He was pretty amazed, in fact. It's not the behavior one expects of one's betrothed. He did say that they smoked occasionally. Cindy especially liked to smoke before they had sex. Dave didn't."

"The old impairment theory, no doubt," Faith

interjected.

"Whatever," Tom continued, "Anyway, Dave insists that dope never did much for him. My guess is a stiff shot of aquavit and a jump in the snow is more in the Svensons' line."

"The police really don't have much of a motive, aside from the fact that he hated her guts. But they do have the fact that he had a quarrel with her shortly before she was killed, a quarrel in the Burger King on Middlesex Turnpike that was witnessed by most of Aleford's teenagers. He also had an appointment to meet her in the place and at the time she was murdered," Tom spoke ruefully.

"What's going to happen now?" asked Faith.

"They'll either formally charge him with murder or keep him as long as they can for questioning. If they don't charge him, they'll have to let him go."

They went to bed early, falling wearily, easily, but not straight, to sleep.

The next morning, Benjamin woke them up at five o'clock, soaked through and hungry. Faith fed and changed him, made a bargain with God that if He would make Benj go back to sleep again, she would try very hard to be a better person, and tumbled gratefully back to bed, God having recognized a good thing when He saw it. Then the phone, not Benjamin, awakened them at seven o'clock. It was Eva Svenson. Dave had been released on personal recognizance the night before, but the police had arrived a few minutes ago to take him in for more questioning. His father had gone with him and they hoped Tom would join them.

Faith went into the bathroom, threw up, washed her

face, and decided enough was enough. She had to get busy.

She made a hasty breakfast for Tom while he was shaving and told him that while he was gone she was going to take Benjamin for a walk and pay a few calls. She toyed with the notion of going back up to the belfry to get some kind of inspiration from the scene of the crime, but she decided she wasn't desperate enough yet for what was admittedly a slim possibility. There was a chance that Cindy's ghost was moving around restlessly until avenged or whatever, but it was more likely to be haunting the parking lot at Friendly's, where her crowd hung out, than the belfry.

No, best to concentrate on the living and she figured she ought to start bravely at the source.

FIVE

MILLICENT REVERE MCKINLEY WAS ALWAYS HOME IN the mornings, seeing to her garden behind the white picket fence surrounding her small, eighteenth-century clapboard house or crocheting endless doilies in an easy chair poised strategically close to her front living room window. Both activities afforded her every opportunity to keep her eye on Aleford and as it was all absolutely necessary work, no one could ever accuse her of nosiness. Was it her fault that her house was smack in the middle of town? That was where her ancestors had built it, or rather moved it. It seemed as if houses were constantly on the move in those days, presumably as neighborhoods or pastures changed, but Millicent's would stay where it was now, thank you, if she had anything to say about it and she did.

Faith approached the gate with not a little trepidation. She knew she had never been number one on Millicent's list of favorites and now after the bell-ringing incident, Millicent regarded her as certifiable or worse. Nor was Millicent, who attended the Congregational church as did her fathers before her, a member of the parish, which might have given Faith an opening. No, the only thing to do was throw herself on the floor (uneven pine) and beg for mercy.

Millicent answered the door with an assumed look of surprise, not a particularly nice surprise.

"Why, Mrs. Fairchild! What brings you to my little cottage so bright and early?"

From her expression, one would have thought it was about six o'clock in the morning and Millicent straight from her four-poster. Actually it was after nine and Millicent had been perched in her window as usual. Faith gritted her teeth and leaned down to take Benjamin from his stroller. Wasn't the old witch even going to ask her in?

"I have been wanting to talk with you since last Friday, Mrs. McKinley, and tell you how deeply sorry I am about the whole incident." Faith assumed correctly that Millicent would know she was referring to the bell and not Cindy.

"I know how upset you have been over the bell ringing and I just wanted you to know that it will never happen again." Faith felt this was a pretty safe promise to make. Another body in Aleford's belfry was as likely as a Benedict Arnold Fan Club.

"Well, that's very sweet of you, dear, but it has nothing

to do with me particularly, you know. Well, perhaps a bit more than some since it was my great-great-great grandfather who cast the bell," Millicent thawed minutely. "Why don't you and your baby (she managed to make the words sound dubious, as though Benjamin might perhaps be someone else's) come in and have some coffee."

Cups in hand, they settled down in her living room with its multitude of candle stands, tilt-top tables, card tables, and whatnots, for each of which Millicent hastened to say, "Please dear, not on that surface, antique, you know."

Faith could have sworn not a few were Ethan Allen, but she balanced her cup on her knees nonetheless and ate some more crow. Finally she managed to steer Millicent onto the murder itself and most particularly onto Cindy. Faith had a hunch that the key to the whole murder lay in Cindy's noxious personality. After all, someone had disliked her enough to kill her. If that wasn't bad personality, what was it?

"Mrs. McKinley," she began.

"Do call me Millicent, everyone does. And I shall call you Faith, or is it Fay?"

"Faith, please, Millicent—or" (She couldn't resist) "is it Millie?"

"Millicent," she snapped. "And you were saying?"

"Yes, well, having discovered the body and since the Svensons are members of our congregation, of course I've been giving Cindy's murder a lot of thought," Faith said, all of which did not fool Millicent for a minute as one snooper eyed the other. Still it sounded good.

"What I've been wondering about is Cindy's other 'friends'. I'm sure Dave was not the only one, and perhaps you saw her with someone else?"

Millicent smiled. It was frightening.

"Oh, I saw Cindy all right. With Dave, of course. On their way to the belfry. *And* I knew what they were up to. But you're right. He wasn't the only one. Most of the others were from the high school or college boys home on vacation. Nobody special. I think they all knew she was going to marry Dave, although for the life of me, I could never figure out what she saw in him."

"Oh?"

Faith suddenly realized that Millicent was perhaps the sole person in town who had some admiration for Cindy. Millicent looked at her sharply.

"Yes, I thought Cindy could do a lot better. She would never have been happy with Dave. She could have had him on toast for breakfast. Not that I liked her," and a scowl crossed her face.

Ah, thought Faith, another victim.

"No, she was mean-spirited and selfish, but she was also bright and strong. And what energy! When she organized anything, you knew it would be done correctly."

Faith remembered that Millicent and Cindy had been the driving, very driving, forces behind that big Patriot's Day pancake breakfast every year that raised funds for the DAR and CAR.

"She was exactly like her great-grandmother Harriet, full of ambition and energy. It's an interesting family, the Coxes—Cindy's great-great-grandfather was Captain Martin Cox and everybody always referred to the family as 'Cox,' even though Patricia's maiden name was Stoddard and they were Eliots before that." Millicent was quick to grab any and all opportunities to show off. Her mind was a familial pursuit Rolodex.

"Harriet wrote a history of the family, which you might enjoy reading. Of course, I can't lend you my copy, but the library has one."

"Thank you, and I wouldn't dream of taking your copy. I'll make a point of getting it from the library," said Faith sweetly. And resolved to add the work to the list of books she would probably never read along with the collected works of Mrs. Humphrey Ward and Sir Walter Scott that stood in leather-bound glory on the parsonage bookshelves.

Returning to her mission, Faith tried to steer Millicent back on course. "But," she insisted gently, "there was never any one boy you saw Cindy with other than Dave ?"

"Not 'boy,' dear," Millicent said archly, "More like 'man,' but that would be telling and I do not believe in spreading idle gossip."

The hell you don't, thought Faith bitterly. This is just to get back at me for the bell again.

Millicent stubbornly continued on her way and was talking about the Coxes again. It had been madness, Faith thought, to think that she could actually direct the conversation.

"Of course the Captain, as Martin was always called, did make a fortune, but I believe Harriet's husband added to it considerably. The Captain's money had all gone to Harriet. She was the oldest. It was some whim of his to keep it all intact. The whole will was distinctly original. The Coxes always were. In this generation Patricia got the house because her sister Polly didn't want it. Polly took the money, though, and it passed to Cindy, or would have."

"Who will get the money now, then?" Faith asked boldly.

"Oh, it will go to Patricia, of course. And just in time, if you ask me."

Which Faith did to no avail. Millicent Revere McKinley was more than willing to drop hints, but as for spreading around any real information of the specific "The British are coming" nature of her illustrious forebear, the answer was "Ride on." So Faith did.

Millicent walked her to the door and continued out down the brick path in front of her house. Faith said good-bye and thanked her nicely for the coffee. She wondered if it was worth it to come back and try again or if Millicent would continue to dangle clues in front of her cat-and-mouse style. Probably the latter. She glanced back over her shoulder. Millicent was picking a few lateblooming roses.

A few pink Sweetheart roses.

Faith's next stop was Eleanor Whipple's pretty white Victorian house. She didn't expect much information here. Eleanor was the soul of innocence and even if she had seen something would probably not know what it meant. Still, her house was at the foot of Belfry Hill and she just might have noticed something, or rather someone.

Eleanor welcomed her warmly and ushered Faith into her cozy parlor. Faith managed to avoid the horsehair loveseat, which always threatened to land her on the carpet, and chose a low-slung sort of folding chair covered with blue and white striped velvet.

"Father always called that the 'Egyptian chair,' whether because it folds in that interesting way or because of the material, I never remembered to ask him and of course now it is too late."

Considering that Miss Whipple's father had been dead for some thirty years, Faith thought it was much too late.

Faith got some nice digestive biscuits with her coffee this time and she was able to set it on a little découpage table in front of her.

"This looks much too fragile to use," Faith protested.

"Oh, that's just an old piece of clutter that Mother made," Miss Eleanor said. "Don't worry about it."

Faith knew it wasn't at all, and managed to find a doily to slip under her cup and saucer. In Aleford, it was usually possible to find a doily someplace—or in certain homes it was, anyway.

She took a sip of coffee; it was good and strong. She thought of the first time she had visited Eleanor and fought to stifle the giggles that always threatened at the memory. It had been teatime and Eleanor had entered the parlor with a heavily laden tray, announcing proudly, "You'll never taste tea like this anywhere else. I make it with my own water," and proceeded to pour a pale, slightly golden stream into Faith's cup. Was she insane? Faith wondered as she eyed the brew. Too much tatting? "Yes," Eleanor continued, "When we modernized the kitchen, Mother made them leave the old pump by the sink. The well is right underneath, in the basement. She didn't like the taste of town water. It's all right for washing, but you don't know what could have fallen in the reservoir and we never drank it." Faith drained her cup and had to admit the jasmine tea did taste delicious. Afterward Eleanor took her to see the pump. She insisted Faith give it a try, although the whole idea, quaint as it was, filled her with repugnance, raising the possibility of blisters and unsightly muscular development.

Faith took another sip of coffee and glanced about the room. It was a shrine to Eleanor's ancestors. There were daguerreotypes perched on the tables and portraits of various sizes hung on the walls. Thick albums covered with velvet attested to still more. Just over Eleanor's head was a faded enlargement of three little girls with fluffy hair, their dresses covered with Fourth of July bunting. Who were they and where were they now? Faith shivered slightly, pondering the probable answer.

Eleanor had noticed her apparent interest.

"I like to be surrounded by my family," she commented, "Of course I didn't know all these people, but I am proud of them nonetheless. Nothing is more important than your family. This was one of my mother's lessons, Faith, and I'm sure you'd agree."

Faith gave what she hoped was an enthusiastic response and managed to work the conversation around to the murder, "Cindy Shepherd was distantly related to you, I understand. What do you think about all this?"

"I think it is terrifically inconvenient for Robert and Patricia," she commented emphatically. That seemed to be the extent of her thinking, although she was willing to talk as much as Faith wanted.

When Faith asked if Eleanor had seen anyone go up the hill on Friday, or noticed Cindy going up on other days, she looked up from the detailed bit of petit point she was working on, "You know, my eyes are not what they used to be, dear, and in any case, I'm afraid even if I had seen someone, I wouldn't have known who it was. I don't know the names of all the young people anymore. Of course I knew Cindy." There was a noticeably acerbic tinge to her voice, "But not her friends."

She returned to her handwork. It was easy to see why her eyes were going.

Faith was forced to concede she wasn't going to get anything from Eleanor, and after some delightful minutes spent with Eleanor admiring Benjamin, she firmly refused lunch—Welsh rarebit—and set off for her third and final stop.

As she sat down at Pix Miller's big kitchen table, Faith had to admit she was there as much for some cheering up as information. Certainly morale was important in any murder investigation.

It wasn't that Pix was little Mary Sunshine exactly and thank goodness. What she radiated was solid common sense mixed with a very funny sense of humor.

She had been a tiny child and her parents had whimsically called her "Pixie"—why do people do these things, Faith wondered, resolving that she would stop calling Benjamin "Punkin" immediately lest it stick with him unto old age. Pixie had solved the problem by shooting up alarmingly in her teens so that at close to six feet, "Pixie" was not only ludicrous, but obscene. Still, old habits die hard and she became "Pix," which seemed to suit her. When Faith finally remembered to ask her what her "real" name was, it turned out to be "Myrtle." After the ground cover with the pretty little purple flowers. Who were these people? So "Pix" it was.

She was the person you called in Aleford if you were looking for another driver for the scouts overnight to Harold Parker State Forest or if someone needed a volunteer to help at the Senior Center kitchen. Pix drove a Land Rover, bred gorgeous golden retrievers, was an expert white water canoer, and had three kids, the middle of which was Faith's trusty babysitter, Samantha. Sam Miller was a lawyer. They had both grown up in Aleford—a high school romance that endured.

Pix welcomed Faith in, automatically gave her some coffee, which Faith had learned they did in suburbia, and took Benjamin lovingly on her lap. Pix adored babies.

"You look full of secrets, Faith," she said, making horrible grimaces at Benjamin, which he regarded with great amusement.

"I wish I were," Faith responded, "This whole thing is a complete mystery."

"Murders usually are—for a while, anyway. But I agree this one is especially deep and dark. The kids are very upset about Dave and everyone is racking his or her brains for some kind of alternative. We all know he didn't do it, but who else is there?"

"Exactly what I tried to find out this morning. Millicent knows something, but she's not telling. Or rather she's not telling me. Maybe she would talk to you?"

"Not likely, Faith. She's never forgiven my mother for refusing to join the DAR. I think she thinks we are some sort of pinkos and you know what she thinks of Redcoats."

They laughed.

"I'll bet there is a Tory or two in her closet," Faith said, "Maybe we can find out and blackmail her into telling us what she knows."

"Faith! My word! You have been taking this more seriously than I thought. What would Tom say?" Pix chided mockingly.

"What he always says, 'Faith, Faith, Faith,' slowly

shaking his head and looking at me with those cocker spaniel eyes. Oh, pardon, golden retriever eyes."

"That's better," Pix propped Benjamin up against one shoulder with a practiced arm and gave a whiff, "Faith, sweetie, give me a diaper—you've got a messy boy here—and while I change him why don't you heat up the lentil soup in the fridge and add anything that comes to mind? Maybe if we eat something we'll think more logically."

The soup was good. Pix could be counted on for certain things, Faith had learned—a terrific chili for a Boston bean and great soups. But then there had been that dinner of chicken covered with pineapple chunks and maraschino cherries. Pix had a fatal tendency to be swayed by the pictures in some women's magazines.

While they ate, Faith told her about her visit to Eleanor and the dry well it turned out to be. Pix wasn't surprised.

"I don't think Eleanor would notice a crime even if it were occurring in her own living room. She'd just straighten the antimacassars and put a blanket over the body, presuming whoever it was was taking a short nap."

"Come on, she can't be that out of it," Faith protested.

"Believe me, she is," replied Pix, "and somehow I hope she stays that way. Something unchanging in this wicked whirling world of ours. You know her skirts will never go up or down and if she's not sitting straight as a ramrod in the third pew from the pulpit on the left-hand side of the church at ten forty-five every Sunday then she's either gone to her Maker on her own or the whole town has been wiped out by an atom bomb or the bubonic plague. I look at her and it gives me strength to cope with my hectic life. At least one person isn't as crazy as the rest of us."

Pix was what could be euphemistically referred to as

"overextended," Faith reflected. In one month she probably put on the equivalent of a cross country journey chauffering the kids and doing errands. She was unbelievably organized, though. There were lists and notes taped to every surface in the house: "Samantha, don't forget your flute" and "Danny, there are cookies in the cupboard, enjoy them while you do your spelling words," and so on. Her laundry room had five separate baskets each labeled with someone's name and standing ready for the clothes as they came out of the dryer. What Faith, and others, did not know was that all this planning and list-making was a cover for Pix's fundamentally disorganized mind. She was the type of woman who asks herself out loud, "Why did I open this drawer?" in order to jog her memory to say, "Scotch tape." She knew that without the mnemonics, life would be hopeless. Where her thoughts wandered was not altogether clear; she could certainly call them back when she needed them, but basically she was a dreamer—night and day. It amused her, and caused an occasional pang of guilt at the deception, that people thought she was so practical and organized. Her husband, Sam, was amused too, but that was because he had observed that over the years she really had become practical and well organized without knowing it. He knew he'd never be able to convince her of that and didn't try. There wasn't any point.

While Faith and Pix finished the soup, they discussed the contents of the tin box. Its existence was not yet common knowledge, but Jenny had immediately called Samantha, her best friend, with news of the find.

"Not the easiest identifications to make," Pix commented. "Can you imagine Charley knocking on doors and asking the man of the house to please drop his drawers?"

They laughed and turned to talk about domestic trials. Samantha wasn't talking to Pix, because said mother had humiliated her by picking up Willy Stergis, a sixth- grade boy, on the way to school.

"Honestly, Faith, you should have seen her!" Pix laughed. "Her entire seventh-grade body was hunched down in the seat and she wouldn't get out of the car at school until poor Willy had gone in the door. I mean who knows what social suicide she would have committed if any of her friends had seen her. And of course, the fact that I had on my flannel nightgown under my trench coat made matters even worse. All I wanted to do was give Willy a ride. It was chilly last week."

They went back to the murder and the various blackmail possibilities, but didn't get any further in their speculations. Faith arrived home to put Benjamin down for a nap with no clearer idea of who could possibly have killed Cindy Shepherd than when she started.

Tom came home late in the afternoon. Wednesday was his day at the VA hospital as chaplain. He was always tired after this and sometimes a little depressed. Today was no exception. Faith fed Benjamin, who rewarded her efforts by giving her the raspberry with most of his meal. Then she made an early dinner for Tom and herself. Afterward they sat in front of the first fire of the season to read.

At nine o'clock Faith realized that she was nodding off and Tom was sound asleep. Rousing him and sending him up to bed, she went into the kitchen and made her- self a strong cup of tea. She could get some sleep when the case was closed.

She went upstairs and whispered in Tom's unconscious ear that she was going out for some ice cream, a statement that would have astounded him had he been awake, since they had a freezer full of Faith's own glacés and sorbets.

She eased the car out of the driveway, knowing full well that it would take several belfry bells, or Benjamin's cry, to awaken Tom, but she thought a little bit of stealth was appropriate to the scene. She wasn't driving a sleek, fully equipped Aston Martin, but a dull, gray, very dependable Honda. It would have to do.

As Faith suspected, the parking lot at Friendly's was filled with kids. Some were inside their cars, but, despite the nippy weather, more were sitting on the hoods, the tips of their cigarettes flickering in the dark. Marlboros and Mocha Chip. Great combination.

Faith sauntered over to the take-out window and ordered a small chocolate cone. It was like eating chicken feet in Chinese restaurants. One had to establish one's credentials in order to get the good stuff.

She recognized one of the church youth group members, Becky Sullivan, perched with a couple of other kids on the hood of a car. Faith walked over to them and they instantly ditched their smokes. It was things like this that forcibly reminded Faith she was indeed the minister's wife.

"Hi," she said, "I got a sudden craving for ice cream. How are things?"

The kids eyed her with unabashed curiosity. The person who had actually discovered the body!

Faith knew it was no good trying to bullshit seventeen-year-olds, not that she had had much luck with any age group. Even if they bought the ice cream story, they

99

would find it hard to believe a conversation in which Mrs. Fairchild first asked them how school was, then wanted to know by the way who killed Cindy. So she decided to be direct.

"Look, you all know that Reverend Fairchild and I are very close to Dave. We're trying to help him. Dave didn't kill Cindy, but obviously somebody did."

"You found her, didn't you, Mrs. Fairchild?" one of the girls said.

Faith had expected someone would ask for an eyewitness account, and she went quickly through it all again. She was rewarded by their rapt attention, and while their eyes were still shining and directed at her, she moved smoothly to the matter at hand.

"What I want to ask you is if you ever saw Cindy with someone other than Dave, especially lately. Or maybe she talked about someone with one of you."

Suddenly everyone was looking at the stars, the thin sliver of a moon, each other, everywhere but at her.

After a long moment, Becky spoke, "Well, Mrs. Fairchild, Cindy didn't have, like a best friend. I mean, like Karen and I tell each other everything." Pause while Karen giggled and some of the other kids said, "Everything ?"etc., etc.

"Anyway, Cindy had sort of friends. We were kind of her friends." Becky seemed at a loss for words.

Faith helped her out. "I don't think she would have been my best friend when I was your age. She always seemed to me like someone who was more concerned for herself than she would be for a friend."

"A back-stabbing bitch," called an anonymous voice from the next car hood.

Nobody denied it. Becky looked uncomfortable and one of the kids slid silently off the car into the darkness.

"So none of you really know anything?" Faith was sure they knew a lot.

One of the boys spoke, "She was older than we are, Mrs. Fairchild, although she did hang out here, but she was usually in a car or with Dave." He stopped, embarrassed at the obvious implications.

Faith nodded and persisted, "When she was in a car was it with somebody in particular?"

A pretty, brown-haired girl spoke bluntly in an angry voice. "Mrs. Fairchild, she was scum. She'd go off just to get Dave upset. It wasn't that she cared about the person and it didn't matter who. Even," she added bitterly, "if it was somebody else's boyfriend."

"So you really don't have any theories about who killed her or why?" Faith sighed. Could it have been a tramp after all?

The kids mumbled vague denials and Faith left them to light up again in peace. She really hadn't expected to get much. It was just another lead to follow. Maybe it was true that they hadn't known her that well, but more likely if they were onto something they might assume she would tell the police. Which she would, wouldn't she?

As she was leaving, she thought of one more thing and turned around. Everyone sat up a little straighter again.

"At the time Cindy was killed, Dave was walking by the railroad tracks and he saw one person, a guy riding a dirt bike. It would help if we could find him."

"I know someone with a bike and he rides down there a lot. He might know who it was." It was the girl with the brown hair.

Faith smiled at her. "That would be terrific, thank you. Would you let me know if you find out anything?"

It wasn't much, but it was the first something she had turned up all day.

She climbed into her car and sat reflecting. They were all trying to help Dave, and the territories were defined. So let the kids do whatever they were doing and she would try to think of something she might have missed.

Not now, though. She was tired and couldn't have investigated her way out of a cardboard box at the moment.

Friendly's was out in a mini-mall near the edge of town and the roads were deserted as she drove back. The darkness surrounded the car and she felt as though she had switched on automatic pilot and the machine was driving her. Gradually she became aware of the sound of another engine. She peered in the rearview mirror. Another car had appeared from nowhere behind her. They were close to the straight stretch of road bordering the Long Meadow conservation land. Faith pressed down on the accelerator. It was a totally irrational impulse.

Faith, she told herself, don't be ridiculous! It's probably some of the kids from the parking lot.

The car behind her speeded up, too.

Don't tell me they think I want to drag! She tried to laugh. Mrs. Fairchild burns rubber on local road.

She slowed down and whoever it was seemed content to follow her lead. She looked into the mirror again and could only make out the driver. If there were any passengers, they were out of sight in the backseat. At this point Faith hoped they were there, no matter what that might suggest. It was infinitely better than being followed by a solitary stranger.

This part of town certainly needs some streetlights, she thought as she drove cautiously in the pitch dark. There was evidently some old Yankee prejudice that if you were not home in bed where you belonged at this hour, you could take your chances. She resolved to call one of the town meeting members about it tomorrow and felt better thinking of that word, *tomorrow*.

Because, she admitted, she was more than a little nervous. She was inching through fright and close to panic.

Why didn't the car pass her? It was right on her tail. She accelerated. Behind her the driver did the same.

Faith was sure now. She was definitely being followed.

She turned left on Liberty Lane.

So did the car behind her.

She glanced out the side window. The passenger side door was unlocked and she quickly reached across to lock it. As she did so, she realized the back was unlocked too. It was just out of her reach. She'd have to stop to lock it. And she didn't want to stop.

All the *Alfred Hitchcock Presents* she and Hope had watched when their parents weren't around to tell them not to crowded into her consciousness. Was there somebody actually in her backseat?

Of course not. And there wouldn't be.

She was crossing the river and would soon be out of these dark, lifeless streets. The lights burning at the parsonage blinked a welcome to her. Faith was almost home.

She started to pull into the driveway, then abruptly turned the wheel in the other direction. Whoever it was could pull right in behind her and she would be trapped!

Calm down, Faith. What do they tell you to do in situations like this? What was it she used to urge those poor defenseless people on TV to do? Drive to the police station, of course.

Her pursuer either didn't know the town or he was a lunatic. He followed her right up to the station.

Faith pulled as close to the station door as she could and the car stopped right behind her. She reached back and locked the rear doors and had started to lean on the horn to attract attention, when someone tapped on the window. After an instant of motionless terror, she slowly rolled it down.

"Good evening, Mrs. Fairchild, out for a little drive?"

It was John Dunne.

Faith was furious.

"Do you have any idea how much you frightened me? What the hell were you doing out there following me that way?"

"I was driving to work, and might one ask what the hell you were doing on Byford Road at eleven o'clock at night all by your lonesome? Parish work?"

"As it happens, I was." Faith thought talking to Becky could qualify and certainly helping Dave was, although Tom might not agree with the definition. "In any case, Detective Dunne, I really don't see that any of this is your business."

He looked at her in mingled concern and exasperation. "Until this thing is wrapped up, you are very much my business, Mrs. Fairchild, and I'll be following you home now, too, if you would be so kind as to start your car and get out of here."

Quick as a flash, Faith asked, "So you don't think Dave did it?"

"That's not what I said. I said it's not 'wrapped up.'"

"Same thing," said Faith smugly as she started to turn her key in the ignition. "Good night, Detective."

"Wait a minute, Mrs. Fairchild. So what did the kids there at the mall tell you?" he asked conversationally.

Faith was momentarily taken aback by this sudden reversion to good cop and decided to tell Dunne the night's events, meager as they were.

"Well, fine, Mrs. Fairchild. Now isn't it time you went to bed?"

"Absolutely. Good night again, Detective."

Dunne got in his car and pulled out behind her. Faith eased into her driveway and got out to open the garage doors. They weighed a ton and swung outward with surprising swiftness. She dodged them nimbly and waved a cheerful good-bye to the detective before driving in. He was still at the end of the drive when she got out to close them. Evidently he was going to wait until she was actually in the house and evidently he wasn't going to help her with the damn doors. She slammed them shut and waved a little less cheerily.

Once inside, Faith took a quick look at Benjamin and was asleep as soon as her head hit the pillow. It was a relief to know that the police weren't convinced that Dave did it. As she drifted off, her restless brain continued to send annoying messages. There was something they were all overlooking. Well, at least now she knew that Dunne knew it, too.

The phone rang late the next afternoon. It had been a

105

particularly frustrating day. Faith was tired after her late-night rambles and Benjamin did not seem to want to eat, sleep, play, or anything else. She grabbed the phone, well aware that whoever it was would hear his screams in the background and she could kiss away her Mrs. America nomination forever.

"Mrs. Fairchild?"

It was the girl from last night.

"I'm, um, Trishia. The one you talked to about the dirt bike last night."

"Yes, I recognized your voice. Did you have any luck?" Faith asked eagerly.

"It was a guy from Byford, but he doesn't want to talk to the police. He said he would talk to you, though."

Faith was surprised. "Okay, how do I reach him?"

"He has supper at the Willow Tree Kitchen every night. It's on the way to Concord."

Faith had seen it, a weathered, gray-shingled roadhouse that looked like a cross between a speakeasy and a farmhouse. There were only a few tiny windows, but they had checkered Priscilla curtains.

"Yes, I know where it is, but how will I know him? What's his name?"

"Oh, don't worry, he knows you." Trishia laughed and hung up.

The goldfish bowl again.

It was four-thirty. Dinner in New England, Faith had learned, could be anytime from five to six o'clock, possibly six-thirty. The first time she gave a dinner party inviting the guests for eight, she discovered later from Pix that they had all eaten before, and assumed they had been asked for dessert and coffee. She shook her head. How would she

106

ever be able to cope with all this?

Of course, she had to talk to this mysterious biker right away. An eyewitness alibi would strengthen Dave's case immeasurably. Besides, if she didn't, she would die of curiosity.

She quickly called Pix, who was always happy to watch Benjamin, and Samantha was there, too. Somehow a rendezvous with a secret informer lost some of its excitement and romance if one arrived with a fussy baby on one's hip.

Benjamin had thankfully stopped crying and was preparing himself for an hour of cuteness. Well, Pix would get to enjoy it this time, thought Faith, as she hastily stuffed enough baby things into the diaper bag for a month-long expedition to the Amazon. She left a vague note for Tom on the kitchen table about running an errand and was off.

Willow Tree was packed to its low rafters with people stopping off for a quick one on the way home or, in some cases, it appeared they were home. Faith looked around the smoke-filled room for some hint of Mr. Motorcycle like a helmet, or a red carnation in his black leather lapel, but all she saw was a crowd intent on which letter Vanna White was going to turn over next or catching the eye of one of the waitresses who were hustling around at the speed of light. True to the Willow Tree's contradictory appearance, the waitresses balancing the oversized mugs of beer looked as if they would be more comfortable at Schrafft's with starched, pleated pastel handkerchiefs coyly peeking out of their uniform pockets. They were all of some indeterminate age and wore sensible shoes. Faith wouldn't have been surprised to see one hand a tract to a customer along with his Budweiser.

There was a smaller room off to the right, which was separated from the bar and booths of the main room by a low divider decorated with wildlife. Real wildlife. Stuffed, slightly worn, patched bobcats," snarls intact and repellent; molting owls; and a stag's head on the wall with just a few antler branches missing. Muskets and other weaponry festooned the rafters. A pair of old snowshoes were crossed above the door, presumably for the pacifists and animal rights advocates who might patronize the place, but somehow, looking around, Faith didn't think there were too many of those. She gazed into the darker, smaller room as the more likely place for a clandestine meeting, if in fact that was what she was having. It appeared to be empty.

Someone tapped her on the shoulder. She turned around.

"You get to like them after a while."

"Get to like them?"

"All the animals. They've been here forever. This little guy is my favorite," he continued, pointing to a dusty red squirrel, "I guess it's because I remember him from when I was a kid. He was the only one who looked like he wasn't going to come to life and rip your guts out."

It wasn't the way Faith imagined the dialogue would go, but it got them to the booth where he had been waiting and they sat down and looked at each other appraisingly.

"By the way, I'm Scott Phelan and if I'm right and you're Mrs. Fairchild, then I'm going to have to start going to church more often."

Faith in turn was stunned. First of all, Scott was not a

teenager. More like mid-twenties. And second, or rather first and foremost, he was gorgeous. Looking at him purely from a connoisseur's point of view, of course, and nothing personal. He was dressed in a gray sweatshirt with a sleeveless blue jean jacket over it. His leather one was on the seat. If from the neck down, he was James Dean, the neck up could only be described as one of Ozzie and Harriet's kids, the boy next door. If you should get so lucky. Dark brown curls, big brown eyes with flecks of gold and a generous mouth curved at the moment in a slightly quizzical smile. What were they doing here anyway?

Faith reeled herself in and got down to business.

"I understand from Trishia that you are the person who was riding down by the tracks last Friday. Do you remember seeing Dave?"

"Yeah, I saw him. Almost clipped him. Not too many people stroll there in the daytime." He waited for her to ask another question and nodded casually to one of the waitresses. Two of them arrived simultaneously.

"Another of these," he pointed to his empty mug, and a bowl of chili." Then he turned to Faith. "I recommend the chili, the chowder, and the beef stew. Starting in the spring, the lobster and clams are good too." He smiled. A girl could get dizzy from that smile. "And I ought to know. I eat here every night." He smiled at the waitress. She dropped her pencil.

"I'll have a cup of chowder," Faith said.

"And to drink?" asked the waitress.

"It's whatever you want, or tonic if you don't drink. But not fancy," Scott told her matter-of-factly. He had obviously brought too many women here who wanted

Black Russians or Strawberry Daiquiris. There was nothing elaborate about Willow Tree and if they wanted the other stuff they could get a frappe at Friendly's and pour a nip in it, which is what they usually did.

"A glass of white wine then, thank you," said Faith and smiled. Faith's smile was pretty dazzling, too, but the waitress was apparently looking elsewhere. She returned almost immediately with the drinks, the chili, the chowder, and a huge plate of baking soda biscuits the size of baseball gloves. Faith was momentarily diverted by the horror of the wine, which came in a small bottle with a twist-off cap instead of a cork. After one sip, which left an aftertaste reminiscent of Dalton's chem lab at the end of a long, sulfurous day, she gently pushed the glass to one side and took a spoonful of chowder. It was delicious. Faith sighed. All these contradictions. It was odd that they had produced such a solid citizenry. Then she recalled that she was here investigating a murder.

"That's why I stick to beer," Scott remarked, "That stuff always gives me a headache."

"It's not exactly grand cru. There are many better wines that I am sure you'd like." Roughly every other growth ever produced.

They were straying again and before she found herself inviting him to the parsonage for a little wine tasting to the accompaniment of Tom's raised eyebrows, she continued the questioning.

"About Dave. Do you know what time it was when you saw him?"

"It must have been about noon, because I get off work for lunch at eleven-thirty. I work at a body shop in Byford. It probably took me ten minutes to drive to

Aleford, then another ten to unload the bike from my pickup and eat my sub. I had ridden a ways up the tracks when I saw him. I turned to go to the hills by the power lines after that. My boss is pretty strict about being on time, so I only rode for about a half an hour. I usually wait to ride until after work, but it was too nice a day to waste."

Except in Cindy's case.

"But I don't understand. You saw Dave and can even pinpoint the time. Why can't you tell the police?"

"It's not a matter of 'can't,' it's more 'don't want to.'"

"But why on earth not? A person's freedom is at stake here."

"Look, Mrs. Fairchild, the cops and me have never been what you'd call buddies. I finally got off probation a year ago and I swore I would never have anything to do with them again if I could help it." He saw the sudden question in her eyes. "Nothing big, no B and E's or anything. Just a lot of little stuff that mounted up—vehicle unregistered, uninsured; truancy, minor in possession. And for the record, since I'm sure you would all like to find a suspect to replace Dave, I barely knew Cindy. Didn't want to. She used to try to talk to me and I would just split."

I'll *bet* she wanted to get to know you, Faith thought. What a notch that would have been in Cindy's garter belt. Suddenly she remembered what Trishia had said about Cindy going after other girls' boyfriends. Maybe she was approaching this thing from the wrong angle. Revenge could provide a pretty powerful motive for a woman scorned.

Scott was still talking. "I don't know Dave much, either. Just to say hello to."

"But you can't let him go to prison simply because you don't have a particular fondness for the police! It's not as if you committed a crime."

"Ah, but you see, that's the problem. Legally speaking, you're not supposed to be riding a dirt bike by the tracks or by the power lines. And it's posted. Everybody does it, but you can get nailed for it."

"For a person who doesn't want to have anything to do with the police, you seem to be taking some rather big chances." Faith was getting annoyed.

Scott looked at her calmly and smiled. Trishia had said he'd like the minister's wife and Trish was usually right. That's why she made such a good girlfriend. She knew him. Ever since they had heard about the murder and Dave's arrest, she had been after him to go to the cops. She was from Aleford and knew Dave. But he wouldn't and then she came up with Mrs. Fairchild—she knew he'd much rather talk to Faith than to MacIsaac.

"Little chances," he told her. "Tiny chances. I never ride there on weekends when people are out walking. And it's not exactly a big city police department. They don't have the manpower to stroll along the railroad tracks every noon on the off chance that Scott Phelan might go for a ride when there are all those traffic tickets to give out and lost dogs to find."

"So you're just going to sit back and let Dave be found guilty of a murder he didn't commit!"

"Now, be calm, Mrs. Fairchild. I never said that. I said I didn't want to and I don't. And here is where you come in, and your husband, since I assume you don't keep secrets from him."

Was he laughing at her, Faith wondered? And of course

she didn't keep secrets from Tom. At least not secrets like this.

"Of course you can just go to the police and tell them what I've told you and they'll come and boot me down to the station for questioning, but what I want you to do is hold off for a day or two. They have a lot of guys working on this case and the police are not the jerks they seem to be, or not all of them anyway. They'll turn some- thing or someone up and then I won't have to get mixed up in it. But don't worry, I'll be a good citizen and if it looks like Dave needs my testimony, I'll come the minute you tell me to. I just don't want to get involved if I don't have to and that's the best I can do for you. Except for one more thing. If you agree to this, I'll work my butt off trying to find out anything else—starting here at Willow Tree. If someone here doesn't know all about it, it hasn't happened yet. If you don't agree, you're on your own. No hard feelings either way."

The smile again.

Faith wasn't sure what she had gained. A partner? A Watson he wasn't and she knew that Tom for one would be appalled by the ethics or lack thereof in the agreement. But somewhere it made a little sense. In any case, it would have to do. She was sure he wouldn't have told her he had seen Dave if he hadn't been pretty sure she would agree to his terms.

"All right," she said, rising to leave, "but not for long and we get to tell Dave."

"That's no problem. I would have told Dave myself, but they've been keeping him pretty busy."

Maybe she was wrong about the ethics, Faith thought.

Scott stood up, too. Really, he was breathtaking.

"Nice to meet you, Mrs. Fairchild," he said, extending his hand.

She took it.

"Nice to meet you too, Scott, and say hello to Trishia for me. She *is* your girlfriend, isn't she?"

Faith looked at her watch. She had been gone almost an hour and had better hurry. Tom might be getting worried. On her way out she glanced into the smaller room and was getting into her car before the fact fully registered that the Moores' son, Robert Jr., had been sitting across from someone in a shadowy corner of the room. Now what was he doing home from college? As far as she knew it wasn't vacation. Maybe he had stayed on for a day or so after Cindy's funeral.

That evening when she told Tom about her conversation with Scott Phelan, he was even more annoyed than she had thought he would be. He was in fact, very angry. He had been angry enough earlier when Faith, in a misguided bid for sympathy, told him about Dunne following her.

"Faith!" he said now as he strode up and down the living room setting off a cacophony of creaking floorboards. "Faith! I thought you were merely going to keep your 'ears and eyes open.' That is a far cry from leaving your house in the middle of the night to tryst with a bunch of teenagers, ending up with a police escort home! And thank goodness he *is* keeping an eye on you, although what he must think of me snoring away while you are all over the landscape, Heaven knows. And now you go off to some shady diner to meet a strange man. Faith, I just can't believe you would put yourself in such danger!"

"Now, Tom, I wasn't in any danger. Okay, I was a little

nervous driving back last night, but meeting someone at a public place—it is not shady and they have very good chowder—is not exactly tying myself to the railroad tracks."

"And what if he had suggested you go examine the exact spot where he had seen Dave? You would have gone. I know you would have. You are the most outrageous combination of blind trust and curiosity of any woman I have ever known!"

"Stop shouting, Tom, you're going to wake the baby. And, how many trusting, curious women have you known? Please give me a little more credit. I do have some common sense. I would not have gone to the railroad tracks with Scott. Especially not at first."

"Faith!"

It took a while, but eventually Tom calmed down and Faith was able to tell him exactly what Scott had said. Which started him up all over again.

"What does this guy look like anyway? I think he must have mesmerized you."

"Honestly, Tom! He's just a kid. A little better than average looking, jeans, leather jacket. You know the type."

"Yeah, Butch Cassidy, the Sundance Kid, and Tom Cruise all rolled into one."

"Tom, we're getting off the subject here. We have a witness. Whatever you may think of him. He saw Dave by the tracks at noon and will testify if he has to and I think he knows he has to. It's that he wants to come in through us and as part of Dave's case rather than through the police. He didn't say not to tell Dave's lawyer, only the police, and we can check with him tomorrow."

But Scott was right. By the next day it wasn't necessary.

SIX

FAITH WAS AWAKENED EARLY NEXT MORNING BY THE sounds of an unusual amount of activity next door at the Millers. She got up and looked out the window.

"Tom! Tom! My God! Get dressed! There are a million police cars next door. Hurry! "

Tom pulled on his clothes in record time and sped over to the Millers. He almost collided with MacIsaac and Dunne, with Sam Miller between them. Faith, watching from the window, could not imagine what was going on. What could they possibly want with Sam? Tom got into the patrol car with them. Faith wasn't sure whether she should go over to Pix or wait to see if Tom called. Five minutes later the phone rang. It was Tom.

"Faith, it's absolutely insane. Sam is a suspect in Cindy's murder! Evidently there are eyewitnesses who saw them together on Friday morning, quarreling. And some of the photos were of Sam. It seems he was having an affair with her. *And* they found a one-way ticket to Puerto Rico in his pocket for a flight tomorrow. You'd better get over to Pix."

Faith for once in her life was absolutely speechless. Sam? Cindy? Who was going to be arrested next? Mr. Brown, the church's seventy-five-year-old sexton?

She got Benjamin ready quickly. She wasn't going to stop for breakfast, she was going right over to Pix. But as she opened her door, there was Pix on the doorstep, red-eyed and slightly crazy. They went into the kitchen where Pix immediately began to weep hysterically.

"Oh, Faith, I hope you don't mind. I didn't want the kids to see me like this. Of course they don't want to go to

116

school, so I can't leave them long. What are we going to do?"

"Have something to eat first and then we'll try to figure it out." It was Faith's credo. "I assume you have a lawyer, right?"

"Lawyers! Yes, we have a lawyer and he's on his way." Pix was starting to hiccup, but it didn't lessen the emotional impact of her words, "Faith, this is all my fault!"

"Now don't tell me you were having an affair with Cindy, too," said Faith, hoping to inject a little humor in the situation. She poured some coffee into two mugs, adding a liberal dose of brandy to Pix's. She cut some thick slices of cinnamon bread, buttered them, and sat down.

Pix raised her head from the table where she had collapsed. "Believe me, Faith, if it would have kept Sam from having one with her, I would have. The little slut. It makes me nauseous to think of it."

She took a large swallow of coffee and continued. "I knew Sam was having an affair and I figured I'd just wait it out. You know how hard he took turning forty. You were at the party."

Faith remembered. The tight little smile and forced laughter Sam had displayed as he opened his "gifts"— bottles of Geritol, *Playboy* calendars, all singularly tasteless, in her opinion. Then there were all the jokes about getting it up—someone had even given him a small toy crane with a long pointless poem about how to use it and when. Somebody else had presented Pix with an elaborate gift certificate entitling her to trade him in for two twenties.

Sam got pretty drunk and went out the next week and

bought a silver Porsche. He said it was his present to himself.

Pix seemed to be reading Faith's mind. "He bought the car and I knew something was going on, but he didn't want to talk about it. It looked ridiculous—our two cars in the driveway side by side—me the big clunky Land Rover, Sam the sleek Porsche. I tried to talk to him about it. After all, I had turned forty last year—very quietly.

"I knew the signs. I read books. Midlife crisis, all that, so I thought I'd try to change, too—bought a lot of lingerie and even tried some of the Total Woman stuff, you know getting rid of the kids and welcoming him home dressed in Saran Wrap and nothing else, but we just laughed too hard. I knew everything would be all right and decided I would just go on as always. Pretend that nothing was the matter. Sex was still good. I wasn't complaining and neither was he."

Faith wondered if all minister's wives had to listen to this sort of confession, and tried to look mature and worldly, as if she had the wives of accused murderers sitting at her kitchen table every day, pouring out the most intimate details of their marriages.

"But if I had known it was Cindy, I would have killed her myself," said Pix vehemently, "Sam is a baby. He was too innocent for her and she must have been driving him crazy. I knew he was tense, but he said it was work. I knew it wasn't all work. There were a lot of unexplained late nights. It wasn't something I liked, but there it was."

Faith reached over and took her hand. Pix gave it a squeeze and sat up straight.

"Faith, marriage is taking turns," she said somewhat didactically. She was on her second mug of coffee cum

118

brandy and her voice was assuming the authoritative tone Faith thought she herself should have. Who was supposed to be comforting whom?

"You go through so many stages. When the kids were little and driving me crazy, Sam would come home and pitch in with the wash or whatever. He was strong for me. Now it's my turn to be strong for him. I certainly wasn't going to throw a perfectly good marriage out the window because he was feeling middle-aged and needed some reassurance. Remember that, Faith. Tom may not have an affair" (better not, thought Faith) "but there will be something, sometime."

Pix started to cry again. This time quietly and that was somehow more desperate than her earlier wails. The anger was gone and the fear was taking hold.

"I've got to get back to the kids and I've got to find out what's going on. You've been a darling, Faith."

Faith gave her a hug at the door.

"Just remember, Pix, Tom and I are here for you any time of day or night—and for the kids, too. Whatever happens, just remember that. We're on your side." Faith felt rather proud of this speech. It sounded like something a minister's wife should say. Then Pix took the wind right out of her sails; in fact, she capsized the craft.

"Faith! You think Sam is guilty!" She looked stunned.

"Of course I don't!" said Faith immediately, realizing that in the back of her mind in fact she *had* believed Sam had killed Cindy in some crazed moment. She was as shocked at herself as Pix was. This was Sam and just because Dave would be off the hook now was no reason to think her obviously innocent neighbor, friend, and fellow parishioner was guilty. It looked as if she wasn't going to be able to abandon her investigation yet.

"Pix! You must believe me! I'm as sure of Sam's innocence as I am, well—of yours or mine!"

Pix looked at her in the eye. "That's better," she said, then added, "but I wouldn't be so sure of mine if I were you."

Faith gasped.

"Just testing," Pix said wickedly.

Faith closed the door and wondered if all her parish duties would end up making her feel like she'd just had one of her mother's talking tos. In any case, she was not sure what she had done for Pix, though Pix had certainly opened *her* eyes on a few things. At least Faith had cheered her up; the Pix who left was quite different from the one who arrived. But then it might have been the brandy. Now the main thing to do was find out what sort of case the police had against Sam. She doubted that John Dunne would figuratively throw the cuffs on someone without pretty solid evidence.

Tom called again at noon. The police were being terrifically considerate. MacIsaac was letting him stay with Sam and Dunne had just gone out to get them all some meatball subs to eat. Faith almost gagged. Talk about cruel and unusual punishment.

Dave had been released and was home sleeping. He had been tearfully relieved before discovering that Sam had been arrested, then he had burst out in an angry denunciation of Cindy. Nobody stopped him.

Before he got off the phone, Tom told Faith that just after they had arrived at the station Sam had confessed that Cindy, parish Young People's President and former record holder for perfect attendance at Sunday School, had been blackmailing him for several months.

And they call New York "Sin City," Faith thought as she hung up.

What had started out as a moment of sweet passion had rapidly turned into a nightmare of lust and a web of deceit for Sam. At least this is the way he thought of it. Faith thought it was an apt but harsh description when she had pieced the whole story together with what she learned from Pix, what Sam told Tom, and even a few details from Charley MacIsaac who couldn't resist a snide comment about people who drove around in highly visible cars.

Sam had offered to drive Cindy home after church one sunny June Sunday when she had complained of a sore ankle. Somehow the silver Porsche had ended up on one of the birch-lined dirt roads near town conservation land and somehow before too long Cindy and Sam were lying under the silver green leaves.

Poor Cindy, thought Sam. She had had a rough time of it, losing her parents so young, and face it, Patricia and Robert were a bit stiff. Not like him. She told him she could talk to him, really talk to him, and thanked him with touching humility for what she hinted was the sublime sexual experience of her life.

Sam didn't smoke, but he had wanted a cigarette as he lay nestled in the ferns with Cindy's lovely head resting on his shoulder, her long dark hair spread down his chest entwined in the dark hair there—sure there were a few gray ones coming in, but that's what maturity meant.

She made him feel seasoned, like fine-grained oak, not old. Hell, not old at all.

By the next week he knew he was hooked. He couldn't stop thinking about her—the sunlight, the smells, the sex. But he didn't call. She was a kid, or if not exactly a kid, she certainly was engaged to be married, and to someone Sam liked very much. Dave had been their babysitter and was like a member of the family.

He pushed the whole thing from his mind and began to go up more often to the house in Maine. Each June as soon as school was over, Pix packed up the kids and the Land Rover and took off for their cottage on Penobscot Bay, where she spent the summer blissfully making beach plum jelly and raising money for the local ambulance corps.

One Friday night in early July, when he went into the garage loaded with his L.L. Bean suitcase plus all the food Pix couldn't find on the island, there was Cindy in a halter top, shorts, and not much else sitting in the front seat of the car waiting for him.

He stopped going to Maine as frequently, or rather he went, but it was further south, to motels in Old Orchard Beach and Ogunquit where they would make love feverishly, then eat lobster on the docks. He didn't know whether he was happy or not about the way things were going, but he knew he was alive. He also didn't know that while he slept Cindy had set the timer on her camera, artfully draped herself around him, and taken several shots which she neatly labeled with his initials, the date, and name of the motel.

Toward the end of July, Cindy changed abruptly. Suddenly she began to make jokes. She started to call him "my old codger" and "Father Time," at first affectionately and then less so. When he was tired, she did not attempt to hide her annoyance. He was no longer the partner in control, the teacher, the wise veteran. He was the supplicant, the controlled. She would cancel dates at the last minute or demand to go back early. He wanted to end things, but for a long time could not bring himself to do it. The memory of the early days was still fresh and Pix was away. Cindy was company, if increasingly bad company.

In early August he decided his nerves could not take it anymore. He was not cut out to cheat on his wife and he had intended all along to go to the island for two weeks. It was a logical time to break things off once and for all.

But Cindy had no intention of breaking things off. She was getting a bit tired of him, she told him, but it was pleasant to have an older man take her to dinner occasionally and as for the sex, she liked to keep her hand in, so to speak. She had laughed mockingly at him. He was furious and his intentions of letting her down gently vanished. So did her lightly amused manner. After he had lost his temper and let her know just what a conniving bitch she was, she had told him in a few pithy sentences that if he ever tried to break off with her, Pix would know everything. Cindy had kept a record of the names and dates of every place they had gone. She said she had taken the carbons from the motels and places they ate on occasions when he was supposed to be out of town on client's business. "And I've got more than carbons on you, something more negative, let's say," she had threatened. She would also make sure his partners knew. Not that they would care much, but he would look like a fool, she said, "Which of course is exactly what you are, Mr. Goodwrench."

She had taunted him all fall, even phoning the house. Thursday afternoon she had called his office demanding that he take her to dinner. He called Pix with a feeble excuse and they had driven to Hawthorne-by-the-Sea. Sam had a theory that in big restaurants you were more anonymous, except in this one he forgot about the loudspeaker system they used when your table was ready. It had never occurred to him at any time with Cindy to use an alias. It would have been no use anyway, he realized later. She would just have had more to blackmail him over.

They sat at one of the windows overlooking the ocean and watched the waves and the skyline of Boston shimmering in the distance. It should have been supremely romantic. Absentmindedly Sam bit into a popover, the house specialty. It tasted like sawdust. He looked at Cindy. She had ordered the most expensive things on the menu and was consuming her oysters Rockefeller with gusto. Sam felt like throwing up.

"I can't live this way. I'm going to tell Pix myself."

"And what about your partners?" Cindy asked mildly.

"They screw around all the time. This isn't going to change anything, and even if it does, I don't care anymore," Sam said wearily.

Cindy just smiled. It made him a whole lot more nervous than any of her threats.

"Just think about it, Sammy. Really think about it. And I need some more wine to go with the lobster."

He was home before midnight and slept with the blessed relief of someone about to be let out of jail.

The next morning Cindy called the house at seven o'clock. Fortunately he happened to pick it up.

"Hello, Sam, is Samantha there? This is Cindy. There's something I want to tell her—and show her."

Sam's throat closed and at first he could not speak. Stupidly, of all the things he thought she could do to him, this was the one that he had never considered. His kids. Perhaps he thought she had had some humanity after all. Defeated, he said, "All right, what do you want?"

"I'll tell you on the lovely drive we we're going to take this morning."

"I'm afraid today is impossible." He was trying to keep his voice neutral. This was a call, just a routine business call for all anyone sitting around the table eating Cap'n Crunch and Lucky Charms could tell.

She cut him off. "Nothing's impossible, Sam, as you've just learned. See you at the corner in an hour. Maybe we should go to the beach?"

Sam hung up. He wanted to kill her, and later that day when he heard someone had, he would have given anything to undo it.

Of course Sam and Cindy had been seen Friday and all those months previously. Millicent knew.

And Jenny Moore knew.

She had come to the Fairchilds' with her mother late in the afternoon, just as Tom was returning from what was becoming an increasingly familiar police station. They had stopped by to invite Faith and Tom—and Ben—to spend the following day at their place in New Hampshire. "The camp" Patricia called it, though Faith knew it bore as much resemblance to the camps of her youth as a Mercedes to a Volkswagen Beetle.

"This is our last weekend before shutting everything up and we plan to spend it quietly. It would be nice to have you with us. Robert hopes to get one last sail in if the weather holds. So bring your long johns."

"Oh, please come," Jenny chimed in, "Then I can play with Benjamin all day!"

Faith looked at Tom. "It's up to you, sweetheart, or rather up to your sermon."

Tom tried very hard to keep Saturdays clear for Faith and Benjamin. It was his day off, if a minister can be said to have a day off, but in practice he was sometimes hastily polishing the next day's sermon. Faith couldn't imagine writing one of these things every week and heartily admired him for doing so.

"There seems to be a lot of food for thought these days," Tom said glumly. "And the sermons are almost writing themselves. There should be no problem about going."

"Good. That's settled then," Patricia said, "We'll see you sometime in the morning?"

Tom took Patricia outside to get her opinion on the wisdom of fall pruning for a line of straggly yews and Faith and Jenny sat at the kitchen table consuming oatmeal cookies and drinking black currant tea. Benjamin had stopped his post-nap fussing and was swinging placidly in the wind-up swing.

Jenny Moore was a small, slender girl with pretty brown eyes and what used to be described in another era as "nut-brown hair." In other words, not many people would have looked at her twice with Cindy in the room.

It was Jenny who brought up the subject of Sam and Cindy.

"You just don't know what she was like, Mrs. Fairchild. Sometimes I think she wasn't really normal. She used to talk a lot about all the guys she had. I couldn't believe it about Mr. Miller at first. I thought it was just Cindy boasting again. She did a lot of that too, but after awhile, she knew too much about the family. Like when they were going to be away in Maine, and stuff. Samantha is my best friend and I haven't been able to go to their house for months. I was afraid I'd see Mr. Miller. How could he do that to them?"

"I don't know, Jenny. I think he was pretty upset about it and wanted to end it. He just got in over his head. It's no excuse, I know, but sometimes even older people do pretty dumb things."

"Yeah, but Cindy. I mean, couldn't he have picked somebody better?"

"I think she picked him," Faith said gently.

Jenny had been dangling an Ambi mirror block in front of Benjamin's pudgy face and said, "Poor Mr. Miller."

"Jenny," questioned Faith, "when I was talking to you at the house I had the feeling you weren't telling me everything. Was there anything else besides this business with Sam?"

"No," said Jenny quickly. Too quickly? "This was what was bothering me. I couldn't tell anyone because of Samantha."

"So there wasn't anyone else Cindy might have been seeing?"

"Well, I think there was someone new, but it was pretty recent. She was still at the hinting around stage. That everyone would be surprised if they knew and how no one was without sin—I thought that was a funny way to put it. Almost like it was a priest or something. Oh my gosh, Mrs. Fairchild, I'm sorry." Jenny put her hand to her mouth.

"That's all right, Jenny, don't worry. I know Tom has plenty of sins, but Cindy wasn't one of them. Of course there are other clergymen in town, or in the greater Boston area for that matter. Cindy didn't always stay close to home, did she?" Faith mused.

"No," sighed Jenny.

This is going to be harder than I imagined, thought Faith. And it always looks so easy in the books. Of course it would be ridiculous to think that Tom ever had the slightest notion of Cindy except as something that crawled out from under a rock.

If Tom noticed the two of them eyeing him with particular intensity when he walked in the back door with Patricia a few minutes later, he didn't let on.

The Moores left and the doorbell rang.

"Does life seem to be taking on a disturbingly frantic quality?" Faith asked. "Not that I'm complaining."

"I'll let you know after I see who it is," Tom replied.

It was Oswald Pearson and as he ushered him into the living room, Tom gave an imperceptible nod to Faith. The last thing he felt like was being interviewed by the press on the day's twists and turns. But Oswald was a loyal parishioner, so he dredged up a welcoming smile. "Nice to see you. We were just going to start a fire. Would you like to join us?"

Faith knew what she was supposed to say and chimed in, "How about a glass of wine or some coffee?"

However, Oswald was not paying a social call. He turned to Tom and seemed a bit embarrassed by the hospitality.

"Actually, I had wanted a few words with Reverend

Fairchild in private." He cleared his throat. It occurred to Faith that now she knew what "harumph" sounded like. Not that she could spell it.

"I'm here on a personal matter," Oswald explained.

Faith looked at Tom bleakly. Don't tell me Cindy was harumphing him too, she transmitted silently and excused herself to go play patty-cake with Benjamin or whatever.

Tom was mystified. Oswald seemed a well-balanced sort. A little smarmy and self-important for Tom's taste, but maybe that was the tabloid influence.

After gazing intently at Tom's bookshelves, Oswald got straight to the point.

"You probably don't know this—not many people do, especially in Aleford—but I'm gay." He paused to gauge Tom's reaction, was apparently reassured, and continued. "I've known ever since I was in college and I'm not here to talk about my decision. I'm comfortable with it, but I feel it is my own private business. I've never felt the need to be active in gay rights, but I'm certainly not ashamed of being a homosexual. It's like the color of my hair or eyes—a part of me and I'm much more interested in having people judge me on my newspaper than on my sexual preferences."

Tom thought he knew where this was going.

"Oswald, did Cindy know about this?"

Oswald looked very tired and the Liberty paisley bow tie under his blue pinstriped collar seemed to wilt.

"She saw me in Boston one afternoon and decided to follow me, just for the hell of it, I guess. Well, she struck pay dirt. I was on my way to meet a friend at a bar on Tremont Street. It's pretty well known as a gay bar. She waited until I came out with my friend, then snapped a picture. He grabbed the camera and tore out the film. She just smirked. 'I don't need evidence, though, do I, Mr. Pearson? You'd find it awfully hard to lie to your mother, wouldn't you?' I wanted to kill her on the spot, but we went to a luncheonette and she told me what she wanted."

"Money?" Tom guessed.

Oswald laughed, a quick burst of laughter that sounded more like a dog barking. "This might be hard to believe, but we're talking about Cindy Shepherd here and she was beyond the scope of the ordinary imagination. She wanted publicity. She wanted to be sure that anything she did—sneeze, cross the street, fart—would be in the paper, and with a picture."

Tom had always been pleased with the amount of coverage the paper had devoted to the Young People's activities. Now that turned to ashes in his mouth. He remembered all the pictures of Cindy. She must have been crazy.

"She had me where she wanted me. My mother would have found a gay son quite unacceptable. Even without a photograph, just the suggestion would have been enough to make serious trouble."

And, Tom recalled, Mother had covered the paper's losses for years, had, in fact, bought the thing for her son.

"But your mother died last summer. Surely you don't think the police would suspect you?" Tom was beginning to wonder what the point of all this revelation was.

"After Mother died, I told Cindy the deal was off, but she wasn't very happy about it. She informed me that she was glad I didn't mind my fellow townspeople knowing and she was sure that I could keep on coaching the youth soccer league."

Tom leaned forward and exploded. "She *was* diabolical, Oswald. I wish I had known what you were going through!"

"I wish I had told you. It never occurred to me that my position in the town would be affected—what people thought of me. So I renewed the contract. I figured she was getting married and after that she'd find bigger fish.

"But it's like she's reaching from the grave. The police asked me to take a look at some photos they're trying to identify. I'm sure you've heard about them. Anyway, they thought because of the newspaper, I might know more people around here than most. Those cameras of hers. I only knew one person—me. It's from the rear and I'm walking next to my friend into that bar. She must have finished her previous roll of film with that first photo. I could take the chance that they won't be able to make a positive identification, although they must have tracked down the location by now. I thought maybe they were trying to trap me into saying something, but nothing has happened. I'm a nervous wreck. Well, I have been since she died. I don't know what to do now. Would there be any point in going to the police? And how would people here react if they knew? Please, Reverend, help me decide what to do!"

Thirty minutes later, Tom poked his head in the kitchen.

"Darling, I'll explain when I get back, but I have to go to the police station for a while."

"Tom ! This is getting ridiculous."

"I know, Faith, believe me, I know." He rolled his eyes upward in supplication or confusion and left, but not before Faith grabbed him for a hasty kiss and whispered in his ear, "Whatever you do, don't eat any more of those submarine sandwiches. I'll have dinner no matter how late it is."

It wasn't too late, and over a mustardy salade lyonnaise, followed by a smoked trout soufflé, Tom filled Faith in, Oswald having decided to let this part of his life be revealed, albeit in as subtle a way as possible.

"In other words," said Faith, "we tell people like Pix, not people like Millicent."

"Precisely. He had to tell the police, of course, and it's bound to get out, so far better to have it originate with him. Somehow, I don't think people are going to care very much. Charley and Dunne didn't bat an eye and after questioning him for a while, just told him to go home and if he had to leave town to let them know."

"There are so many suspects at the moment, if we count all the guys in the pictures, it's almost an embarrassment of riches. Well, Oswald makes more sense than Sam, although both are ludicrous."

"I'm not sure I see how he makes more sense and I don't want to. My brain is so foggy now, I need a beacon to find my way upstairs."

"Follow me, Tom. Anyway, we can talk about this on the way to the Moores' tomorrow."

"Swell," he said and flicked off the kitchen light.

The next morning as they drove north through Newburyport and Salisbury to the Moores' house perched on the coast with virtually one room in Maine and one in New Hampshire, Faith thought she would always remember this fall as one of the most beautiful and horrible ones of her life.

The town of Aleford was completely panicked. Sam's interrogation had stirred even more indignation than Dave's. Sam had been a Town Meeting member practically since he came of voting age and he had been talking recently of running for selectman. Wives eyed their husbands furtively. If Sam had fallen, what about Dick or Harry? Perfectly innocent men looked full of guilty secrets. But no one except possibly Millicent believed Sam had killed Cindy and that meant there was a murderer among them.

In the car Faith had told Tom about her conversation with Jenny and he had laughed until the tears ran down his cheeks. It was a moment of great comic relief.

"Of course she was always sniffing around me, Faith, particularly when I first came to town. I know she wanted a parson to add to her list, sort of like the Mile High club or whatever it is where two people somehow manage to copulate in one of those airplane toilets where I have trouble just getting myself in to pee. Anyway, I was firmly avuncular and more lately positively nasty to her."

"Sure, sure," chided Faith. She could imagine Tom's idea of nastiness. "You probably told her she couldn't have the weenie roast when she wanted it or something like that."

"A very apt choice of activity, I may say," said Tom, "but actually you're pretty much on the mark. I was challenging her quite openly at the recent meetings. You know I've always wanted other kids to take charge and not let Cindy run the show. Last month I said something about a new president and she was very upset. I guess it hadn't occurred to her that once she was married, she wouldn't be the president or in Young People's anymore. Of course there would have been plenty to do in the couples group, but Cindy never liked to let go of anything."

"Exactly. She always had to be in control. Look at Sam and Dave, and now Oswald. And the way she ran things in town—all those pancake breakfasts. You know she didn't give a damn about any of it, it was just to be in charge. Maybe it was losing her parents at such an early age—she was afraid to let things out of her hearty little grip. You know, love, maybe she did have some deep-rooted psychological problems and we've been a tad insensitive."

Tom and Faith looked at each other.

"Naaaaah," they said simultaneously.

"But that explains the hints about a man of the cloth. She was really more angry at me than I supposed. Probably she thought I should make her some kind of president for life."

"I shudder to think what she had up her sleeve. Some kind of whisper campaign complete with scarlet letters addressed to the parsonage. But eliminating Dave, Sam, Oswald, and you leaves me without a suspect again."

"Don't worry. I'm sure you'll come up with a new theory soon. Theory, Faith, no more sleuthing, unless you take me too. You know, like 'You must never go down to the end of the town, if you don't go down with me'"?

"I promise, James James."

They had felt pretty optimistic, almost normal, for a few minutes, then concern about Sam and the Miller family occupied their conversation.

Faith hoped John Dunne was dissatisfied with Sam as a

suspect. Sam had been allowed to go home, but was summoned back bright and early that morning for more. The ticket to Puerto Rico in his pocket had in fact been for a client, just as he had asserted when they found it. Still he did not deny that he had been with Cindy until eleven-thirty Friday morning, when she had suddenly demanded to be driven back to Aleford, and casually jumped out of the car when he stopped for the light in the center. Her last words to him had been, "So long, sucker." Faith privately agreed with Jenny that Cindy was definitely not normal. She seemed to be possessed by Mae West, Mata Hari, and Scarlett O'Hara all at the same time.

They were almost to the Moores' house. Faith was looking out the window. Tom had a tape of "Prairie Home Companion" on and Garrison Keillor's hypnotic voice made her feel suspended and sleepy—and safe. A beautiful fall. That was the ironic part. All this was happening in one of the most beautiful falls to hit New England in a lifetime. The air was balmy; sometimes Faith even thought she could smell an ocean breeze and tropical flowers in downtown Aleford. Each morning started in gentle darkness and gave way to brilliant sunshine. The leaves did not seem to want to fall from the trees and when they did, they arranged themselves into exquisite bright mosaics of yellow, orange, and red on the lush green grass. It really was too much, Faith thought. Like Keillor's voice it lulled one into a feeling of safety and security. It made it too easy to forget what was really happening.

There was some banjo music on now. Faith had missed the hootenanny era, but Tom loved bluegrass and she was trying to educate herself for his sake. It was quite an effort. She found it hard to listen to most music. Despite her mother's rigorous training at Lincoln Center and Carnegie Hall, as soon as Faith heard the opening bars, be they Scarlatti or Scruggs, her mind started to wander.

Soon after, they turned off the main road onto the first of many little roads that would eventually land them on the Moores' peninsula.

Patricia had steaming bowls of chowder waiting for them. Robert was anxious to get out on the water before the tide turned, so they sat down to eat right away. After the house in Aleford, the camp was always a surprise.

This was Robert's house. He had discovered the spit of land jutting out just south of Kittery while sailing one day and had fallen in love with it. They used to camp on it when the children were young. At that time, the only structures were a dock and boathouse. Then five years ago they had built a magnificent contemporary house. The architect had been a client of Robert's and Robert had liked him immediately. When he saw the man's work, he knew this was whom he wanted to build his house. This house contained, rather than the hodgepodge of generations that furnished the Aleford house, Robert's collection of twentieth-century photographs; sleek, sublimely comfortable Italian furniture; and some of the beautiful Amish-type quilts Patricia had started making lately. The huge glass windows brought the pines and granite rocks into the house and at times it was hard to tell if you were inside or out.

They were eating on the deck. Patricia ladled the soup into chunky pottery bowls with which they could pleasantly warm their hands. This was followed by a big salad and more sourdough bread, which was Faith's contribution. Jenny had made a blueberry cobbler with blueberries frozen the past summer to finish the meal. It was perfect. Faith would have been content to sit and bask in the sun all afternoon, but Robert was plainly eager to get going.

"Come on, come on," he complained, "We're going to lose the wind and the tide will be turning before we're started."

"Good, Daddy," said Jenny. "Then we can clam!"

He turned to her in mock disgust. "Some sailor."

Jenny was going to watch Benjamin and at the last minute Patricia decided to stay behind and work on her latest quilt. Faith suspected she wasn't as ardent a sailor as Robert and only went to keep him company.

The three of them set out and before long the house was a pinprick in the midst of the dark green line of pines stretching far up the coast.

Robert let out a sigh of pure animal pleasure.

"Sometimes when I'm out here I wish I never had to go back to shore."

Clearly he was in a pensive mood. Tom said something noncommittal about wishing things like that himself sometimes. Faith knew his technique well enough by now. He would draw Robert out, unraveling the thread of his discontent, then help him knit it all back up into a more wearable garment. He really was a very good minister. She let their voices play about her and closed her eyes.

Presently she heard Robert say, "I've been pretty stretched to the limit, Tom, what with the two houses to keep up and Robby's tuition. And the wedding was going to set me back a good deal. I won't pretend that the money isn't damn handy."

Faith kept her eyes closed. She had the feeling that if she showed signs of being awake, Robert would stop talking. They were tearing across the water now at a terrific clip. Robert's voice picked up and the words came faster.

"It sounds horrible, especially now, but I've always hated her. Maybe I resented her coming into the family when she was a child, but I like to think that if it had been a different child, I would have loved it. From the beginning she did nothing but cause trouble. When Jenny was born, I actually feared she might harm the baby. She was about seven years old then. She knew what she was doing. We had a nurse at first and she left the room for a moment when Cindy was there playing. When she came back a few minutes later, Cindy had taken Jenny from the crib and was balancing her on the windowsill. She said she wanted to see if she could fly like baby Superman, but that was just Cindy covering up. Obviously she resented having another girl around, try as we did to avoid playing favorites. Patricia really has been a saint.

"Cindy never bothered Rob much. Well, he was a little boy to her and she was only interested in older boys. He wasn't any kind of threat to her, although she used to tease him cruelly. I had to speak sternly to her on several occasions and she would look very sorry, then start in on him again when my back was turned. You didn't know him when he was Jenny's age, but he was a bit chubby and Cindy drove him crazy. She had all sorts of names for him. You can imagine."

Tom could and, remembering a similar phase in his own adolescence, wondered why Rob hadn't killed Cindy then.

Robert had made some minute adjustments to the sail and was back at the tiller. The Moores had an assortment of boats—the inevitable Boston Whaler; rowboats, canoes, and dinghies for the kids to mess around with; Robby's boat, a Snipe, his pride and joy, which he raced, with his father as crew; then this old Dark Harbor sloop lovingly restored and cared for by Robert. Cindy had not been interested in boats, or in New Hampshire much.

"I was glad that Cindy didn't like to come here. She never wanted to rough it, which was all right with us. She didn't have to and she seemed happy to go to camps with less primitive accommodations instead. Maybe we were two families: the Moores and the Moores plus Cindy. We certainly didn't intend it to be that way in the beginning. Patricia's mother was still alive when we took Cindy and she warned us not to expect her to be like Rob. 'She's been badly spoiled from the start,' she said, 'Just do your Christian duty and run for the cellar when trouble comes, because she's going to bring you plenty.' Her grandmother was the only one Cindy minded and I think she was afraid of her."

"It's too bad she couldn't have taken her then. Maybe that's what Cindy needed—the old-fashioned 'spare the rod and spoil the child approach.' Not that I think it's right," Tom said.

"She didn't want her. She knew she didn't have too many years left and I think she wanted to have some peace and quiet. She liked her little house on the corner by the river. We would have been happy to have her in the big house—she had been born there and raised her children there, but she said she wanted a change and her own place. A remarkable woman. Patricia's a lot like her—they look soft, but underneath there's that native bedrock. Besides, Patricia wanted Cindy very much. We had been married for a long time before Rob came along and Patricia always wanted lots of children. We hadn't seen a lot of Cindy. They lived in California, you know. Patricia was terribly upset about losing her sister and she had just had a miscarriage, but here was a ready-made daughter and she was excited about having her. I have to admit I was too, at first. But it didn't last, especially for me."

He grew quiet and it seemed the conversation was at an end, but then he seemed to painfully drag an unbidden thought to the surface.

"You know, Tom, I'm sure that a man is involved in this business." Cindy had no scruples when it came to men. It's crazy to think it's Sam, but she could have driven him to it. Hell, she could have driven me.

"I've never told Patricia this, but Cindy used to try to get me interested in her. It's abominable and I told her exactly what she was doing and why. Just like Sam, she wanted to have something on me. Several times when Patricia was up here with the other two and we were alone, she'd come into the study with next to nothing on and put her arms around me. It makes me want to vomit when I think of it now.

"I felt sorry for Dave. He didn't know what he was getting into, but it was the happiest day of my life when she told us she was getting married and leaving home. My God, she didn't even leave to go to college, just took a few courses at Chamberlayne. You can't know how much I wanted to get rid of her."

Behind her closed eyes, Faith seemed to see the words in boldface type. **Get rid of her.**

Tom was murmuring something about the burden Robert had carried and carried alone. The boat was still speeding along, faster than ever—one side almost planing out of the water. The wind was tremendous and now that Tom was speaking Faith couldn't hear clearly any more. She looked at Robert through half-closed eyes. His face was slowly being drained of the angry contortions of a few minutes ago, but his hand was still tightly clenched upon the tiller. He was a large man, a powerful man. Faith felt obscurely afraid and wished they were back on dry land. Surely they were going too fast? It was impossible to distinguish the shoreline anymore, just a blur of greens and grays.

Suddenly she heard Robert shout to her, "Faith, are you awake?"

She sat up, "Yes, do you want me to do something? Lower the mizzen mast or hoist the boom?"

He laughed. And there they were, just three friends on a pleasant autumn sail. "Well, do you think you could move to the other side of the boat? Pretty tricky, but I think you can manage. We're coming about."

Faith knew what that meant and scampered over to the other side as they swung around. Robert handed the tiller over to Tom and went to get the thermos Patricia had sent along, which proved to be filled with strong, sweet tea, Lapsang Souchong, Patricia's own favorite, which she drank all day long, scalding hot and strong enough to dissolve the cup. There were chocolate chip cookies too—big chewy ones with plenty of walnuts.

The rest of the sail was uneventful and after a while they headed for home. The afternoon lay stretched out as flat as the calm water that filled the inlet by the point. The wind was a breeze and they sailed slowly into port.

Back at the house, Patricia was sitting on the deck swathed in bulky cardigans, stitching away at the quilt in her lap. It was almost finished and Faith admired the beauty of the colors—deep purples, smoky blues, and celadon greens with touches of scarlet. The stitching was so fine, it was hard to believe the human hand could accomplish it. Faith thought of her own tribulations with buttons and a ghastly failure at hemming a skirt once.

"I'd love to be able to make something like this." Faith sighed. "Or rather I think I would, but in all probability I'd try it and hate it. It's like thinking how nice it would be to live on a farm, one of those tidy Scandinavian ones with the white geese, like Carl Larsson's pictures, but I know deep inside I'm not that kind of person. It's the same with quilting."

"Nonsense," said Patricia briskly, "Well, maybe not about the farm—I know I always have visions of the same sort that conveniently leave out all the hard work. But about the quilting. You could start with a small hanging to get the idea, then go on from there. If you can do a running stitch, you can quilt. And if you can do the piecing on your machine, it goes quickly."

Faith didn't dare to tell her she didn't own a sewing machine, but agreed a hanging might be within her range.

Robert came out with two mugs of hot mulled wine. He and Tom were going to a neighbor's to inspect their new superinsulated Trelleborg house. They would be back soon. Jenny was reading inside and Benjamin was still asleep after an afternoon of unmitigated delight. He clearly adored Jenny, and Faith had high hopes of many happy babysitting hours ahead.

Patricia and Faith sat in companionable silence watching the lengthening afternoon shadows against the pines. The wine was delicious, and just as Faith was wondering if it would seem either piggy or inappropriate behavior for a minister's wife to ask for more, Patricia got up and took her cup. "I don't know about you, but I could do with a little more of that concoction."

Faith smiled. "You read my mind. Thank you."

"Are you too cold out here, Faith?" Patricia said, returning with the steaming mugs.

"No, it's lovely to drink hot things when it's a bit cool."

"This is my favorite time of day, not time to think of cooking yet—which I must admit I don't love the way you do—and too late to start any new jobs. Just time to put up your feet and read something frivolous."

They talked some more about what constituted frivolous reading. Patricia thought there should be a subcategory called "Hairdresser Reading," which was frivolous, too, of course, but more trivial.

"*People* magazine," offered Faith.

"Exactly," agreed Patricia, "Whereas real frivolous reading is like taking one of Jenny's Nancy Drews."

"Or a good murder mystery with no hidden literary value," suggested Faith, realizing as she said it that it was not the most appropriate remark for the occasion.

"We don't really need to read murder mysteries these days—literary or not," Patricia said grimly. "Which reminds me of something I wanted to say to you, Faith. It is undoubtedly none of my business, but I will claim an older woman's prerogative and speak anyway.

"I know you have been upset over the arrests of Dave and Sam and have been doing a little inquiring on your own, but I think you should stop and leave it to the police."

Faith was quite surprised—not that Patricia knew she had been asking questions; this was, to be sure Aleford—but that Patricia would feel strongly enough about it to tell her to stop. Patricia had never spoken to her in this way before.

"You don't always know what you are getting into when you start to try to uncover things," Patricia continued, "and you may hurt people you care about. What I mean is that there may be aspects of all this that are better left alone."

Was there something in Cindy's box that Patricia wanted to remain hidden? Robert was having financial problems and the girl had been goading him and his family for years. Given the width of her sward, was she blackmailing them, too?

The wine was making Faith feel mellow and benevolent. So be it. Patricia wouldn't be raising all this without a very good reason and certainly these people had suffered enough. What was one murder more or less?

"I know you would never do anything intentionally to hurt someone or the family," Patricia went on. "Not to mention that there could be some danger to yourself. We have only known you a short time, Faith, but we love you very much and are so happy Tom lured you to Aleford."

Patricia paused and looked down at her quilt as if expecting to find the text of her remarks stitched there. She looked up again.

"Of course the shock of finding the body was horrible and I can understand that you might feel you have a responsibility to get to the bottom of things. But please,

Faith, leave it all alone now. Detective Dunne and Charley will handle it."

Definitely there was something having to do with Robert. Faith was feeling even tipsier and everything suddenly seemed to make sense, although she did have the vague notion that once again the tables were turned. She had thought she was supposed to be consoling Patricia and perhaps offering a few well-chosen words of advice to the bereaved, but this was rapidly becoming the same kind of down-the-rabbit-hole conversation she had had with Pix Miller. Just who was the minister's wife here, anyway?

"I would never do anything to hurt anyone, especially not your family, Patricia," she promised solemnly. She could out-Whipple Eleanor on family in this one, she congratulated herself.

"Good. Well, that's that then. Now we do have to think about food and put all talk, frivolous and otherwise, aside for another time." Patricia looked at Faith gratefully, "You know, Faith, I haven't decided what to do with this quilt and if you would like it, I'd like you to have it. Maybe it would be an incentive for you. To quilt, that is."

"Patricia! I'd love it, but I couldn't possibly accept such a gift. It's taken you ages to do it."

"Not really ages and I'll start another one the moment this is finished. Besides, I didn't know you when we gave you a wedding present, so it was a bit impersonal. This is really for you." She gave Faith a slightly wry smile. "The name of the pattern is Sunshine and Shadow."

Faith thanked her profusely and followed her into the kitchen, where she tried very hard to dismiss the nagging thought at the back of her head that whispered "bribery." And what had she meant about an "incentive"? Quilting indeed.

Neither one of them heard Jenny tiptoe back to her room and then emerge as if she hadn't heard every word the two of them had been saying for the last half hour.

"I think Benjamin's awake," she reported.

"You've been reading in dim light again," her mother commented, "Come here and let me see; your eyes are all red. No, don't rub them! That just makes it worse."

"I'm fine, Mom," Jenny replied, and to prove it gave a very wobbly smile.

After a delicious supper of bluefish caught that morning and crisply fried in Patricia's huge old iron skillets, the Fairchilds drove back to Aleford. The Moores were staying until the next night. Faith knew Robert had to get in just one more sail and hoped the weather stayed as fine as it had been all day.

She told Tom what Patricia had said and also that she had been eavesdropping on the boat.

"I know," he teased her, "I couldn't imagine you sleeping through such a confessional. But," he continued seriously, "what was it all about? Don't tell me you've added him to your suspect list. You might as well put Robby down too and be done with it. Some smoldering adolescent jibe ignited recently? Nothing easier than to slip into town when everyone thought you were at school." Tom shook his head. "Will you listen to me! I'm getting as bad as you!"

"Remember what Charley said, anyone can kill, although I don't see Robert bothering to attach a rose to the body."

Faith leaned back into the seat, then sat bolt upright, "But wait a minute—Patricia might! Do you suppose they did it together? That would make sense, one as a lookout and Patricia adding the rose to throw in a red herring."

"Faith, fun is fun, but this is too crazy to even think about," said Tom wearily, "I mean these are my parishioners, God-fearing people. Although I *am* pretty puzzled about what Patricia was getting at. Maybe she's just concerned for your safety."

"Then why didn't she put it that way? It was almost like a threat. No, threat is too strong a word. A hint, a very strong hint."

"I think I should call on her next week on some other pretext and give her a chance to talk. Robert certainly seemed to want to and we'll have to get together again. Cindy really led them quite a life and I'm sure they have some guilt about the relief they feel. And that's all it can possibly be, Faith."

"There should be a club, a support group for all the people who were tormented by Cindy when she was alive and now feel guiltily blissful that she's gone—Dave, Sam, Oswald, probably Rob and Jenny, the Moores, of course, and Pix. And those are just the ones we know."

"Exactly, Faith, the ones we know and somewhere there's someone we don't know who wanted this relief enough to kill."

"And what makes you so sure it's someone we don't know?" Faith asked softly.

The car was moving steadily down I-95 in the darkness. There weren't a lot of other cars, not like in the summertime when you inched along at the Portsmouth Bridge. It was quiet and Tom took so long in answering that Faith thought he hadn't heard her. Then he spoke.

"I can't believe otherwise, Faith. It's too difficult. My

intellect tells me all is possible, but my heart and my faith dictate otherwise and for the moment I'm going with them."

"Well, then I'm coming too," said Faith and wished she didn't know how dangerous it was to travel with your head on the driver's shoulder.

The next morning in church Faith found it hard to stick to her promise. Her eyes kept scanning the congregation and her thoughts were sinfully secular. The weather had turned colder, but the sun streamed in the high arched windows, making the mums on the altar shimmer like gold. She tried to find a comfortable spot on the thin scarlet padding that was all that separated one from the austere wooden pews. The Women's Alliance had a slowly growing fund for new cushions, but Faith had a suspicion that they felt uneasy spending money for the comforts of the flesh when there were so many more important projects to support. At the moment, with a growing numbness au derrière, Faith would have liked to donate the whole sum herself—anonymously, of course.

They stood up to sing a hymn—what blessed relief! The church was almost full. Whether this was a tribute to Tom's popularity and a growing congregation or an unusual number of uneasy souls, Faith did not know, but church was where she wanted to be today. She needed to think.

She knew Tom was right and they couldn't allow themselves to believe it was someone they knew. She scanned the upturned, open-mouthed faces once more as they sang praises to the Lord. All those well-scrubbed, innocent faces.

But if not someone they knew, then who? She felt

hopelessly confused as she sang, "Amen," sat down, and bowed her head.

The afternoon passed busily. Tom had calls to make and Faith took Benjamin out into the sunshine while she tidied up the garden. He practiced his baby push-ups on a blanket under one of the maple trees and shrieked with delight every time a leaf fell. It felt good to be outside and have the cobwebs blown away.

They didn't talk about the murder at all on Sunday, and when Faith's mother called that night to find out how they were, Faith realized with a start that she had almost forgotten to tell her the latest developments.

She was up early on Monday, resolved to do as Patricia asked, not so much because she had asked but because the conversation with Tom had convinced her that practically speaking, and spiritually, she couldn't continue to go around Aleford casting baleful eyes on all the inhabitants and expect to have any peace of mind—or after a while any friends.

Tom was walking out to the Parish Office and Faith went down the front walk with him to get the mail out of the box. Monday's mail was usually a bit sparse and there was only a flyer from Sears and a plain envelope that had not gone through the post with Faith's name rather childishly scrawled on it. She opened it with a smile, thinking one of the children from the Sunday School where she sometimes helped had sent her a drawing.

Tom had gone through the gate and was suddenly startled to find Faith grabbing him desperately, barely able to speak.

"Tom, look!" she cried in horror.

He looked.

Inside the envelope folded in a sheet of white paper was a pressed rose. A pink rose. Just like Cindy's.

SEVEN

FAITH LOOKED OUT THE WINDOW AND WATCHED Boston rapidly assume the look of one of those relief maps made for a school project: The Charles River carefully painted brownish blue by unsteady hands and Beacon Hill a glorious wad of papier-mâché crowned by the State House's golden dome. Afterward there would have been an argument over who got to keep it, or rather which attic, closet, or basement it would grow dusty in before someone's mother heartlessly threw it away.

It seemed only seconds had elapsed between Faith's finding the rose and finding herself enveloped by a Newark-bound 737 securely buckled in with Benjamin clutched on her lap and a scotch and water clutched in her hand. Normally she didn't drink on planes, or rather not since Benjamin was born. She liked to keep alert, and after discovering that parents traveling with small children were not allowed to sit next to the emergency exits, there was all the more reason. As a matter of course she further protected her urchin by sitting one row back from the door and explaining to one of the people in the row ahead that if they had to evacuate the plane Faith would be passing her baby to him or her. The few startled looks she got were worth the peace of mind and possibly Benjamin's life, she repeatedly told Tom, who always pretended not to know her at these times and flatly refused to sit ahead of her himself and be the receiver. Anyway all this had been accomplished and Benjamin's rescuer was a rather serious-looking young man who was reading Kierkegaard, so Faith was pretty sure he wouldn't be too caught up in the plot to notice the plane was on fire or crashing.

She leaned back, put one of those tiny cushions stuffed with plaster of paris behind her head, and let the reel of the day's events pass before her eyes.

After she had handed him the envelope with the rose, Tom had been like a maniac. He dragged her into the house, shielding her with his body as if there might be an army of machine gun-toting assailants in the shrubbery. He slammed the door, locked it, and called the police all in one motion. Detective Dunne, this time without Charley MacIsaac, was there in minutes.

Faith remembered sitting bolt upright in the wing chair and agreeing automatically that now was a good time for her to visit her parents. She heard herself speaking in a normal tone of voice and wondered why she wasn't screaming. After all, someone seemed to want to kill her.

She decided to mention it to Tom and Detective Lieutenant Dunne, who seemed unduly preoccupied with flight times and at that moment were arguing over Newark versus Kennedy as an airport. They stopped and looked at her in amazement.

"Faith, sweetie, we just finished talking about all that. Don't you remember? Oh, my God, I'd better come with you for a while," Tom had cried.

Faith honestly could not remember the discussion. She knew they had all been talking for what seemed like years, but somehow the gist of it had passed her by. So they started again. This time with hot coffee and sandwiches quickly thrown together by Tom. Faith noted that somewhere along the line, it had become "Tom" and "John," but she was still "Mrs. Fairchild."

Dunne took a bite out of his ham sandwich, thereby consuming all but a small part of the crust, "Now, Mrs. Fairchild, this business could be any number of things—a prank by someone with a very warped sense of humor or a forcible hint from someone who genuinely cares about you and is afraid you might be too involved.

"However, we can't rule out that it could be from the murderer, who may also think you are too involved, but who might possibly not have your best interests at heart."

Faith appreciated the attempt at humor and also the way Dunne's voice dropped several octaves, putting it somewhere in the basement of C below low C, when he mentioned the last possibility.

He continued, "It has not escaped our notice that you have been asking people questions and in general hinting around that you'd like to find the murderer yourself."

He looked at her sternly.

Not another talking to, thought Faith, I just can't take all this advice.

Dunne's expression lightened up to a mere threat of showers, "Not that I'd mind someone else solving this. It's no secret that we aren't satisfied with the case against Sam Miller and even if we were, the entire law profession of the Greater Boston area has been bombarding us with so many calls, threats, and writs that it would take years to try the damned thing. But I'd prefer the someone else to be a police officer. It looks bad if the Spensers, Peter Wimseys, and Miss Pinkertons of the world show us up too often."

Faith was surprised. "I never would have guessed that

you read mysteries," she said, momentarily diverted by the idea of John Dunne tucked up in an emperor-sized bed eagerly trying to figure out whodunit.

"I don't, but my wife does. She says it's more interesting than my job and she thrives on crime."

Tom jumped in. He knew his Faith and the moment Dunne had said "wife" her eyes lit up. The next question was bound to be size-oriented or worse. "Faith, you see why it makes sense for you to leave now, don't you? Aside from easing my mind about your safety?"

Faith knew what he was doing and shot him a glance that said "later" all over it.

Now that she was calmer and fed, parts of the previous conversation were coming back to her. She agreed. "Yes, of course—to make the murderer, if that's who sent it, feel secure and relaxed, thereby committing some kind of blunder, like mentioning in the Shop and Save that he or she killed Cindy.

"If it wasn't the murderer, it doesn't matter so much, but don't worry. I would just as soon absent myself from the scene at the moment. Not," she added hastily for Dunne's benefit, "that I was ever so involved in it."

He looked at her and raised one eyebrow skeptically. This was a man who had definitely gone to the right movies as a kid.

Then Faith remembered what she had wanted to ask him. "Why did you say before that it would be virtually impossible to trace the letter?"

"Well, first of all the stationery is sold everywhere— in CVS or places like it. You've probably got some yourself to use when you pay bills."

Faith didn't, but that was neither here nor there.

"Then there's the handwriting. Of course, we'll give it to the analysts, but I'll bet you a jar of Ubet's syrup that it was written with an ordinary #2 Ticonderoga yellow pencil with the left hand. Pretty impossible to trace, short of demanding a handwriting sample from everyone in Aleford. And the person may not even be local. We've discovered that the field of Cindy's, shall we say 'acquaintances,' ranged pretty much over the greater Boston area. She was luckier than we've been, though; they all seem to have alibis and pretty good ones."

"So you still suspect someone local?" Tom asked quietly.

"We do. Of course we'll take handwriting samples from Sam Miller and Dave Svenson, Oswald Pearson too, but I doubt they'll prove anything."

"I really wish you wouldn't bother them. It's ridiculous to think one of them did this. Even if he was worried, Dave or Sam would come right out and tell me—or tell Tom."

"Please, Mrs. Fairchild, Faith if I may, let us go about this in our own way."

"Yes, you may—call me Faith that is, but I still don't like the idea of your grilling my friends and neighbors."

"Well, we'll try to make it more of a saute," Dunne quipped.

"Not funny, John," said Faith, but she was smiling. He really was a charmer when he tried. She wondered what his wife was like, probably five feet tall and a pistol.

"Before you get ready to go, let's go over everyone you've talked to about the murder again, in the last few days especially. Maybe we can figure out who got the wind up."

That reminded Faith of the sail on Saturday. Should she tell him about the conversation with Patricia? And what about Robert's confession in the boat? She looked at Tom uneasily and he understood.

"He means everything, Faith, this isn't a time to hold back, thinking you might be betraying a confidence. I certainly don't intend to."

"Good," said John, eyeing Tom appreciatively. He'd never been involved in a case with a minister before and he hadn't known what to expect. It had been a long time since he had been in church himself.

Sitting in the plane, thinking about it all, Faith felt far removed and as light as the air she was speeding through. It almost seemed to have happened to someone else, or in a book she read. She sipped her scotch slowly. Benjamin wasn't asleep, but he wasn't really awake either. She had given him a bottle at takeoff so his little ears wouldn't hurt and since then he seemed content to stare out the window and listen to the muffled roar of the engines.

She returned to her thoughts. They had gone over everybody without any significant results and finally she had hurried upstairs to pack, which roughly meant putting everything Benjamin owned in a bag with a few things for herself. Until she had a baby, she never realized how fast they went through clothes. She had expected to change a lot of diapers, of course, but Benjamin turned out to be a champion at what one of the books coyly referred to as "projectile vomiting"—like something from the space program. He was pretty much out of the stage now, but while it lasted Faith began to think his childhood would be one long laundry cycle.

Tom had been downstairs phoning the airlines. They had decided that Faith could go alone after all. She had felt better and had longed for the relative safety of the Big Apple; besides, she hadn't known what she would do with Tom in the city, since her plan was to fill out her winter wardrobe. She had also thought he should stay in Aleford so he could tell her what was happening. As he called her mother at work she could hear his voice while he tried to explain to her that her daughter had just received what amounted to a botanical death threat in the mail. Well, if anyone could do it, Tom could, Faith thought, and realized she was going to have to keep a firm nonhysterical hand on herself.

Detective Dunne had left with the letter carefully wrapped in some kind of plastic envelope. Faith supposed they would test it for everything in the world—fingerprints, sweat, and so on. She had pointed out to Dunne that, as with the murder, the most logical suspect was Cindy herself. Poison pen letters or the equivalent were certainly in Cindy's line, but she was undoubtedly in no condition to go around pressing flowers these days.

Dunne had wished her a good trip and told her to bring back some decent corned beef. Although they hadn't really gotten anywhere, at least something had happened and that seemed to cheer him up. Just pack little Mrs. Fairchild off to her mother's, solve the case, and then she could come home again.

John Dunne had been born and raised in the Pelham Bay section of the Bronx. When his father died, the whole neighborhood, plus relatives on both sides, jumped in to fill the gap. John knew his Bronx wasn't the Bronx of his mother's childhood—she was constantly lamenting the passing of certain landmarks—but it was a good place to grow up. The fires that would erupt later were just beginning to smolder and a long subway ride away in any case. Orchard Beach and City Island were nearby and if he wasn't at one or the other for a family picnic, he was there to swim and hang out with his friends. Everybody knew everybody else in the few blocks that constituted his world. Then he learned to cross the bridge and discovered Manhattan. By the time he graduated from high school, there wasn't an inch of that island he hadn't explored.

He met his wife while she was on her senior class trip to New York City, the culmination of thousands of bake sales, car washes, and raffles. Betsy was from the potato fields in northern Maine, a stone's throw away from the Canadian border. It took Dunne months to understand everything she said and years to decipher her family's accent. On the New York trip, she had become separated from her classmates and had no idea where she was, so she walked into the closest police station, as instructed by Mrs. Greenlaw, the chaperone. Mrs. Greenlaw's greatest fear was to lose one of her charges to the white slave trade and she understood that the latest tactic was using grandmotherly-looking old ladies in gloves and hats to lure unsuspecting girls astray.

Out of all the police stations in New York, it had to be Dunne's. It wasn't that Betsy was particularly beautiful, but she had something that appealed to him immediately. It was his first year on the force and his mother was after him to settle down. When Betsy walked in and asked how she could find the hotel they were staying at, he knew he'd be taking her there personally and buying her lunch on the way. Later she told him how intimidated she had been. He assumed she meant by his size, or because he was a policeman, but she confessed it was because he had been to college. His size never bothered her and if anyone thought they looked mismatched—Betsy *was* just a little over five feet and indeed a pistol—it wasn't something they said to John's face.

He sent Mrs. Greenlaw a dozen American Beauty roses the day they got engaged.

He'd never regretted marrying Betsy, even though she wouldn't live in New York. She made him laugh, was a terrific mother, and understood him better than anyone ever had. But there was scarcely a day he didn't miss the city. It wasn't Faith's city he missed, although a few of the quadrants intersected; it was one of the other hundreds of New York Citys people construct for themselves. He was sorry Faith had to leave Aleford for the reason she did, but he had to admit he'd like to have been on the plane with her.

Faith's scotch was almost gone and they would be landing in Newark soon. She was on the wrong side of the plane to see the Statue of Liberty as it descended but she did get a pretty impressive panoramic view of the New Jersey Turnpike.

She tightened the seatbelt, which she had never removed, and took the cushion from behind her head. She was thinking again about who could possibly have put the envelope in her mailbox—or rather she had been thinking about it all the time except on the rare occasions when another thought managed to creep through. Not Dave. Not Sam. So who else? That was the question that kept nagging at her. Maybe she should have taken the Aleford phone directory and gone household by household.

Faith had ruled out Patricia after classifying her under the heading of interested worried friend. Patricia wouldn't have spoken to Faith the way she had on Saturday if she had planned to scare her off the case with the rose.

Pix ? It just didn't seem to be her style.

Style was the key to it—style and personality. It was someone who read too many bad novels. Someone with time on his or her hands. Someone like Cindy or someone who liked Cindy? Faith was playing around with the words. Someone like Millicent Revere McKinley?

As Faith brought this to the front of her mind, she realized it had been lurking behind the parlor curtains for a while. Millicent was the type, all right. She didn't like Faith and certainly wouldn't mind alarming her, but was it such a strong dislike? And how to classify her? Murderer? Worried friend? Nut?

Faith couldn't believe Millicent was the murderer; she had been one of Cindy's few supporters, but as for sending the rose, it seemed just up her white-picket-fenced alley. And not because she was worried about Faith. Nor did Faith think she was nuts—well, maybe a little nuts. No, Millicent resented somebody else having a poke in her pond. This conclusion made Faith feel a lot better and she resolved to call Tom as soon as she got to the apartment and ask him to tell Dunne—somehow she still couldn't think of him as "John." It was too simple.

Faith's father was waiting for her at the gate and until she saw his tall, calm figure looking completely out of place in the airport chaos, she hadn't realized how happy she was to be out of things for a while. To let go and be a child again. He caught her up in a bear hug that

159

threatened to squish Benjamin and said, "Faith, what on earth is going on up there?"

She spent the trip into the city filling him in on the Peyton Place details that had become everyday life in Aleford, while also keeping a sharp eye on his driving. The Sibley car stayed in the garage for weeks at a time, since they didn't use it in the city, and Lawrence had a tendency to forget that he was driving and not riding in a cab.

They swung down the ramp approaching the Lincoln Tunnel and Faith feasted her eyes on the skyline, now becoming sadly crowded with banal glass and concrete boxes, but still the most exciting sight in the world. The Chrysler Building, her favorite, was gleaming like something from Oz in the late afternoon sunshine. At the bottom curve of the ramp there was the same enormous billboard that she remembered from her childhood. It always seemed to be advertising some kind of alcoholic beverage related to outdoor activities totally inappropriate to the surroundings—alpine skiing or Hawaiian surfboarding.

They pulled into the tunnel and Faith automatically looked for the tiles proclaiming the New York/New Jersey line. When they had gone to the Sibleys, it had been a contest with Hope to see who would spot it first. Were all children so competitive or just in her family, she wondered? There were the tiles now. She had seen them first.

She continued talking to her father. Some of their best and/or most momentous conversations had taken place in the car as he either drove her to or fetched her from the airport. They seemed to be able to communicate best when not face to face, yet still in some physical proximity.

160

Faith had asked her psychology professor at school about this one time, prodded no doubt by finding herself in an elevator with her. The class they had just left had touched upon father/daughter relationships and, carefully couching her question in nonidentifying terms, she revealed herself in the elevator. Her professor had smiled and remarked that many of her closest conversations with her father had been on similar occasions, something about a captive audience and enforced closeness. That made sense, but it also had to do with the lack of interruptions—Hope, her mother, the phone. Her father had always been a very busy man, except when he picked her up or drove her to the airport.

Before long they were at the apartment. Her mother had just gotten home from work and she folded Faith in a long, close embrace that left Faith smelling slightly of Arpège. Hope arrived a few minutes later. She had moved into her own apartment the summer before and from the contented look lurking below the expression of concern, Faith suspected she might have a "fella" at last. She resolved to get her alone for a sister-to-sister talk after dinner.

It was lovely to be back in the apartment with everyone wrapping her in cotton wool, admonishing her not to talk about "it" unless she felt like it, and then asking a lot of questions. She began to cheer up.

Just before dinner, Faith called Tom to tell him about Millicent.

"I really don't know why it didn't occur to me before, Tom. But it could be tricky getting a handwriting sample. Maybe Dunne could get his wife to pretend to be doing a survey. They could also check the envelope for her perfume, Mary Chess. There can't be too many people wearing that anymore. She must have bought a crate of it."

Tom had been equally enthusiastic, but he quelled the suggestion about the survey by saying that the police had their methods.

"Honestly, Tom," Faith retorted, "you're beginning to sound just like them."

"Glad you are feeling so much better, dear," he had replied sweetly.

"At least tell them about the perfume," she pleaded.

"That I will and I'm sure they will be very grateful for your highly educated nose."

"I miss you, Tom. This is our first long separation. Did you realize that?" said Faith, just realizing it herself.

"Of course, and you can't imagine how empty the house feels, not to mention how empty the bed is going to be."

"And better be."

"Actually this would be a good time for me to fool around. Everyone's so caught up with the murder that they wouldn't notice if I had twenty chorus girls living in the parsonage."

"I don't think men fool around with chorus girls anymore, Tom. They'd be pretty hard to find, and I wouldn't sell the town so short. I think the residents of Aleford are more than capable of concentrating on several scandals at once, so give it up."

And after some more nonsense and a good-night gurgle from Benjamin, they hung up.

After dinner Faith went into her old room to nurse Benjamin. He had taken wholeheartedly to solid foods and she knew she would be weaning him completely soon. He loved his little "teacher beaker" cup and it would not be long before he would use that full time. Then he'd be off to college.

She looked around at the familiar surroundings. The walls were a soft gray, the trim white, and the carpet one of her grandparents' cast-off Orientals with beautiful shades of rose. Rose! She shook her head—better make that pink. The room had gone through several metamorphoses from a Laura Ashley bower in her childhood to an ascetic black, white, and chrome cell in adolescence to its present incarnation, which had been gently demanded by her mother after Faith had been at college for a year and which was spurred no doubt by the nightmares of the guests who occupied the room in her absence.

She thought she had taken all her books with her to Aleford, but on the top shelf of the bookcase a few still lingered, an incongruous mixture: Judy Blume and C. S. Lewis, Camus and Agatha Christie. There was a thick volume of Jane Austen, which she thought she might take to bed that night as a pretty poor second best to Tom. Faith had always found Jane Austen's heroines comforting in times of physical illness or when her mind was diseased. Wondering whether the army was going to stay in town for the winter season, deciding what to wear at the Pump Room in Bath, or the gentle settling of all the complications and humiliations of matchmaking always made Faith feel her problems were small stuff. It also tended to put her to sleep.

She did miss Tom, though, more after speaking with him, and she wondered if he had spoken with Dunne or

Charley MacIsaac yet.

She had her answer an hour later. Hope had gone home early, after arranging to meet Faith for lunch the next day. She said she was tired, but Faith thought it more likely a late date with whoever this new man was. Her parents always went to bed early and she was just getting ready to settle down with the Bennets when the phone rang.

It was Tom. He had not been able to reach Detective Lieutenant Dunne, but Charley was at the station. He had listened to Tom carefully and thanked him, but expressed a cautious disbelief.

"I've known Millicent for over thirty years," he told Tom, "And I'm not saying she doesn't have a few screwy ideas—hell, a lot of screwy ideas—but this isn't like her. She'd be more likely to write to *The Aleford Chronicle* complaining about Faith than stick a dried-up old rose in her mailbox. Still, somebody's behaving peculiarly and we can't rule anyone out."

He said he'd get through to Dunne at home and be in touch in the morning.

"And tell Faith to go to bed," MacIsaac added before he hung up, "You too, Tom."

So they did.

For the next two days Faith basked in the late autumn New York sunshine and walked her feet off pushing Benjamin up Madison Avenue to see what was new in the boutiques, then down Fifth to the department stores. She even managed to squeeze in lunch with an old friend at a restaurant she wanted to try while Ben stayed with a sitter.

On Wednesday she and Hope got enormous sandwiches and hot coffee at the Carnegie Deli and took a cab to the park. It was chilly, but not too cold to eat lunch out in the sun. Faith wasn't interested in eating in a restaurant with Benjamin at this stage and the sitter the other day had cost what good Beluga was bringing. Wait until he can order for himself, she told Hope, who had generously offered to take Faith to Bellini's.

They sat on a bench by the lake and Hope went first. She was in love—and so desperately that she had even started doing crazy things at work like almost forgetting important meetings! Faith realized this must be serious. Missing a meeting for Hope was tantamount to waking up one morning to find Tama Janowitz had taken over her body sometime in the night.

Hope and her beloved had met at the tie counter at Barney's, which further proved Faith's adage, "Bergdorf's with your mother; Barney's with a man." Hope had been selecting a tie for a co-worker's birthday. Quentin (that really was his name) had been buying for himself. Advice was sought and given. Then lunch. Then dinner. The next day it was the squash court and now only a matter of time before they were head over heels in prenuptial agreements.

It was relaxing to sit in the cool October sun and listen to her sister outline their plans—not hopes and dreams, but plans. Faith was attending with part of her mind while the rest wandered foolishly around con- structing names for the happy couple's brokerage—Hope and Hopemore; Hopeful and Lee—when she realized that the child screaming was hers. Benjamin had grown tired of the entire contents of FAO Schwartz strung in and around his MacLaren Baby Lie-Back Buggy and wanted a new diversion. Hope picked him up and he rewarded her with a grin.

"Quentin wants children, of course, and so do I; but

not immediately." She paused. "And Fay, maybe we should wait until Benj is a little older before the two meet. Quentin hasn't actually seen many babies. He thinks 'Thirtysomething' is a figment of some fiendish television executive's imagination and it might be best if the whole thing were approached gradually."

"I'd say Benjamin's high school graduation should be soon enough if we want to be sure of halfway civilized behavior and even then we might be taking a chance," Faith replied and they laughed. But it wasn't unreasonable. The last thing you want a would-be spouse and father to observe is a screaming infant who will not be quiet no matter what the entire room full of intelligent loving adults do—an infant who carries some of the same genes as your own would.

Hope asked Faith some questions about the murder, but Faith was reluctant to think about recent events and regaled her sister instead with some of the funnier adventures she had been having as a minister's wife, like Eleanor Whipple's water and, last month, Mrs. Lawton's Siamese cockfighter's chair.

Mrs. Lawton was a globetrotter and had brought back numerous exotic souvenirs, which she had been proudly showing Faith. She had pulled forward an elaborately carved thronelike chair with a compartment underneath saying, "And here we have a cockfighter's chair, the man sits here," she sat, "and keeps his cock down here." She ducked her head down and slid the compartment open, leaving Faith gasping for a moment as she sought to stifle her hysterical laughter. She could give way to it now with Hope.

When Hope went back to work, Faith decided to sit a

while longer. Benjamin was lying back in the lie-back and she thought he might go to sleep. She watched her sister walk purposefully across the park. A woman with a definite place to go and definite things to do. How could two children in one family be so different? They even looked different. Hope was tall and dark, like the Sibleys. She had rather exotic green eyes, which didn't come from anyone in the family. Faith had always thought they were some kind of attribute dreamed up by Hope herself. Faith wouldn't have minded having those green eyes herself. She was sure Hope had been turning heads on Wall Street and not just rolling them, but Quentin was the first man her sister had ever been serious about. He'd better be good to her, Faith thought fiercely. If it took a BMW to make her little sister happy, then so be it.

Faith and Hope had one of those typical close sister relationships: love, hate; defense, attack; pride, jealousy. Today was a loving, protective, admiring day and Faith was happy. Someday she'd find a way to tell her sister how much she loathed being called "Fay." Fortunately, Hope was the only one who did so.

Benjamin was asleep. As Faith sat on the bench watching passersby, she mused about families. "For better or worse" should be on one's birth certificate as well as in one's wedding vows. All those inextricable—or was it inexplicable?—bonds. "Family" brought her back to Aleford, where these ties were not only tight, but sacred. More than a birthright. Generation after generation defined by who you were: "One of the Appletons" or "I'm a Forbes, you know." Quiet pride, or in cases like Millicent's, something a bit more extreme. In Aleford even the skeletons in the closet were reverentially dusted, although usually years later. Faith realized she was feeling a slight twinge of nostalgia for the town's leisurely pace, which she quelled immediately by leaping to her feet and heading for Bloomingdale's.

That night she decided to call her Aunt Chat and see if she wanted visitors the next day. Charity Sibley was Lawrence's oldest sister and lived in Mendham, New Jersey. She had been divorced for so long that Faith couldn't remember what her husband had been like. Chat had retired some years ago after a highly successful career on Madison Avenue, breaking in at a time when few women were working there. Eventually she had started her own agency, which she sold when she retired for Tom's veritable "beaucoup de bacon." Now, when she wasn't traveling, she lived in the country complete with horses, pond for swimming, and a tennis court she didn't use. "But people always want to play," she explained to Faith, who had been surprised to see it the first time she visited. Aunt Chat's idea of vigorous exercise was a stately breaststroke across and back some small body of water.

Charity said she would be delighted to see Faith and Benjamin the next day for lunch. Faith hung up and started to prepare dinner. Hope was coming and Faith had promised to get her out in time for her date with Quentin.

She began to deftly fill some wonton skins with a mixture of finely ground smoked turkey and scallions, which would serve as their first course, floating in a light broth with creme fraiche for those who wanted a dollop. As she worked, she began to think about Aleford, which had receded to the background these last few days, except for the feeling of unease with which she awoke each morning, not altogether explained by the absence of

168

Tom's familiar warm body in the bed beside her. He called every night and there was nothing new to report. Dunne had been more interested in Millicent as a possibility than MacIsaac had, and planned to pay her a visit. Faith wondered where on earth he was going to sit, if he could even get in the house.

Faith planned to stay in New York until Sunday night or Monday morning. She didn't want to miss seeing her Sibley grandmother and the whole family was going out there on Saturday. It was good to have had a break, but she was getting restless in exile. And she missed Tom.

The wontons were done and Faith took out the rack of lamb she had bought as a surprise for her father. It was his favorite and Faith was pretty sure he wasn't eating it every night for dinner, her mother's idea of nourishment being a piece of fish and a nice salad.

As she rubbed the lamb with a clove of garlic, she wondered what Aunt Chat would have to say about everything tomorrow. Chats with Chat had been a childhood joke, but very important to Faith. Her aunt had also been one of her main supporters when she wanted to start *Have Faith* and everyone else thought she was crazy.

She washed some greens for her mother's salad and made a gratinée of winter fruits with calvados to be whisked under the broiler at the last minute. There was still plenty of time before dinner to play with Benjamin and nibble at his tiny toes.

Faith had hoped her father might be free to go with her to Mendham, but at dinner he told her he couldn't get away, although if she stayed around and kept cooking the way she was, he might be unable to refuse her anything.

It was a slightly uproarious meal, especially for them,

169

Faith reflected. They indulged in some gallows humor at Aleford's expense and Tom's, what with his parishioners in a revolving door situation at the police station and worse. Faith felt better than she had in days. It really did seem a long way away and not of such earth-shaking importance at that.

Benjamin reclined in his little tilted seat. Faith never knew what these things were called—baby holders? bundle boards? or wasn't that for some other purpose? He smiled and waved and bore a striking resemblance to the Queen Mother, except without the hat. Of course, if Quentin had come to dinner the resemblance might well have been to Jekyll and Hyde. Children were nothing if not mysterious. Like those paper balls you had as a child. You'd unwind yards of tissue paper and end up with a plastic whistle that didn't work or a beautiful ruby ring you could swear was real. Every day with a baby was like opening a prize ball.

The next morning Faith and Benjamin made their way alone out to Mendham; Faith getting lost almost as soon as she crossed the Hudson just like any other self-respecting New Yorker. They arrived at Aunt Chat's at around eleven. She was in the garden reading, quite buried under a huge hat and a mountain of coats and shawls.

"Faith! Benjamin! How dear of you to come all this way. Do you want to sit outside? I couldn't resist, it was so lovely and warm."

Faith, whose lips were beginning to turn blue despite the sunshine, declined. Chat, though quite unathletic, was as hardy as the rest of the Sibleys. It took a minute or two for her to collect all her things—glasses, paper, book, throws, Thermos of tea. The Thermos reminded Faith momentarily of Patricia. It was like the one she had sent along with them on the boat. Faith wondered how she was and realized that last night's flippant Aleford humor had not dispelled her deep unease about it all. Patricia's ambiguous warning, the rose, the murder itself.

"Do I hear a sigh? How uncharacteristic. Come on, Faith, let's go inside and I'll light a fire to warm those little bird bones of yours and you can tell me everything while I cuddle Benjamin. And I won't even mind if he throws up all over me like last time."

"He doesn't do that anymore, Aunt Chat, or at least he hasn't lately," said Faith, slightly aggrieved at the mention of any imperfection in her offspring.

They moved indoors and settled down before the fire in the big stone fireplace that dominated the living room. The house was a complete mishmash. Parts of it dated to the late 1700s, while others were added on in what the owners somewhat benightedly thought was the same style. Rooms trailed on, one after the other, petering off in balconies or stairways. The kitchen had been added on most recently and was enormous. The room they were in now was adjacent to it, but was one of the original ones. Yet somehow the house seemed all of a piece, or maybe it was Chat's sense of design that unified it. It was American Comfortable—lots of quilts thrown over tables or hanging on the walls, bright fabrics covering soft chairs and footstools, bookcases everywhere, some with books and some with Chat's collection of folk art animals from all over the world. You assumed she had lived in the house for a lifetime, but it had actually been purchased after her retirement when she had moved out of her New York apartment to the accompaniment of dire predictions of loneliness and vegetation from all her friends. In fact she was seldom without company, except when she chose. The house had every comfort, including sauna and whirlpool. The gardens were lovely and people tended to look at Chat's as a kind of ideal vacation spot. As did she.

Faith stretched her legs toward the fire, glancing out the window toward the paddock where the horses strolled picturesquely.

"This really is wonderful, Chat. But who would have thunk it? I never pictured you as a country girl."

Her aunt laughed. "You forget I grew up in the country, Faith. Besides I wanted more space so I could finally get everything out of storage. I can't imagine how I lived in that tiny apartment all those years."

That tiny apartment had been an entire floor in one of the San Remo towers, but Faith supposed compared to this sprawling place it was tiny.

Benjamin was cozily ensconced in Chat's lap—a pretty roomy one. Like all the Sibleys she was tall and was discreetly referred to by the family as a "big girl." Her hair was almost completely white and very thick. She had dyed it while she was working and afterward the tidy dark bun had gradually given way to an equally tidy white one.

"Lunch is all made, Faith, or rather bought. And you will probably hate it, seafood quiche from the local gourmet shop and some kind of salad with lots of things in it, but I'll give you a glass of wine and you'll be polite enough not to notice."

Faith was sorry she had the reputation for being a food snob, but work was work and standards were standards.

"So, love, what the hell is going on in that parish of

172

yours? Are you sure it's not Salem or Stepford or one of those places? New England is always so unpredictable. You never know what they're going to do—vote for the most radical or the most conservative candidate; secede and start a new country. Anyway, I'm rambling. Start from the beginning and go to the end."

Chat looked increasingly serious as Faith related the events of the last two weeks. At some point she put Benjamin down on the floor to give Faith her undivided attention. Faith told all. Well, maybe she glossed over Scott Phelan a little, but then he wasn't really in the picture now that Dave was out of the running and her aunt just might react the way Tom had and once was more than enough. When Faith told her about finding the rose in the mailbox, Chat stood up and said, "Lunch. I want that glass of wine now and so do you."

At the table over what turned out to be pretty good quiche and really quite a good salad, Faith finished the tale. "So you see it's not over yet. It won't be until they find out who killed Cindy, or as far as I'm concerned, who sent the rose."

"Or maybe both," said Chat.

"Exactly. That's really what's worrying Tom—and me too, of course, but it all seems so improbable."

"Faith, honey, the whole thing seems improbable. If I didn't hear it from your own lips, I would say it was some kind of plot for a novel, a rather farfetched one at that. Really—Millicent Revere McKinley and an oversized detective named John Dunne."

"His mother liked poetry," Faith replied automatically.

"Fine, but there are limits. No, the whole thing is crazy and the craziest part is that you are mixed up in the middle. And a lot of it is your own fault."

Heavens, thought Faith, another talking to?

"You don't have enough to do up there, so you're bored and when a body literally falls into your lap, you treat it as a heaven-sent opportunity for excitement, instead of the dangerous mess it is. Now, do admit Faith, I know Benjamin is a darling, in fact the most darling baby in the world, but don't you find all these hours with him the teensiest bit enervating?"

You could never hide much from Chat, Faith reflected as she answered her aunt.

"Of course it's boring, but it's also wonderful and besides it's not for long. In fact it's for too short a time. Already I can't remember what he was like the first few weeks. And of course I feel guilty for being restless. Yes," catching the slightly triumphant look in her aunt's eye, "you are right, I am. I do admit it. I would like to have my fingers in a pie again, preferably one of my own making. But Chat, this is the choice I made and it's the right one. All my friends with babies either feel guilty because they are home or because they're not. It's a completely no-win situation, so you just have to accept it."

"Now say you're glad you don't have to work because you wouldn't miss this for the world," said Chat all in one breath.

"No need to be nasty. It's true. And everything else is true, too. I miss New York, and the little part of New Jersey that is forever you, and I miss working, but I wouldn't miss this for anything." Benjamin at that moment was fortuitously most engaging. He rolled over and babbled up at them lovingly from the quilt Chat had spread on the floor. A patch of sunlight hung over his head like a halo and Faith felt vindicated.

"I know all this, Faith, and I'm glad I didn't have to make any of these decisions myself. I never missed having children. I had you and Hope whenever I wanted and not when I didn't. Maybe the best of all worlds, but, you muddleheaded thing, you, all this work or not to work, guilt, and so on is not the real issue here."

"What do you mean?" Faith asked, feeling truly muddled by Chat's conversational leaps.

"The problem is that when you nipped into the belfry, you stumbled onto something, or somebody thinks you did, and it's very likely that you could be in real danger in Aleford. Playing amateur sleuth didn't help either and I suppose that's why I am yelling at you."

"Oh, is that what you're doing?" said Faith.

"I think the only sensible thing for you to do is to come with me to Spain next week. My friends have rented a large villa in Cadaqués, which is warm and sunny this time of year. You and Benjamin can come back all nicely browned and in one piece when this business is over. There's plenty of room and I plan to stay until late November anyway. That should give John Dunne and all his troops plenty of time to solve the case." Chat spoke emphatically and Faith knew she had already made the extra reservations, sent a wire to her friends, found a nice baby nurse from the village, and arranged the schedule for baths in the time it took Faith to answer.

"Oh, Chat, that would be lovely, but I can't leave Tom, especially now. And besides I think you are overreacting to the rose business," said Faith, forgetting her own sheer panic on Monday.

"I knew you'd say that at first, but I want you to

promise me that you will at least talk to Tom about it and not say no until then."

"I promise," said Faith, putting her arms around her aunt's neck, "and you know if Tom really thought there was any danger, he'd be the first one to get me out of town. And not just for a week."

"I know, Faith." Chat paused. "We could stop in Paris and eat and shop," she continued, dangling the possibility before Faith like an especially delicious *carotte.*

"Not fair! You really are too much. Tom will be so proud of me for resisting all this temptation. Maybe I am turning into a minister's wife after all," protested Faith.

"What makes you think minister's wives are any different from other wives?" asked Chat, "Don't tell me you see solving Cindy's murder as some kind of colossally good parish deed?"

"No, no, of course not. I don't know what I see it as anymore. Maybe you're right about the boredom stuff, but once you get involved in something, it's hard to stop. And I don't *think* minister's wives are different from any others. I know it. Remember, I've had a lot of opportunity to observe them over the years."

"Well, then, you drew the wrong conclusions." Chat dismissed the whole thing summarily. "We'll have to deal with all that another time if you're going to beat the traffic back into Manhattan."

Faith hadn't realized how fast the day had gone and quickly changed Benjamin for the trip. Chat gave her a little carved lamb from Equador for Benjamin's room and the last thing Faith heard as she drove away was, "Think Paris. Think Spain."

It took a long time to get back into the city, since she

got lost again. All the highways in New Jersey seemed to be eighty something and led to the turnpike. She ended up crossing the George Washington Bridge, or rather crawling across, at six o'clock listening to the "Eye Over Manhattan" helicopter reporter describe the traffic as "jam and cram," "stall and crawl." She got so interested in his rhyme schemes that she was home before she knew it.

Her mother had dinner ready—a nice piece of fish and some salad. Faith was happy to go to bed early and fell asleep before she could think too much about what Chat had said. When Tom had called, he had heroically urged her to go to Spain, but was not displeased when she said it was absolutely out of the question. She was very touched by Chat's offer, but it was back to Aleford, and any sun she got would be raking leaves outside her own little clapboard *casa*.

Friday Jane Sibley took the afternoon off from work and spent the time with Faith. She was sincerely worried about her daughter, but trusted Tom to assess the situation. Faith herself had not seemed upset after the first night and Jane was inclined to ascribe the rose in the letter box to some crank. Something about minister's wives seemed to attract a lot of slings and arrows of an outrageous nature and Jane had had a few herself.

They took Benjamin to the Children's Zoo in Central Park, more for themselves than for him, and had some nice sentimental moments together while Benjamin and the monkeys made faces at each other. Afterward Faith found a winter coat at last, at Bergdorf's, and they got back to the apartment with an armload of packages at five, weary but with a sense of accomplishment.

The phone was ringing. Faith reached it first and,

slightly out of breath, said, "Hello?"

It was Tom.

Patricia Moore was dead. Poisoned.

Robert had found the body in a small room off the kitchen when he came home from work. There was an empty mug lying on the kitchen floor and the teapot had been laced with enough weed killer to destroy several generations of Moores.

And Dave Svenson had been there all morning working in the garden—mulching the roses for winter.

"I'll take the nine o'clock shuttle," said Faith, hung up, and burst into bitter tears.

Tom met them at Logan and they drove home almost in silence. Faith could not stop crying and when they reached the parsonage, they went straight to bed. It was too terrible to talk about yet.

Few people were sleeping easily in Aleford that night, but one head drifted off almost as soon as it hit the pillow, smiling drowsily in self-congratulation at one last thought. *It had been ridiculously easy. That teapot just sitting on the kitchen counter. Well, better go to sleep. After all, there was still one more to go.*

EIGHT

ALEFORD HAD GONE TO SLEEP IN PROFOUND SHOCK ON Friday night and awoke to another on Saturday morning. Dave Svenson had been taken to the police station again.

Erik and Eva Svenson arrived at the parsonage wild-eyed and almost incoherent and Tom rushed off to the station with them. They got there not long after Dave, with Patrolman Dale Warren glued to his side, had been taken from the squad car and hustled into the station past a curious crowd.

While it had been ludicrous to think of Dave killing Cindy, there was at least a possible love/hate motive. But the idea of Dave, or anyone else, killing Patricia Moore was obscene. He had worked with her in the garden for as long as anyone could remember, learning the names of the plants the way some little boys learn the names of cars. It was she who had first given him his love of the soil, and between the two of them they had made the Moores' garden the beautiful place it was.

Dave had been overwhelmed with grief when he heard she was dead. It never occurred to him that he might be suspected. Mulching the roses was something he had done hundreds of times. When he wasn't at school or home, he was always in the garden. Yesterday he had been in and out of the shed where the Moores kept their gardening tools and supplies. The same shed the police later stripped of all the weed killers and fertilizers for analysis.

Dave had heard all this without connecting it to himself. When they came for him early the next morning, it was like hearing the news all over again. Like the worst bad dream he had ever had and something that could not possibly be happening to him. To be accused of her murder was like death itself.

The entire town was suffering from the same combination of grief and disbelief. But fear was abroad and the fact that someone, anyone, was arrested meant that at least something was being done. Little by little throughout the day, news leaked out and spread through Aleford like a particularly noxious gas.

It seemed Patricia had called the police station on Friday morning and asked to speak to either Charley MacIsaac or Detective Lieutenant John Dunne. Neither was available, but Dale Warren told her he could reach them easily. They were up at the county courthouse. She asked him to have one or both of them drop by that afternoon as she had something of particular importance relating to the case which she had decided to tell them.

Her exact words were, Dale recalled later, "I have decided to tell them something which may help clear things up." Accordingly Dale left a message with the secretary at the courthouse and told her it was urgent. But somehow it didn't reach Charley until close to dinner, arriving just before the message of her death. He had in fact been in the cruiser on the way to the Moores' when the news came over the two-way radio.

The police were speculating that Dave overheard Patricia's conversation with Dale and killed her to prevent whatever it was from coming out. Everyone knew how fond Patricia was of Dave and it was not unlikely that she might have been shielding him in some way. Just as he had killed Cindy in a moment of passion, he killed again.

When Robert found Patricia, she was sprawled out on the floor, a few feet from the phone. Her coral twin set was covered with vomit and one hand was still grasping her mouth in an expression of intense pain. The small daybed in the room was in disarray, the pillows flung to the floor. When the coroner arrived, he told Dunne that she had probably gone to lie down, feeling unwell, then convulsions started. She managed to get up to try to get help, but it was too late and she may have gone into a coma.

They had the answer soon.

Metaldehyde, administered in the strong, hot tea Patricia was so fond of drinking, a habit all Aleford knew about.

Metaldehyde—an unpleasant last meal for snails and slugs. An excruciating one for humans.

So it was Dave again. He met all the classic tests: means, motive, and opportunity. The snag was personality and Charley tried hard to convince himself that indeed anyone could kill, as he had so emphatically told Faith.

Dave had, by his own report, left the Moores' at noon, which was the approximate time the poison was administered, according to the coroner. Friday noon for Cindy and Friday noon for Patricia. Could it be simply coincidence?

Dave had gone home, eaten lunch, and left for an afternoon class. Just a normal day. The next morning he was hauled in for the murder of the woman he had loved best next to his own mother.

When Dave entered the police station, Charley could hardly bear to look at him. He tried to put a comforting hand on Dave's shoulder, but it was shrugged away—not so much in anger as sadness. Charley thought he had never seen anyone look more tragically defeated than Dave sitting slumped over, his eyes fixed on the concrete floor, waiting.

Tom and the Svensons arrived and Dave broke into noisy sobs. But they didn't last long. The lawyer came soon after and tried to talk with him, but Dave wasn't saying much. It was as though he was afraid that if one word escaped, a whole torrent would gush out and he'd never regain control. Finally a statement was taken.

Tom turned to the Svensons. "Why don't you go home for a while? The others will want to know what is happening and I'll stay with Dave. I'll call if there's anything new to report. We *know* Dave didn't do this, so it's a question of sitting tight until the police find the real murderer."

The Svensons reluctantly left and a few minutes later Dunne asked Dave and his lawyer to come with him to review and sign Dave's statement. Charley and Tom looked at each other wearily.

"Thanks for getting rid of the Svensons, Tom. The way Eva was staring at me, I was beginning to feel so guilty I almost confessed myself just to get that look off her face."

"I know," Tom agreed, shaking his head. He was sitting in a swivel chair across from Charley's desk. He was becoming horribly familiar with the decor of the Aleford police station and it left a lot to be desired. The calendar from the Patriot Fuel Oil Company appeared to be the only thing that wasn't gray or dark green.

"Charley, I know this probably isn't necessary to say, but I hope when I have to leave, you'll keep a close eye on Dave."

The chief looked surprised.

"I don't think he's going to try to escape," Tom said. "Or at least not in the way you're thinking. I'm afraid he's so depressed now, he might try to take his own life."

"It's crossed my mind, too, Tom. He's never been a high-strung kid, but Lord knows what's happened in the last two weeks would do it to anyone. Dale has known him for a long time and I'll make sure he's with him all the time. Once he starts to really talk, the danger will be past. I've seen it before."

"Maybe he'll talk to Dale. Of course the one person he would have opened up to isn't here." Tom looked grave.

"You know, Tom, I simply can't make any sense of this one. Patricia Moore was just about the finest woman I've ever known and if it does turn out to be Dave, it would have to have been insanity. Maybe Millicent is right and there is some sort of lunatic loose. Last night I was awake all night. What did Patricia have to tell us and why didn't she tell us sooner? Why didn't she tell Robert, her own husband? He says something was definitely bothering her lately, but when he asked her what was wrong she told him it was something she had to work out herself. It all ties in with what she was saying to Faith last weekend, too. Obviously she knew something, but what? I know it wasn't Dale's fault, or the secretary's. We were in closed court, but dear God if only she had called yesterday—I was at the station all day. She might be alive now."

Tom had never heard Charley speak at such length. He got up, went around the desk, and put his arm around MacIsaac's shoulder. Charley didn't shrug it off.

"Charley, don't forget the strain you're under, too. The answer will come in time. The pieces are all here in Aleford in front of our noses, I'm convinced of that."

"So am I. I just hope Dunne and I can put them together without breaking the town up too much."

Charley was verging on metaphorical, Tom thought. It looked like he was being stretched to the limit.

"I'll be going now. Faith is meeting me at the Moores'. She wants to take Jenny back to our house for the next few days and maybe that would be the best thing for her. You can reach me there if you need me."

"We'll be in touch, Tom, and thanks for all your help."

Faith was waiting at the foot of the Moores' driveway. She wore a black wool dress quite unbecoming to her and her eyes were puffy from crying, yet there was a kind of wild beauty to her and Tom was momentarily startled. Faith was very, very angry.

"Everything is different now, Tom. Somewhere in Aleford there is a completely amoral, degenerate person who must be stopped. We could treat the whole thing with Cindy a bit lightly, but I understand now that it was just as bad. It was the taking of a life. I know you think I should stay out of it, but I cannot. Patricia was a dear friend. I'm not going to lock the door and hope whoever it is confesses."

Tom took her in his arms and held her tightly. "Faith, Faith, my darling. I know. I feel that same way. Patricia stood for a lot of things for me, and not the least of them was her own personal courage and unselfishness; but Patricia herself was worried that something might happen. She didn't realize it might happen to herself and not you. Still, she must have had a good reason for thinking it might be you, and what good will you be to me and Benjamin dead?"

"I'm not going to die, Tom. What I am going to do is be very, very careful. You are the only person I am going to tell this to. As far as everyone else is concerned, including Dunne and MacIsaac, Mrs. Fairchild is scared silly and minding her own business."

"So what do you plan to do then?"

"Just watch, Tom, just watch."

He looked at her resolute face and they went up to the Moores'.

Patricia's house when Patricia had gone from it was like

the husk of one of the milkweed pods in the nearby meadow when all the strands of shiny silk had blown away in the wind. Faith walked down the hall past the familiar ship pictures, the Queen Anne lowboy on which Patricia had placed a huge bowl of chrysanthemums only yesterday morning. They were as fresh as when she had gathered them and bore the mark of her own distinctive way of arranging flowers—tendrils of ivy and wild flowers mixed with their more cultivated neighbors.

Faith knew she was going to start crying again.

Robert took them into his study. He was shivering and Tom immediately lit the fire, which had been laid but not started. Faith went into the kitchen to make some tea. She filled the kettle, put it on the stove, then reached for the teapot before remembering that of course it wouldn't be in its usual place. She opened a cabinet to look for another one and felt totally overwhelmed at the sight of Patricia's neat shelves, her blue and white cups hanging from their hooks. Faith found it impossible to believe that she wouldn't ever sit down and look across one of these cups at Patricia. She closed the door and went into the dining room for some brandy instead.

When she returned, Robert's head was bowed and he was mumbling to Tom. She left the decanter and went to find Jenny.

She was in her room with Rob. Both of them were momentarily cried out and sitting silently by the window leaning against one another. Jenny ran to Faith and put her arms around her and started to sob. There was really nothing Faith could think of to say, so she just sat and held the girl, stroking her soft hair. After a while, Jenny was calmer and Faith looked over her head at Rob still sitting in the window seat and apparently engrossed by the design on the cushion.

He looked up at her and spoke first, "It's not Dave, Mrs. Fairchild. You believe that, don't you?"

"Yes, I do."

"But who? It had to be someone who knew her pretty well—and knew the house.

Jenny's room was flooded with sunlight and Faith was stunned by a sense of unreality as she sat with these two children talking about murder amidst Jenny's collection of foreign dolls and horse books. Their mother's murder.

Rob continued to speculate. Faith realized he was trying to cope with the whole thing by organizing it like a term paper. She half expected him to produce a card file—and maybe it wasn't such a bad approach.

"The thing to figure out is what linked Mom with Cindy? Did she see something or did somebody tell her something? She was in town at the Museum of Fine Arts that day, so she couldn't have actually seen anything. I think it had to have been something somebody said later and Mom realized it didn't sound right.

"She's been pretty tense lately," he continued, "And talking a lot about not judging people harshly. I thought she meant me, because of how I felt about Cindy. I know it is horrible, but I was almost glad she was dead. But maybe Mom was talking about somebody else."

"Did she have any visitors lately? Especially anyone who didn't come normally?" Faith asked, addressing the question to Jenny. Rob wouldn't have known who had been there that week.

"Jenny and I have been all over that." He smiled for a moment and Jenny managed a faint replica in turn.

"Mom always had a lot of visitors. This house is like the Grand Central Station of Aleford. You know that. Her quilting group met here on Wednesday and it was their turn for the Bridge Club Thursday night. This doesn't include all the people dropping in and out."

Faith knew it was true. She had been in the habit of dropping in herself when she was up that way, to see Patricia, walk in the garden and likely as not leave with some flowers or a jar of jam. On paper Patricia would have sounded too good to be true. In real life you thanked God she was.

Faith offered to take Jenny for the next few days, but as she suspected the kids wanted to stay together and with their father.

"You know we don't have much family. Dad was an only child and now there's no one left in Mom's family, so we have to stick together," Rob said matter-of-factly, then added in a voice a little less controlled, "Dad has been pretty bad and he doesn't want to see anybody but us. We don't want to leave him."

Faith had only met Rob a few times before and although she had been slightly amused at the refined punk image he had adopted in defense against the preppiness of Williams, she didn't have much impression of him. Now she felt that he was going to keep things under control here. The numbness of grief would come later, but first there was anger and a lot to do.

With Jenny it was different. She looked completely devastated and Faith noticed that she was almost unable to speak. When Rob walked downstairs alone with Faith, she was glad to hear that Doctor Kane had given Jenny a tranquilizer the night before and had been checking in on them throughout the day. Jenny was going to try to sleep a little now—it was the best escape Faith could think of for her.

"If you need anything at all, Rob, please call—or just come over. For a meal, or talk, whatever helps."

"Thanks, Mrs. Fairchild, we will; although, it won't be for a meal unless we bring the food. If I could get all this stuff in the freezer, we'd have enough for a year or two. Plus the Minuteman Café phoned this morning and offered to bring a hot meal whenever we wanted. And of course none of us can eat a thing."

They went into the study. Robert and Tom were sitting before the fire. Robert looked a little better and Rob went over to his father and put his arms around him.

They left father and son soon after and went out to the car. As they were getting in they heard an insistent tapping on the upstairs window. It was Jenny. She was struggling to lift the heavy sash. Faith called up to her, then, realizing she couldn't be heard, went back in the house and up the stairs. Jenny was standing in the doorway of her room, her arms filled with a quilt—Patricia's last quilt.

"Mom wanted to give this to you. It's not finished. She was going to add another row of these quilted feathers . . ." Jenny could barely say the words.

Faith held her closely. "Oh, Jenny, it would be one of my greatest treasures, but I think you ought to keep it."

Jenny interrupted her as fiercely as her shaky voice would allow, "No, Mom wanted you to have it!"

"Then I will take it with great thanks. It is very beautiful, like your mother, but I am going to leave it with you to keep for me—just for now." Faith took Jenny's hand and led her back into her room, tucked her into bed, and spread the quilt over her—the deep blues and purples with flashes of red were like jewels in the sun and she hoped it would blanket Jenny with a little of the warmth and comfort of that other irreplaceable warmth. She closed the door softly and let herself out without disturbing Robert and Rob, noting as she did so what an easy house it was to slip in and out of unnoticed.

On the way back to the parsonage Faith told Tom what Jenny had done.

"Of course you know what this means?"

Tom knew exactly. "It means she was listening."

"Got it in one, sweetie. And it means she probably heard the whole conversation on the deck, not just the part about the quilt."

They swung into the driveway next to their house, a maneuver that had to be done decisively with one sharp turn of the wheel, since the drive itself was about the width of a footpath and bordered on one side by the Miller's arborvitae hedge and on the other side by their own protected-by-the-Historical-Society stone wall. Faith and Tom had each dislodged a stone or two, which they hastily and guiltily replaced. So far the arborvitae stood untouched.

Having safely reached the garage, Tom stopped the car and felt free to say what had been on his mind since the turn from Main Street.

"And yours may not have been the only conversation she overheard."

They entered the house, paid Samantha for babysitting after hearing what a perfect doll Benjamin had been, and then collapsed in front of their own hearth—a cold one, which Tom quickly filled with a roaring fire. He leaned back in the big wing chair and Faith sat on the floor, her head resting against his knees. He put his hand on her hair and absentmindedly twisted the strands between his fingers. Benjamin was on the floor next to Faith and Tom thought they must look like a scene straight out of Norman Rockwell—which was the whole point. What was going on beneath the surface of tranquil Aleford bore absolutely no resemblance to the picture on top. In one case, the discrepancy was deadly.

Patricia's funeral would be on Monday. Robert had left all the arrangements to Tom, as he was in no shape to plan anything at the moment. Tom thought he would go back to the house after church the next day and speak to each of them briefly with some suggestions. The children in particular might want something read. He already knew what Patricia had wanted; Aleford would have to listen to Wordsworth again, this time for real.

Faith told him about her talk with Rob and Tom was glad to hear he was taking charge of his father and sister. Then she stood up and stretched before bending down to scoop up Benjamin in her arms.

She turned to face Tom. "Now it's time to really talk and we need something to eat, so let's move into the kitchen."

Tom was completely exhausted and had planned to spend the evening as close to the position he presently occupied as possible, with perhaps a brief foray into the kitchen for some kind of sustenance, preferably something that took less than three minutes to prepare.

Faith looked at him sympathetically. "I know, I know—you're very tired, but we'll rest when the whole thing is over. Now we have work to do."

She put Benjamin in his beloved swing, wound it up, and made a mental note once more to nominate the inventor for the Nobel Peace Prize. Benj smiled up at her and began to move sedately to and fro.

When he was born, Faith swore she would make all his baby food and never buy the jars; but after she discovered how much it was costing her to puree pears out of season she succumbed and only made applesauce and vegetables. She reached for a jar of apricots now and quickly made some cereal and warm milk which she handed to Tom. A shadow crossed Benjamin's face when the swing was stopped, but as soon as he saw his little Peter Rabbit dish, he began to wave his hands in greedy anticipation. "Ah, my little gourmand, my *petit chou*," cooed Tom. He loved to feed his son. It was so direct and satisfying.

Faith meanwhile was bustling around, putting together a rich béarnaise sauce for the steaks and layering potatoes for a hasty Pommes Anna. "We need rich food, Tom, and a good Côtes-du-Rhône."

Tom could see Faith meant business.

An hour later Benjamin was asleep in the swing and Tom and Faith were savoring the last mouthfuls of Jack Savenor's steaks and what Faith had done with them.

Tom noticed that a yellow legal pad had materialized by Faith's side and she was starting to make a list. Tom didn't know whether it was the wine, food, or what, but he had begun to think that Faith was right. Between the two of them, they had a great deal of knowledge about the town and the case. Maybe if they went at it in a systematic way, they'd hit on something everyone else had missed.

Patricia's death had changed everything. It wasn't amateur sleuthing any more. It was his—and he unwillingly conceded, their—responsibility to try to find the killer.

"Now I know this sounds a lot like a novel—you know, the heroine sits in her bedroom in some drafty country house, writes down a list of suspects, realizes that the only one that makes sense is the very man she's in love with, then wakes up the next morning to find out the butler did it, of course."

"But," interrupted Tom, "the man you're in love with is sitting here and nobody in Aleford has butlers, so we'll just have to go on with the list."

"Exactly," said Faith, "There must be something to it, since you keep reading about it all the time and even Dunne carries that notebook."

"Let's start by treating the two murders as one," Tom suggested. "We'll list all the possible suspects and see who was where at the time of each and what motives exist."

"And what about the break-in? I think we have to assume that the murderer was looking for something in the tin box."

"Good point, and since it occurred while we were all in church, we should be able to remember where everyone was."

"Two things are wrong with that theory, Tom, although we have to try it. One, the murderer may not have been acting alone, and two, it's very hard to recall if someone was in church or not, particularly if he or she attends regularly. We're so used to seeing someone there, that we assume they were."

"And three, my love, the person who broke into the house may not be the murderer, but merely one of Cindy's pigeons."

"Tom, if we're this confused before we even start, we'll never get anywhere. Let's stick to the two deaths and go on from there."

Accordingly, Faith folded the paper in three lengthwise columns and wrote, "Suspects," "Murder 1," and "Murder 2" at the top of each column. Somehow it wouldn't have bothered her to write "Cindy's Murder," but it would to write "Patricia's." If she started to think about Patricia, she knew she would never be able to write anything.

By the end of an hour they had exhausted the possibilities and the paper looked a little sparse:

Suspects	Murder 1	Murder 2
Dave Svenson At the scene	At RR tracks;	seen by Phelan

Motives: Cindy was driving him crazy with her cruel behavior and what amounted to sexual blackmail. Despite his denial, was she blackmailing him about something else? Was he more drug involved than he admitted and she had further proof? They thought they knew Dave and it seemed unlikely, but he had already surprised them. Patricia knew he had killed Cindy and maybe even why, so he had to kill her, too. As for means, he could have done both easily; although, as MacIsaac had revealed, whoever killed Cindy must have been lucky or had some rudimentary medical knowledge to get the knife exactly where it was.

Sam Miller alibi	Unverifiable alibi	Airtight

Motives: Cindy was definitely blackmailing him and would no doubt keep escalating with further demands and humiliations. He hated her, but enough to kill her? Patricia had discovered something that definitely linked him to the murder, so he had to kill her too.

His alibi for Murder 1 was pretty slim. His car was seen near the center at 11:30 the day Cindy was killed and she was next to him. No one saw her get out at the light as he claimed. He was seen later at D'Angelo's Sandwich Shop in Bedford, but this was at 12:30, plenty of time to get up to the belfry with Cindy, kill her, and get down again. But where was his car? No one had seen it parked in the center (no one being Millicent McKinley and Eleanor Whipple, both of whose houses commanded a bird's-eye, or in Millicent's case, an eagle's-eye view of the approach to the belfry). And there was no way even a Porsche could drive up that hill.

Sam did have a strong alibi for Murder 2. He was in court at the time in full view of judge and jury. Faith suggested that the poison could have been put into the empty teapot the night or morning before, but Tom reminded her that Patricia always scalded it with boiling water before she made the tea and the poison would have been rinsed out. Still, they made a note to ask MacIsaac or Dunne if enough could have remained.

Virtually anyone in town had the means to kill Cindy: Easy enough to slip a knife from the kitchen drawer and Sam might also have known just where to place it. His hobby was medicine and he not only read the Harvard Medical School Healthletter from cover to cover each month, but had rows of medical texts in his study. Faith once asked him why he hadn't become a doctor and was surprised at the simplicity of the answer.

"I can't stand the sight of blood," Sam had replied.

No blood with poison, and Cindy's wound had been remarkably neat.

Pix Miller   No alibi for Murder 1 or Murder 2

Pix reported that she was shopping at the mall at the time of Cindy's death. She had been buying shoes and the saleswoman had remembered her, but not the exact time, other than that it was after lunch and before break. When Patricia was killed, Pix had been doing housework, always a solitary and unverifiable occupation. It was only noticeable when one didn't do it.

Motives: She discovered what Cindy was doing and killed to protect her husband's reputation and their marriage. Again she killed Patricia to prevent her from linking the Millers to the original crime.

Oswald Pearson   No alibi for Murder 1 or Murder 2

Pearson claimed he was in and out of his office both days working on stories. Faith remembered passing him on her way to the belfry, so he was in the area.

Motives: Cindy was definitely blackmailing him, but with his mother's death, it had lost most of its force. Unless there was more to it than he revealed. Again, she was leaving town soon and would be out of his thinning hair presumably for good. The only motive for killing

Patricia was if she had known he killed Cindy.

Millicent Revere McKinley (this was Faith's contribution). No alibi for either day, or any other day. She was certainly in close vicinity of the belfry on the day of Cindy's murder and had easy access to the roses, as did anyone strolling by her fence, but Millicent no doubt had them counted. Any murderer would certainly bring one along rather than risk the wrath of Millicent before even getting to kill Cindy. Faith made a note to check the roses in the Svenson's and Miller's gardens. And since Millicent didn't attend the Fairchilds' church, her absence would not have been noted. She could have broken into the Moores' house.

Motives: She was crazed by the use to which Cindy was putting the belfry, Dave apparently not being the only one to enjoy its timbered pleasures, and then she had to kill Patricia to prevent her from revealing what Millicent had done? Tom grudgingly agreed to include her in the list, but felt it was a pretty weak reed.

Robert Moore. Faith wrote this and looked at Tom. "It doesn't seem possible that he would kill Patricia, but maybe he killed Cindy and someone else killed Patricia?"

Tom disagreed. "I think the same person killed both of them, and I know Robert doesn't have alibis for either time. Few people would—it was lunch time, hard to prove you were someplace as opposed to being in your office with your secretary or whatever. And we don't know the extent of his money worries. I'm not saying I consider him a strong suspect." Tom ran his fingers through his hair in a gesture of fatigue and irritation. "Holy *merde,* Faith, I can't seriously consider any of these people as suspects, they're my friends, not to mention parishioners, except for Millicent."

Faith said skeptically, "I'm not so sure I would actually call her a friend either. But as for Robert, we have to put everything down. We do know he wasn't terribly grieved over Cindy's death. Patricia inherited everything and now it goes to him. Maybe he has a secret life. A cozy mistress on Beacon Hill?

"You know, Tom," she continued, "I'm convinced that Jenny knows something. Of course she would be reacting this way simply on account of her mother's death, but I can't help but feel that there is something more. Something she overheard maybe and then there was that strange remark Patricia made about family. Family, now what does that remind me of? Something Rob said." Faith shook her head impatiently.

"Don't worry, you'll remember," assured Tom. "Now, for the life of me, I can't think of anyone else to put on the list."

"Well, there are the quilters, bridge club members, and friends, but I don't see how any of them would have benefited from either or both deaths. Sam seems to have been the only prey for Cindy in town. At least that we know of to date.

"Pix is a member of the Bridge Club and I'll ask her for the names. Casually, Tom," she emphasized, seeing Tom's expression, "Believe me, I am not risking life and limb, or your peace of mind by going around asking a lot of questions. The words are 'low profile.'"

She wrinkled her forehead. "I wonder if there could be

anything in what Trishia said? You know, some girl who lost her boyfriend to Cindy going berserk and stalking her. But then how would Patricia fit in? Still, maybe I should talk to Scott again." She smiled wickedly. "With Trishia and anyone else you might want to have along to keep an eye on me."

"That's a pretty loose definition of 'low profile,' but as it happens I think it's not a bad idea. And since it's our only idea, I think *we* can follow it up. Scott called the Svensons, incidentally, and has talked to the lawyer."

"I knew he would come through." Faith felt somewhat vindicated.

Benjamin was snoring softly in his swing; lying in lopsided comfort. Faith reached across the table and took Tom's nice warm hand.

"I really can't think of any other suspects. Well, there's us, MacIsaac, and Dunne, but we can't get too crazy. Besides, if Cindy had had something on Dunne, he would have been more likely to tan her hide than kill her, and the same goes for Charley."

"What about the way they were killed? Cindy's was quick; she wouldn't have known what was happening after the initial stab of pain, but Patricia's death was truly agonizing. Unless," he stopped and appeared even more puzzled, "unless the murderer thought the poison would just put her to sleep. A gentle death. But in any case a death he or she wouldn't have to see."

"That would tell us that it was Robert or Dave. Someone who loved her."

Tom looked at Faith and drank the last of his wine.

"Robert or Dave—or one of her kids?"

Faith stared back at him. She had a sudden image of

Rob at the Willow Tree. She had forgotten all about it, assuming he was there on a date or whatever. But it wasn't a usual haunt for Aleford kids. Much more likely to be a place you'd go if you didn't want to run into anyone you knew. This and Jenny's hysterical grief smacked into her consciousness. It was like walking into a door. She told Tom about it and he was inclined to dismiss it, but added the information to the sheet.

"All right, put them on the list," Faith said, "And then let's burn the damn thing."

Tom didn't burn it, but put it carefully into one of his files. Then he followed Faith upstairs where she was changing Benjamin's diaper. He got out a fresh sleeper and they found some solace in the everyday routine of putting the baby to bed.

They got into their own bed and Faith snuggled up against Tom. "I don't feel much like a heroine," she said.

"Just wait a moment," he replied.

Overnight, winter descended on Aleford. By Sunday morning the trees had dropped all their remaining leaves in unsightly heaps, which a freezing wind made impossible to rake up. At eleven, as Tom was stepping into the pulpit, a heavy rain splattered against the windows like a barrage of gunshots. The congregation stiffened and it seemed to Faith that no one relaxed again during the rest of the service. Not that church was necessarily a place to relax, but it was as if they had all gasped collectively and then did not let the air out.

And it was freezing, at least it was to Faith, and she was sorry she hadn't worn her new winter coat. She had noticed last winter that New Englanders seemed to take some sort of perverse pride in how long they could go before they turned on the heat and, having done so, how low they set their thermostats. It was a common cocktail party conversational gambit, "Turned the heat on yet?" She fully expected to hear someone tell her one of these days that they had gone until January. Now she sat and shivered her way through the service, finding it hard to pay attention to even Tom's sermon. She felt out of sorts, as if she was coming down with the flu, but it was a flu of the mind, of the soul, and she didn't doubt that she shared it with most of the people in the church. When Tom mentioned the time of Patricia's funeral the next day, several handkerchiefs came out, and despite the atrocious weather, few lingered to talk to their friends at coffee hour. For once, no one wanted to exchange news. All the news was bad.

The Svensons' usual spot, six rows back and to the right, had been conspicuously empty. Dave had been arraigned late on Saturday at the District Court and taken to the Billerica House of Correction. His parents were working to arrange bail and meanwhile one or the other of them tried to be at his side.

The Moores' pew had been empty also. Tom found himself staring at the space in the middle of the second row where Patricia always sat, her face turned upward in expectation. It was hard to get through the sermon.

By Monday the rain had stopped, but the cold had settled in. There had been a killing frost during the night that left all the remaining flowers blackened stalks. It was hard to believe that only two weeks ago they had gathered in the same cemetery in light clothing surrounded by lush gold and scarlet leaves. Faith felt vaguely thankful to whatever meteorological quirk had ordained the change. It was all in keeping. Nature was mourning, too, with providentially gray skies blocking out the sun.

The church had been filled and afterward a large crowd gathered around the open grave. Patricia had known so many people, and not just from Aleford. Faith saw John Dunne's mountainous form looming over the crowd. He was wearing a well-cut black topcoat and she was surprised to see how sad he looked. She assumed cops weren't supposed to show their emotions. Charley was different. He had known Patricia since his first day in Aleford and Faith could understand why he was so upset, but Dunne?

In fact John Dunne was thinking of Dave Svenson. Dunne was remembering how startled the boy had been the day of Cindy's funeral when he came upon him on the ridge above the cemetery. He knew how Dave felt about Patricia. It had come out during the questioning about Cindy the first time. Dunne shook his head. The whole thing stank. He looked over at Charley and then at Faith. It never feels good to have one murder follow another and in this case it had felt worse than usual. Patricia was a close friend of Charley's and he had taken it hard, felt responsible. And maybe he—and Dunne himself—were.

Rob Moore had read "A slumber did my spirit seal" at the church service and said a few words about his mother. He was remarkably composed, but Faith noticed when he went to sit down between Jenny and his father, neither of whom were able to speak, he took their hands in a viselike grip. She wondered when he would break down and let some of the pain he was feeling out. Some of the Moores' friends had read things, Tom spoke, and they sang Patricia's favorite hymn, "For the Beauty of the Earth."

Now at the grave, Faith heard her husband reciting the words for the burial of the dead in a voice filled with sorrow. She seemed to be hearing everything from far away as though she were standing in a tunnel, then certain phrases would leap out assuming sudden clarity: "Thou knowest, Lord, the secrets of our hearts, shut not thy merciful ears to our prayer." What secrets had been in Patricia's heart, the hearts around her?

Tom's voice had momentarily lost its ceremonial tone and sounded almost conversational.

"My friends, I want to pause at this time so that we may have a moment of private prayer, but before we do I want to say good-bye to Patricia with a few more lines of her favorite Wordsworth—lines that remind me of her, her deep love of family, friends, growing things, and all this world can offer."

It was the last section of "The immortality ode" and when he reached the final lines,

"Thanks to the human heart by which we live,
Thanks to its tenderness, its joys, and fears,
To me the meanest flower that blows can give
Thoughts that do often lie too deep for tears."

There were tears.

After the silence, a long one in the cold grayness, they threw the clods of earth on the coffin, which so impossibly held the body of the woman most of them had seen a few days ago busily preparing for the church fair or buying groceries at the Shop and Save or answering the hotline at the drug crisis center.

They listened to Tom as he repeated the phrases that

were so familiar, but to which no one ever became accustomed—"earth to earth, ashes to ashes, dust to dust . . ."

Then it was "Our Father" and they turned away quickly, reluctant to stay, whether from cold or disbelief, Faith couldn't tell. She looked up and just as the trees had so rapidly dropped their leaves, the cemetery was empty of its mourners.

The Moores were the first to go. Jenny had started to scream when she saw the earth hit the coffin and her father picked her up in his arms and took her to the car. Rob followed at the end of the service with slow steps, unwilling to let go of even that much of his mother that still remained on earth.

There were no sherry and sandwiches this time. Those who had to hurried off to work and others went home. A few gravitated toward the parsonage and Faith found herself sitting in the living room with Sam, Pix and a few other parishioners. The Svensons, she knew, were going to see Dave. They were spending as much time as possible with him, trying to share his unshareable nightmare. Tom was at the Moores for much the same reason.

Faith had made some coffee and put out an assortment of things from the refrigerator: cheeses, some smoky Virginia ham, chutney, and duck rillettes. She had baked bread the day before and kept some of the baguettes out of the freezer, thinking at least the Millers would come back after the funeral. Pix brought over a huge pot of thick pea soup. There was plenty to eat, but so far no one had touched a thing. They were drinking a lot of coffee, though, and Faith was just about to get another pot when the doorbell rang.

"Pix, could you get the door?" she called. A moment later John Dunne and Charley entered the kitchen. Somehow she wasn't surprised to see them. They were so much a part of this whole cast of characters that any gathering seemed odd without them.

"Hello, Faith," Detective Dunne said, "Could I have a cup?"

"Of course, and please help yourself to some lunch. It's on the table in the dining room."

"It was a beautiful service, Faith," Charley said. He still had a catch in his voice and looked very, very tired. Faith remembered trying to pump him for information after Cindy's funeral. Dave had been the chief suspect then, too. She had the feeling she was repeating virtually the same words. "You can't honestly believe that Dave killed Patricia—or Cindy either." Faith faced them both squarely. "I really don't understand what's going on. Are you trying to smoke somebody else out? Is that why he's been charged? If so, it's a cruel and immoral thing to do."

Charley didn't say anything. Dunne looked at her sadly, "Faith, you must understand there's a great deal of evidence against Dave. In Cindy's case, he had a powerful motive; she was certainly driving him close to insanity and his alibi for the time in question is dependent on someone the police do not regard as a reliable witness. In the case of Patricia Moore, we are assuming that he overheard her call and knew he faced exposure. He was at the house at the time of death and had access to the poison used. Perhaps he couldn't bear for her to know that he had killed Cindy, but that's getting very speculative."

"I'm sorry. I'm not buying it at all." Then, as she caught a glance between the two, she hastily added, "Oh, don't worry, I'm not getting my magnifying glass and fingerprint kit out. You can do the job yourselves." She moved toward the door into the living room with the pot of fresh coffee. "Just do it, is all I ask," she tossed over her shoulder.

"Let's have a sandwich, Charley," Dunne said.

"Good idea, then I suppose we'd better get back to work before Faith reports us."

John Dunne smiled. He had heard about Faith's cooking and if the coffee was anything to go by, what was in the dining room should be pretty tasty.

Charley returned to the living room first and took a seat next to old Daniel Eliot, who had settled into the wing chair for the winter. Charley wasn't surprised to see him. Dan never missed a funeral. He was close to ninety and lived at the Peabody Home near the center of town. You had to be somewhat hale and hearty to stay there. It wasn't a nursing home so much as a residence for elderly people who didn't want to cope with a house. Daniel had never liked his house much and was only too happy to move his pared-down possessions into a bed/sitting room and let somebody else worry about what to cook. This had been twenty years ago and he'd been worrying about what to cook for a good twenty before that after his mother died. Daniel had never married and he was proud of his misogyny.

"How are you doing, Dan?" Charley asked.

"About as good as you, I expect," he replied.

Charley tried a different tack. "A very sad business." He sighed.

"Yup, the women in this family are going like flies. Her mother—she was my cousin, you know—just the other day and now Patty. Well, they always did want things their way. It's a lesson, Charley." Daniel nodded emphatically.

MacIsaac had no idea what the old geezer was talking about, but he nodded in return. Patricia's mother had died over ten years ago, which was not exactly last week. Might be an opening at the Peabody House soon.

He spotted Dunne with an empty plate motioning to him and he excused himself. They said good-bye to Faith and slipped out under her gimlet eye.

When Faith tumbled into bed that night, the last thing she would have thought was that she would have trouble falling asleep, but she did. Normally she carefully arranged herself in a fetal position under the duvet, put her head on a big square down pillow and was instantly asleep. Now she tried reading, got some warm milk, which she loathed even with nutmeg in it, and was still wide awake. She wandered around the house, checked Benjamin an unnecessary number of times, and finally settled onto the couch in front of a lifeless fireplace.

They had done some good thinking there, as well as other less cerebral things, for she knew why she couldn't sleep. There was something she had said or someone else had that she was sure was important, but she couldn't remember. She had driven Tom crazy all evening trying to dredge it up, but now perhaps if she just closed her eyes and let her mind drift it would come of its own accord. She thought of all the people, the scenes—funerals, kitchen table confidences, the sail in New Hampshire, the Moores' house.

All right, it was something to do with the Moores' house. She went room by room, then suddenly clear as a bell she heard Rob say, "Dad was an only child and now there's no one left in Mom's family."

Faith sat up with a start and ran upstairs to shake Tom's peacefully sleeping shoulder.

"Tom, Tom, I've got it. What we've been missing!"

"Oh, Faith, can't it wait until morning?"

Well, it could have, Faith thought guiltily. She had been so elated she had forgotten how exhausted Tom was.

"I'm sorry, sweetheart." She looked so crestfallen that Tom reached out and pulled her under the covers.

"Come on, tell me, otherwise I know I won't be able to sleep."

"*Family*, Tom, it has to have something to do with family. We've been concentrating on sex and money, admittedly more interesting in most cases than family, but we've lost sight of the fact that Cindy and Patricia were members of the same family. There's got to be a tie-in that way, not through Dave, Robert, and company."

" I'm not sure I get you, honey. Don't you think the police have explored this angle?"

"I'm not sure I get me either, Tom. It's a hunch, but it feels right. Maybe I have been living in New England too long, but it seems more in keeping with both crimes— roses and poisoned teapots instead of love nests and murder for hire like in the *Daily News.*"

"Okay, I see your point, but don't be too quick to stereotype Aleford. I'm sure there are plenty of love nests around."

"That's a relief," Faith said, curling up into her own.

NINE

JUST AS FAITH DROPPED OFF TO SLEEP AT LAST, SHE remembered the book Millicent McKinley had mentioned, a family history by one of Patricia's ancestors. She resolved to go to the library as soon as possible to get it. She also had to figure out a way to get a look at Patricia's will—and Cindy's, if one existed.

Accordingly, the next afternoon after Benjamin's nap, she strapped him into his Snugli for the short walk, dropped a goodly supply of zwiebacks into his diaper bag and set off for the Aleford Public Library, or rather the Turner Memorial Library, named after Ezra Turner who had given it a much needed boost around 1910 by leaving his extensive private library to Aleford rather than Harvard. After stocking the hitherto sparse shelves, the town sold off some of the more valuable works, most of them to Harvard, and everybody was happy. Well, maybe not Harvard, which did not like to buy what it could have received for nothing, not to mention tacitly acknowledging the foolhardy practice of non-Harvardian bequests.

At the moment, Faith was standing under the imposing portrait of Ezra that dominated the reading room, talking to Peg Bartlett, the head librarian. Ezra looked like Thomas Carlyle with more neatly combed hair and Peg looked like a Scottish farmer's wife who has just come in after delivering a calf with not a wisp of hair out of place or a wrinkle in her tweeds. She was a terrifically enthusiastic person who took her vocation, the dovetailing of person to book, with the utmost seriousness. Whenever Faith asked her to recommend something to read, Peg would cock her head to one side and eye Faith reflectively as if measuring her for a dress and murmur, "Maybe the Iris Murdoch, no wait, there's a new Anne Tyler," until she would suddenly straighten up and lead Faith to the exact book she wanted. Faith thought she was rather extraordinary, although a little intimidating. When Faith wanted to read a Judith Krantz, she would slink surreptitiously to the counter and slide it to one of the high school kids to check out.

Peg was replying to Faith's query about the book Millicent mentioned.

"Certainly I know the book, *A Ship Captain's Daughter,* by Harriet Cox Eliot. She was Patricia's grandmother and the literary one of the family. She wrote quite a few books, mostly about her family and local history. Harriet was the oldest of the Cox girls, as they were called all their lives. Captain Cox used to take his family with him on board his ships whenever he could. He wasn't at all superstitious and never had a ship go down. Harriet's book is all about her travels and includes a great deal of family history. Her mother was Persis Dudley, you know."

Faith didn't know but somehow with a librarian she found it easier to admit ignorance than with other people. They were so used to answering questions.

"I'm sorry, Peg, who was Persis Dudley?"

"No, *I'm* sorry, Faith, I keep assuming you've lived here all your life."

My God, thought Faith, momentarily panicked, has the Big Apple bloom rubbed off already?

"Not that anyone would mistake you for a New

Englander," added Peg with an eye on Faith's agnes b. outfit, "But it just seems you belong here."

"Thank you," said Faith, she knew not for what.

"Anyway, as a young woman, Persis Dudley was a close friend of Lucy Stone's and an ardent worker for women's rights. I'm sure she would have been terribly annoyed at Harriet's choice of title had she lived to see the book. But Harriet also wrote a reminiscence of her mother, *A Daughter Remembers,* which reprinted many of her mother's speeches. Persis was quite in demand as an orator and was evidently quite effective in stirring up an audience. She was also a Lucy Stoner."

This was something Faith did know. "Oh, so she kept her maiden name?"

"Yes, she was always known as Persis Dudley, never Persis Cox, although the children were named Cox.

"And of course there was her will. Really she was quite advanced for her time. The money was left in trust to the women in the family for five generations. She thought men could make their own money and by leaving money to the women of the family she would give them some independence. She hoped that after five generations women would have the same opportunities as men and the stipulation wouldn't be necessary."

"So when she died the estate passed to her daughters and not her sons? "

"Well, there weren't any sons and I have the feeling that if there had been, Captain Cox might not have agreed to have his hard-earned money left the way it was, but yes, it went to the eldest daughter. He did insist that the estate not be split up. He made provisions for each, but the bulk went to Harriet, lucky girl. There's a chapter on the will and its meaning for women in her book. She was, of course, pretty enthusiastic about the idea."

"I'd like to read the books, Peg, could you tell me where they are?"

"Of course," and she led Faith to a shelf set aside for local history.

"Now that's odd. I saw them both just the other day when I was shelving some other books and now it seems they're out. Let me just double-check that, Faith."

Peg went to the desk and Faith sat down to wait, quite disappointed. This had been her big brainstorm and she wasn't sure what she would do next. Although aside from the will, there didn't seem to be much more to mine in stories about ocean voyages or reprints of women's rights speeches.

Peg was back in minutes, "I'm afraid you're out of luck. They have both been checked out, but I can put a reserve on them for you."

"Thank you very much, Peg, I'd appreciate that."

Faith left the library and slowly walked down the wide front stairs to the street. So somebody else was interested in Patricia and Cindy's roots. Who could it possibly be?

She walked along Main Street toward the green and thought about begging Millicent to lend her her copies, but she knew just what would happen. She, Faith, would grovel all over the threadbare Orientals and Millicent would find a way to say "No" with the suggestion in her voice that it was because Faith would break the bindings or spill jam all over the pages.

Faith looked across the Green and tried to decide what to do next. As if in reply, Eleanor Whipple's house snapped into focus and Faith realized she could ask her if she had copies of the books. Eleanor was related to Patricia somehow and perhaps it was on the Cox-Dudley side. And if that didn't work out, she would have to go into town to the Massachusetts Historical Society or Boston Public Library.

It was a beautiful day and Faith strolled across the green basking in the late afternoon sun. She took a deep breath of Aleford fresh air as she crossed the street to Eleanor's. Missing the crunch of people on the crowded sidewalks of Manhattan—and the store windows everyone was trying to look at—she still felt a surge of well-being. She would have to be careful, she realized. Aleford was growing on her. Like some tenacious lichen.

She walked down the front path and climbed the stairs to Eleanor's porch. In the summer, one pot of red gera- niums stood neatly at the end of each step with two Bar Harbor rockers facing each other in unvarying positions on either side of the front door. All these things were presumably spending the winter in Eleanor's potting shed to appear like clockwork on the first of May.

Faith didn't doubt that Eleanor was home, probably working on one of her projects for the church fair. She didn't go out much, just to church and occasionally to a friend's. Eleanor didn't drive, but then Faith knew quite a few New Yorkers who had never learned either. The reason was the same—they didn't need to. Eleanor walked to the center every day or so and bought her groceries at the Shop and Save. Faith had never heard her talk about buying clothes. They looked like they had grown on her and Faith imagined she just replenished them with similar ones from the trunks in her attic, adding a little of her own tatted lace here and there, those "touches of white at the throat and cuffs" so beloved of ladies of a certain class and age. Every few months someone drove her to the hairdresser's for the permanent that kept her short white hair in soft ringlets. Faith thought of her as a very old lady, but as she rang the bell, she realized Eleanor might not be that old, probably not much older than Aunt Chat. It was all in the way one dressed. Faith gave a small interior nod as one of her most basic beliefs was yet again confirmed.

Eleanor answered the door immediately.

"Faith—and Benjamin—this is a nice surprise! Come in and have a cup of tea with me."

Eleanor was so glad to see them that Faith felt a twinge of guilt at not coming more often.

Poor soul, she's probably very lonely, she thought as she followed her down the hall.

Eleanor brushed aside Faith's offer to help and told her to make herself comfortable in the parlor instead.

"I won't be a moment, dear."

Faith sat down, glad to loosen the Snugli. She suspected Benjamin might be getting ready to cut his first tooth. He had been drooling a little more than usual lately and was apt to get fussy if moved from one comfortable position to another not immediately rewarding, so she kept him on her lap and let her eyes wander around the room. Eleanor's parlor was a little like the Moores' in that you felt nothing that entered the house had ever gone out again. The big difference was in the kinds of things that came in. Where Patricia's sideboard held a well-rubbed and often used Georgian silver tea service, Rose Medallion bowls, and a bevy of Battersea boxes, Eleanor's Victorian veneer table set in front of the bay window held a few large pieces of cut glass and a small case of what looked like some souvenir spoons from vacations long past. An intricate arrangement of wax flowers and stuffed birds in gravity-defying poses beneath a huge glass dome stood in solitary splendor on a marble-topped sideboard. There was a slightly pathetic dignity to the room. It tried very hard and sought to cover up any mistakes with antimacassars and embroidered centerpieces.

A bookcase that looked to be the major repository of the Whipple book collection stood against one wall. Advice on gardening elbowed Hawthorne and Thoreau. There was an exhaustive edition of Joseph C. Lincoln, which looked well read, and scores of old children's books. Between *Rebecca of Sunnybrook Farm* and *Lad, a Dog,* was *The Ship Captain's Daughter.*

Faith felt a little thrill of discovery. She called out to Eleanor, "May I look at one of your books?"

"Certainly," she replied, "help yourself. We're almost ready. I don't know why it should be true that a watched pot won't boil, but it is. I hope Lapsang Souchong is all right?"

"Yes, of course," she answered, shivering slightly, because it wasn't. She knew she would never be able to drink the tea without thinking of Patricia.

While she was waiting, Faith stood up and took the book from the shelf. She was just opening it when Eleanor appeared carrying a tray with the tea things. By now Faith had mastered the art of managing the tea strainer, hot water pitcher and all the accoutrements that accompanied tea in Aleford. At first she had tended to make a cup that was either hot water or pure tannic acid.

Eleanor put the tray on the table in front of Faith.

"Would you like me to hold Benjamin while you pour yourself a cup? That way you can make it the way you like it."

"Thank you." Faith smiled and started to close the book she had been holding when her gaze was pulled down sharply by the frontispiece. It was a reproduction of the three ship paintings that hung in the hallway at the Moores'. The *Nina,* the *Pinta,* and the *Santa Maria,* Patricia had said they called them when they were children. But that wasn't what they were called at all. No, they were the *Harriet,* the *Elnora,* and the *Rose.* Another rose. And *Elnora.* Another Eleanor?

Eleanor Whipple was looking at her speculatively. Faith felt suddenly uneasy. This wasn't Peg Bartlett's genial musing, but more like the look a poker player casts across the table before asking for a card.

She's wondering what I have in my hand, Faith thought in surprise.

"I see you've been looking at Aunt Hattie's book," Eleanor said carefully.

"Aunt Hattie's book?" Faith countered.

"Why, yes. Harriet Cox Eliot was my aunt."

The whole thing is going to be clear in a moment, Faith thought, but I'm not sure that I want it to be. And with the feeling of a person who finds himself alone in an unfamiliar bog at midnight, tentatively squelching along trying to avoid the holes that will engulf him, Faith stood up slowly and tightened the straps of the Snugli around her shoulders.

"Eleanor, if you don't mind, I'd like to take a raincheck on the tea. I'm suddenly feeling a little tired and I think I'd better go home."

"I'm terribly sorry, Faith," Eleanor replied gently, "but I think you had better sit down again. You see, I'm afraid I can't let you go now."

"What on earth do you mean?" Faith was genuinely aghast.

"You may not have figured it all out yet, my dear, but you are so clever that I'm sure you will and I really can't have that. You never should have taken the book down." She eyed Faith reprovingly much as she would have if Faith had been caught taking pennies from her purse.

"Well, really, Eleanor, I can't imagine what you are talking about and I only took the book because I am getting interested in local history and heard it mentioned. Now I really must go. Tom will be wondering where I am." Faith walked toward the door firmly, but was stopped by the sound of a drawer opening followed by a small steely click and the even steelier tone of sweet Eleanor's voice.

"Faith, if you don't sit down, I'll have to shoot you. And Benjamin." Faith managed to make her way back to the chair where her wobbling legs collapsed beneath her. This couldn't really be happening. She was in Aleford, sitting in Eleanor Whipple's sunny parlor, facing a tiny but menacing-looking gun firmly clutched in the hand of the woman who held the record for top sales of needlework at the church bazaar. It had to be a dream.

"It's father's gun. He always believed a house should be armed, though he never had occasion to use it himself."

Eleanor's poker face was gone, yet the one Faith knew so well, the gentle, slightly bemused pleasant face she was accustomed to see in church, was not in evidence either. Eleanor looked tired, a little sad, and very determined.

Faith realized she had absolutely no idea in the world what to do. Screaming was useless. She couldn't pretend that Tom was arriving soon as she had so fatally revealed that he didn't know where she was only a few minutes before. She remembered you were supposed to try to keep an attacker talking until help arrived and, failing anything else, she figured she might as well try it.

"Eleanor, don't you think you could put that away or at least hold it lower?"

At the moment the gun was aimed just where Faith's eyebrows met, or would meet but for assiduous tweezing. Slightly hysterically, Faith wondered if she would ever tweeze her eyebrows again, before forcing herself to concentrate on getting out of the parlor alive. Eleanor lowered the gun, but did not loosen her grip.

Would Eleanor really kill her? Faith wondered. And an innocent little baby? Was it worth the risk to make a run for the porch? Unfortunately Eleanor's house was set far back from the sidewalk and further obscured by a tall Canadian hemlock hedge. But surely she wouldn't shoot them both? Maybe the gun wasn't really loaded.

Of course, Faith reflected, as the numbing realization that Eleanor had already killed two people hit her, two more murders at this stage might not seem to matter much. She decided to stay where she was for the moment and play dumb.

"Perhaps you'd like to tell me what you imagine I know? Eleanor, really, I don't know what is going on and things seem to be getting a little out of hand."

"Now Faith, you do know what it is about and I will excuse the minister's wife from a lie in view of the circumstances, but I do so wish you had not interfered in

217

all this. I will miss you at our Alliance meetings."

Eleanor sounded a bit peevish and the allusion to missed Alliance meetings had not escaped Faith. And by now Eleanor was right. Faith knew exactly what was going on.

First Eleanor had killed Cindy, then two weeks later Patricia, and now Faith and Benjamin had ingenuously walked into her parlor to be the third and fourth victims. Spilled curds and whey were nothing compared to what Eleanor had in mind.

Eleanor was thinking out loud.

"It's a shame I never learned to drive. It really makes things awkward." She paused.

Faith could feel her heart beating against her chest. She was surprised it didn't send Benjamin bouncing up and down. Talk. She must keep Eleanor talking. Murderers always liked to discuss their crimes, she had read. So be it.

"Eleanor, can you really be saying that you killed Cindy and Patricia and that this is what I have figured out?"

Maybe she would deny it and this whole business would turn out to be some sort of passing dementia. Faith half expected Eleanor to laugh and hand over the fun. But only half.

"Why, yes, Faith. You see, I knew you knew," Eleanor sounded triumphant.

"But why? What possible reason could you have for killing them?" Faith found herself looking forward to Eleanor's explanation in spite of everything, although the circumstances were not what she would have wished. Better to have had Eleanor explaining from a straitjacket.

"Why?" Eleanor sounded puzzled, "For the money, of course. I thought you would realize that. For

Grandmother's money."

Faith realized she had missed an episode.

"Grandmother's money?"

Eleanor sighed. Faith had not been as clever as she thought.

"You see, Faith, my grandfather and great-grandfather made rather a lot of money with their ships. My grandmother was a very forward-thinking woman who realized that men make much more money in this world than women do, so she had better take care of her female descendants. Unfortunately Grandfather didn't want to have his estate divided. He wanted the money to go with the house, so whoever had it would always be able to keep it up. As if there wasn't plenty," Eleanor gave what could only be described as a snort of disgust.

"Yes, I heard all this," Faith said, "But forgive me, what does it have to do with killing Cindy and Patricia?"

As she spoke, Faith suddenly understood exactly what it had to do with killing them. She knew what Eleanor would say now. She owed Tom a dinner. And the sooner the better.

"My grandmother always intended the money to be shared equally, no matter what the will said. But when she died Hattie got everything. Elnora, for whom I am named, never married and lived with them, so she never needed any money. I suppose in a way she did get her share. But my poor mother, Rose, didn't get anything much." Eleanor was beginning to speak a bit dreamily. Faith watched and waited for her chance.

"You know I didn't grow up in Aleford, Faith. Oh, no. My father was just a poor country doctor who worked hard every day of his life for us. We had to move to this house when he died. It belongs, or I should say, belonged to Patricia. We have life tenancy. Tenants!" Eleanor spat the word out.

"You never knew Mother, of course. She was much more suited for the Captain's house than the Moores. After Hattie died, it should by rights have gone to her and that was what grandmother had intended. Patricia and Polly's mother, Phoebe, was nice enough, but she wasn't a real lady like mother. And her husband, Lewis, was just a common boy.

"Mother died two years after we moved here and I think part of what caused her death was seeing what had happened to all her things and having to live in this pokey little house. Then everything went to Polly, but she just wanted the money. So much for Grandfather's idea. She was happy to let Patricia and Robert live in the house while she and that husband of hers flitted all over the place. I remember when my sister Rose and I heard the news that they had been killed. Rose just looked at me from where you are sitting now and I knew what she meant. There is some justice in this life after all." Eleanor sat up straighter with a complacent smile on her face.

"You know I am a very devout woman, Faith, but it did give me just the tiniest bit of pleasure to kill Cindy. She was an extremely wicked girl and she hurt Rose's feelings terribly one time. No, it was necessary to kill her so I could inherit, but it wasn't exactly a disagreeable thing to do. I used to see her go up there," Eleanor waved the gun toward the belfry, then swung it immediately back toward Faith.

"That Friday when I saw her, I knew she would be meeting somebody and I'd have to go quickly, so I just nipped off one of my roses and slipped out the kitchen door. She was inside on one of the benches and didn't even bother to get up when I entered."

Eleanor was indignant and Faith resolved if she ever got out of this to teach Benjamin all the social amenities. One never knew when manners might save one's life.

"Really," Eleanor sounded surprised, "she made it so easy. I didn't have to think. I just stabbed her. I have been studying father's medical books, so I could get it right and I did," Eleanor sounded proud. "The rose was in memory of Rose, and Mother too, of course. I wish I had thought to do all this when they could have been here to enjoy it with me. I know Rose especially would have been glad that Cindy was dead."

"But Patricia? I thought you liked her?"

"Of course I liked Patricia. She was a very good woman, but Faith, dear, don't you see, I wouldn't get the money if Patricia was alive. I didn't want to hurt her, so I just put the snail killer in her tea. Dave Svenson was in the back talking to her about her garden. Not that he ever thought to help me with mine. I knew the police would suspect him again. It was really very lucky."

Faith saw everything now and spoke aloud a thought better left alone, "So you plan to kill Jennifer as well?"

Eleanor was quiet for a few moments.

"I don't think you ought to be asking so many questions. You know I saw you go up the hill that day and was glad we hadn't met. I certainly never intended for you to be involved in all this. And sweet little Benjamin. It never concerned you." Eleanor looked at Faith reproachfully, using the tone of voice she might have if Faith had been asking her for whom she was going to vote

221

in the next election.

"And now it's too late."

"So you sent me that rose to stop me from getting involved," Faith said, hoping to distract her from the implications of that last remark.

"Rose, what rose? I never sent you any roses, Faith, although it was a splendid year for them." She glanced out to the garden where the stalks stood stripped of leaves and flowers in lethal thorniness.

"You didn't put a pressed rose in my mailbox!?"

Eleanor looked at Faith kindly, "No, of course not. What an odd notion!"

Odd notions seemed to be on a rampage.

Faith could not resist one more question before she acted.

"But why do you need the money?"

Eleanor looked at her as if to say, You of all people.

"Why does anyone 'need' money? I want to buy nice things and travel and mostly get out of this house. You have no idea how noisy it is living so near the green and the center. Plus it's very damp. No, the Captain's house is much healthier."

At the word "healthier," Faith seized her chance. She leaped up suddenly and overturned the loaded tea table directly onto Eleanor's lap. Then she sprinted for the door. As she raced down the hall to the front door she could hear Eleanor's enraged cries behind her.

At the door, she grabbed the lock, twisted the bolt free, and reached for the ornate brass door knob. She turned hard, heard a click, but the door wouldn't budge. In vain she pulled with all her strength as she realized that Eleanor must have locked the door with another key and taken it.

There was still the kitchen door, which might not be locked at all. Faith turned and ran down the hall. Eleanor was presumably buried under a mound of broken English ironstone and soggy digestive biscuits, but it wouldn't be for long.

She quickly pulled the kitchen door behind her. Damn, there was no way to lock it. The outside door was also locked, but Faith could see through the door that a key hung conveniently on a nail under the porch eaves, well within reach if she smashed the glass. Eleanor's shadowy backyard and Belfry Hill behind it never looked better and she grabbed an iron skillet from the top of Eleanor's stove to break the pane.

It was too late. Eleanor, wet and furious, strode rapidly across the room and shoved the gun against the small of Faith's back. It did not feel pleasant and Faith began to sob in fear and frustration.

"Put that pan down, Faith. You have made a horrible shambles and broken some of my treasures. Now it appears you are about to cause further damage." She nudged Faith toward the other end of the kitchen. Faith put the pan down on the table, abandoning any thought of using it to smack Eleanor over the head. The gun would surely go off and the bullet travel straight through her body into Benjamin's. Eleanor herself seemed to have grown a foot and any previous hint of frailty had disappeared. Faith began to suspect Eleanor was both a lot younger and a lot stronger than she had thought.

"I should have done this immediately and not let you sit and talk so long. Now, open the door on my left slowly and go down the stairs," Eleanor said in a commanding voice, "Remember, I will shoot you both if you try anything else."

Faith was crying again as she moved toward the door she knew must lead to Eleanor's basement. There didn't seem to be anything else to do, although she had little hope of melting Eleanor's heart with her tears. Slowly they moved down the steep wooden stairs.

Faith figured she had nothing more to lose and when they got to the bottom, resolved to throw herself against Eleanor and try to get the gun. But at the foot of the stairs, Eleanor suddenly leaned forward and turned on a light switch. Faith was momentarily disoriented and it was enough time for Eleanor to push her along into another room.

The basement was a rabbit warren of rooms, each for a distinct purpose: the laundry room, the lumber room, the trunk room, the furnace room, and so on. Before she could think what to do and with Eleanor's pistol jabbing her in the back, Faith was standing outside a sturdy-looking door with the key in the lock.

"I told you I didn't enjoy the killing part, Faith, and have no wish to shoot you and dear Benjamin."

Faith couldn't believe her ears. Hope sprang anew.

"But you will have to die." Eleanor sounded unpleasantly definite.

She turned the key and pushed Faith into a pitchdark closet.

"Now dear, I have to go upstairs and clean up all the mess you made."

It looked like that was to be Faith's epitaph. Eleanor Whipple had locked them in her airless preserves cupboard and left them to die. She wasn't going to kill them. She would let time do it for her and since this was perhaps the last place anyone would think to look in the search that would undoubtably take place, time was on her side. Faith felt her palms sweat and a dizzy nausea overcome her as the terror of the situation became real. She was alive, but as good as buried. Buried! How would Eleanor get rid of their bodies? Then she remembered the well. There was nothing funny about it now.

Eleanor would never crack. No, she would be as genuinely concerned and grieved as she had been at Patricia's funeral. She would no doubt help, tramping through the woods, making pots of tea, and offering advice about where to look. It would never occur to anyone that this sweet little old lady was well on her way to mass murder.

Benjamin was awake and babbling. In spite of the absolute darkness Faith knew exactly what his face looked like. Would she ever see it in the light again? Hopelessness took over as she pictured their lifeless bodies falling down the well and she began to cry.

Somewhere around the fiftieth sob, she stopped suddenly. It didn't seem possible to be in any greater fear, but here it was.

There was a sound in the tiny room and it wasn't coming from her or Benjamin or the countless jars of rosehip jelly, pickles, tomatoes, and corn relish.

There was something or someone else there. The sound was breathing. Very heavy breathing. Faith put her foot out cautiously in the direction of the sound. Nothing. Then she remembered she had the diaper bag with her purse in it. Matches. Picked up last week, only last week? in New York, so she could remember the name of a restaurant, Bouley. She reached into the bag and pulled them out. She lit one and the warm glow filled the room, bringing a momentary sense of safety.

There were no mysteries lurking in the corners now, only rows and rows of tidy jars filled with the fruits of summer, and under one shelf, sprawled in what must be a drugged sleep, was Jenny Moore. The match flickered out and Faith stumbled over to the child.

She didn't know whether to be relieved that Jennifer was still alive or in despair at what lay ahead for them all. She sat down on the cold earthen floor and cradled Jenny's head in her lap.

There wasn't long to wait. Jenny woke up slowly and understandably it took a moment for her to grasp that Faith and Benjamin were in Cousin Eleanor's pantry with her. After a while she was able to tell Faith what had happened.

"I came home from school and the phone was ringing. It was Cousin Eleanor. She wanted me to come over to get a pie she had baked for us and some of her preserves. I didn't want to go, but Mom always told us to be especially nice to her, so I said I would be right there. She gave me a glass of lemonade. She always does and I hate it because she never puts in enough sugar, but this time it was really sweet."

To mask the drug, Faith thought. Eleanor had really been very clever. Nothing to make Jenny suspect any-thing, just a visit to Cousin Eleanor's like any other, except there wouldn't be any other.

"I was really tired and wanted to go home, but she insisted that I get the preserves, so we went into the basement and in here. She began to put a lot of jars in a basket and I don't remember anything after that."

Jenny began to cry. She was completely conscious now.

"What's going on, Mrs. Fairchild, why did she put me in here and what are you and Benjamin doing here?"

Faith put her arm around Jenny and pulled her closer. She felt as if the three of them were huddled on a raft.

"Jenny, everything is going to be all right and you mustn't be afraid, but Eleanor is the person who killed Cindy and your mother. She put me in here too, because I found out."

Jenny shrieked. "Cousin Eleanor killed Mom! Why? She must be crazy!"

Jenny was frantically struggling to get up and Faith held her tighter. "Eleanor is very, very crazy and she got the idea that if she murdered all the women in your family, she would inherit the money and the house."

Jenny pulled out of Faith's grasp, "You mean she wants to kill me, too? Oh, Mrs. Fairchild, we've got to get out of here!" She stumbled against Faith as she tried to find the door in the dark.

"Jenny, sit down. We can't panic"—at least not yet, Faith thought. " Eleanor has locked the door, so we have to concentrate on finding a way out or staying in and keeping her out until someone finds us."

A brave hope, but not totally impossible. Faith realized she had been momentarily diverted from her own terror. Having another person to take care of, especially one who could speak, was doing a lot to quell her fears. Someone had to be the grown-up—and there weren't too many candidates.

Faith lit another match. The closet was about nine feet square and lined with deep shelves from just above the floor to the ceiling. The door was between two narrower shelves and opened in. When Faith held the match to the keyhole, she could see the key was in it. But even if they succeeded in pushing it to the ground, there was no room for it to pass under the door. It was a tight seal, guaranteed to keep the jars cool and dry. The door itself was backed with tin. The match started to scorch her fingers and she blew it out. It was depressing to be back in the darkness again.

"I think the best thing is for us to sit to one side of the door, so we would be behind it if she opens it."

"Yeah, and then we can knock her out with one of these jars," Jenny responded enthusiastically.

Ah, for the optimism of youth, thought Faith. Because there was very little to be optimistic about. The tour of the room had shown her what she had feared from the moment Eleanor closed the door. There was no way for any air to get in and when what they were sharing now was exhausted, they'd be dead. She squeezed her eyes shut on her panic. This was no time to hyperventilate.

She insistently pushed any calculations about how long it would be before they used up the air in the room back to the word problems that had plagued her in Algebra I. "Two women and an infant are locked in a closet. A train traveling to Chicago passes the house. What time will it be in Milwaukee when there is no more oxygen left for them to breathe?" Instead she tried to remember Biology I.

"Jenny, just in case it takes some time for them to find us, I think we should try to use as little air as possible. So that means we shouldn't talk much or move around. But first let's see what we have here. You take Benjamin and I'll open the diaper bag."

It was a veritable bonanza. This will teach Tom to laugh at all the stuff I put in here, thought Faith. It was nice to be right, although she might not have the chance to tell him.

There was a rubberized pad for changing Benjamin, which they spread on the cold floor with one of his receiving blankets over it. In addition there were a bottle of juice, a bottle of formula, a banana, zwieback, a package of baby wipes, diaper pins, two disposable diapers, a complete change of clothes for Benjamin, an apple, some toys, a cloth diaper, a bib, two fairly large slices of pumpkin piñion bread with cream cheese, and miraculously a small penlite flashlight Benjamin's doctor had given her. It was from some drug company and Faith resolved to write a fervent note of thanks to the president when and if she ever saw the light of day. It was for checking Benjamin at night and Faith pressed it and turned it on him now. He was smiling happily in Jenny's arms. Faith rapidly concluded her inventory. She had tucked her small purse in the outside pocket of the bag, along with a novel she was reading. The novel could wait, but she checked her purse: comb, lipstick, blusher—at least her looks wouldn't have to go—about fifteen dollars and some change, not enough to bribe Eleanor when she was going for the big money, the matches, her Swiss Army knife, a clean handkerchief—mother would like that—and a small notepad and pencil, which someone had brought her from Florence and that she carried because it was so elegant, but rarely used. She could leave a note for Tom. A note he would never get. She felt a lump in her throat and quickly turned to Jenny. They were in the dark so as not to waste the penlite battery, but she still didn't want to transmit her deep fears. Fears as deep as a well.

"Jenny, do you have anything in your coat pockets?"

Fortunately they both had their coats, Eleanor wouldn't have wanted them hanging in her hall. Jenny evidently had never taken hers off and Faith had picked hers up when she'd first tried to leave. So they weren't cold—not yet anyway.

"I'm sorry, Mrs. Fairchild, I just ran out of the house quickly. All I have is my house key, some tissues, and half a Milky Way."

"Well, you might as well eat that if you want and when we get out of here, I'll give you some really good chocolate."

Obviously the Moores had not been teaching their children much about food. Today's Milky Ways were too sweet. Faith would get her some Côte d'Or chocolate to start. Starvation was not their problem in any case. Aside from their own provisions, there were all these jars. Faith hoped she would live long enough to be forced to open a few. She might even choke down some watermelon pickles.

"Jenny, you keep holding Benjamin—he's not messy, is he?"

"No. At least I don't think so."

"You'd know it. I'd just as soon wait as long as possible before changing him. I'll have to feed him soon, though. But maybe there's a window behind one of the rows of jars. It's dark now, so we wouldn't see the light. You sit still and I'll look."

Before she tackled the shelves, Faith examined the door. She took the awl on her knife and poked the key to the floor. No light was showing and she realized the amount of air that was admitted through the tiny hole was negligible, but it made her feel as if she was doing

230

something and slightly less claustrophobic. Then she dug away at the earth at the bottom of the door to see if she could let in more air, but she came up against cement almost immediately. It was as if Eleanor had had the closet especially constructed for their imprisonment.

She turned to the shelves. It was not an easy task. They were built onto the wall and didn't move. Faith concentrated on taking jars from the top of the shelves down to the middle. It wasn't likely that there would be a window on the bottom. After thirty minutes of fruitless effort, but more than enough fruit, she stopped to feed Benjamin and rest. She knew she was moving around too much, but she had to try.

"How can she possibly eat all this?" Faith wondered aloud.

"I don't think she does. She just likes to have it. And it's all really terrible. I hope we don't have to eat any. She doesn't put enough sugar in the jam and she puts too much salt in the tomatoes. Oh, I don't want to think about it! I'm beginning to get hungry."

Faith was hungry too, and Benjamin was eagerly sucking away. They could eat the apple, banana, and bread for now.

Jenny was calmer, Faith noted. She seemed to have no doubt that Mrs. Fairchild would find a way out and Mrs. Fairchild did not intend to disabuse her of this notion, a notion that was fast becoming an impossible one.

They ate and Jenny began to confide in Faith, "It's kind of a relief to know Eleanor did it. I mean it means it's not who I thought it was."

Faith was puzzled. Surely Jenny couldn't have suspected her father.

"I know this doesn't make any sense, but in the beginning I thought maybe Dad had killed Cindy by accident. There were a lot of things going on. I heard him arguing with her one night and she was threatening him. It was horrible. Mom was crying and Cindy was screaming. Dad didn't want to pay for the wedding and he wanted Cindy out of the house. Then after Cindy was killed, Mom seemed afraid of something. And Rob was acting weird, too."

Her voice became slightly muffled, "I put the rose in your mailbox, Mrs. Fairchild. I read about somebody doing it in a book once and I was afraid you'd find out that it was Dad who killed Cindy."

Faith felt irrationally relieved. So no one had been trying to kill her after all. At least not then.

"But you couldn't have thought your father had anything to do with your mother's death," Faith said gently.

Jenny started to cry—grief, fear, and exhaustion.

"Never. I thought that it must have been a maniac." She cried harder. "I don't know what I thought, but not Dad."

They finished eating. For a short while it had seemed cozy and warm, as if they were on some sort of Girl Scout camp-out. Jenny giggled when Benjamin gave one of his mighty burps and if they could have just turned the latch and walked out, the whole thing might have seemed a perverse sort of fun. One of those "My Most Unforgettable Experiences."

Faith began to systematically take the rest of the jars off the shelves. It appeared that the closet was built into the side of Belfry Hill. Still, she figured she might as well look.

There was nothing else to do.

Jenny was rocking Benjamin and crooning softly to him. Faith looked at her watch, thanking her stars that she had worn it today, although she wasn't sure why it was so important to note the passing of time. It was eight o'clock. She had arrived at Eleanor's doorstep about four o'clock. They had been locked in for over three hours, Jenny for four. It seemed like weeks.

"Jenny, do you want to take over for a while?" Faith struggled to keep her voice calm. The thought of all these jars suddenly overwhelmed her and she thought if she had to lift one more, she would start throwing them instead.

"Sure," replied Jenny.

Faith sat down and pulled Benjamin onto her lap. She was very tired and wished she could sleep, but there was always the possibility that Eleanor could catch them un-awares. She might have changed her mind about the "killing part." A few shots followed by a speedy descent in that well would tie up all the loose ends and the money would be hers. "Why, what a surprise! Do I get all this?" Faith was sure she already had stacks of travel brochures and charge account applications tucked away in some lavender-scented drawer.

As she thought this, she realized she was getting slightly hysterical. She patted the two quart jars of dill pickles they had placed close to hand and wished desperately for the chance to hurl them at Eleanor. It was becoming sickeningly clear that unless Eleanor *did* come in, they had no chance of getting out.

Jenny wasn't having any luck with her search either. "Mrs. Fairchild, what if there isn't a window? What are we going to do?" Her voice rose in alarm.

"There are a lot more shelves, Jenny. Let me take over again," Faith said wearily.

By nine-thirty, Faith gave up searching for a window.

There wasn't any.

The brief feeling of coziness vanished. In its place desperation and a particularly pungent diaper of Benjamin's, which she had changed an hour before, gave an acrid scent to the air. The earthen floor that had re-minded Faith of what was just outside and freedom now called forth only thoughts of entombment.

Benjamin suddenly and emphatically decided he was tired of this game and wanted to go home. Faith tried in vain to stop his cries. It seemed as though each wail used up half the remaining air. Finally he cried himself to sleep. She had some idea that there would be more oxygen at the top of the room and cleared a shelf for him to sleep on, barricaded by the jars, but now she didn't want to move him. In any case, what was the point? He might live a little longer than they would, but what good would it do him?

Jenny was nodding. Faith made her a pillow of the diaper bag and held the girl close until she felt her limbs relax in slumber. The sweet escape. Then she slipped Benjamin from under the receiving blanket and lowered him into the Snugli, strapping him onto her chest. They were both warmer that way and thank goodness he didn't wake up. She put the tiny blanket on Jenny. The minutes began to crawl.

She went back to the door and tried desperately to chip away at the concrete with her awl. It snapped off and she tried with one of the knife blades. Finally she leaned up against it and sobbed.

She could hear the two children's regular breathing and felt complete despair.

They were all going to die.

A few feet away, Scott Phelan stood in Eleanor Whipple's backyard looking up at the sky. It was a clear night and the stars shone brightly. He could see other beams, flashlights, darting through the trees of Belfry Hill behind him. They had all started together at the top and systematically were searching their way to the bottom. It was very quiet. The flickering lights were moving steadily. No one was stopping for a closer look. No one was calling for the others to come.

Nothing. No sign of them. Not a button off a coat or a bent branch to show some struggle.

He decided to go back to the church, where they had set up a command post, to check in and find out if there was any news. There had to be. Three people couldn't just disappear. He looked to the moon for a clue.

Where the hell could they be?

TEN

FAITH SAT UP WITH A START. SHE HAD FALLEN ASLEEP. Her heart was racing madly and a scream rose in her throat.

She knew where she was.

She covered her mouth with her hand and bit her palm. It hurt. So she must be alive.

The children were still asleep. She could hear them and dug into her pocket for the light to shine on their faces.

There wasn't much point in trying to save the battery anymore. Then she looked at her watch. It was six o'clock. Morning.

The tears began to stream down her face. Dawn was breaking. But not for them.

There was still some zwieback left and she took one, savoring each crumb. The darkness began to look a little less dark and the top of her head was feeling lighter. She knew that it must be the beginning of the effects of the lack of oxygen, but for the moment it felt good. Just float. Eat and float. Food. That was something she knew about. Something she had accomplished. She must be hungry. The zwieback had gone straight to her stomach and was saying, " Send more. Send better."

All those meals she had cooked. Even the failures weren't bad. Like Mrs. Haveabite's quiche. She knew her mind was wandering. There wasn't anything else to do except follow.

It was in the business's early days and Faith had been thrilled to get Mrs. H. as a customer. She was a wealthy parishioner of Faith's father and one of those ladies who lunched—and gave lunches. Soon Faith was catering all of them and the nickname arose out of the lady in question's irritating habit of hovering over a perfectly arranged platter, asking as she picked up the choicest morsel, "Oh, Faith, this looks delicious! May I just have a bite?"

The woman's other habit was worse. In those days Faith had charged by the job and not by the person. It was Mrs. Haveabite who changed her policy. A select luncheon for ten dear friends usually meant twelve and Faith would use up all the reserves she had brought. Then came the day when the ten turned into fourteen and no matter how she sliced it, the main course, *tarte à l'oignon,* was not going to stretch. Mrs. H. had thoughtfully told her about the additional guests when she arrived, so there was time to make another *tarte,* and that's what she did, using Mrs. Haveabite's own frugal supplies—margarine crust and yogurt instead of heavy cream. She made sure the hostess got a hefty slice of the emergency dish. She followed up the lunch with a polite note explaining the change in billing. She wasn't asked back until Mrs. H. realized she had lost the hottest caterer in town and by then Faith seldom had an opening.

There had been other times as well. Like going into the wilds of Connecticut with her staff and after unpacking the van discovering that three perfect *charlottes aux poires* reposed in the refrigerator in New York, leaving them with absolutely nothing for dessert. She had dashed out to the 7-Eleven for inspiration and come back with vanilla ice cream, baking chocolate, heavy cream—all the ingredients for old-fashioned hot fudge sundaes, complete with nuts and maraschino cherries (horrid, but authentic) in bowls for those who wanted them. And everybody wanted them. After that the sundaes became a specialty. A big success. Some evocation of childhood? Forbidden calories? She never could figure it out.

She was dreaming, though not asleep.

And all the triumphs. That dinner at the U.N. with not one or two, but six exquisitely authentic cuisines.

She began to smell mushrooms—big, juicy porcini mushrooms, gently simmering in butter. Succulent mushrooms. Sexy mushrooms.

Someone was screaming.

It was Jenny.

"No! No! No! I don't want to die! I don't want to die! I don't want to die! I don't . . ." Faith turned the dimming beam of the penlite on the whirlwind that was Jenny. Jenny sweeping jars from the shelves heedless of the wreckage. A stench of rotten vegetables and overripe fruit. She grabbed the girl's flailing arms.

It took all the strength she had left to pull Jenny down to the floor again, where she collapsed sobbing on Faith, and on Benjamin, who was awake and wailing himself.

"Oh, Jenny, darling, please, please try to stop. We have got to try not to give up. We can't! Come pray with me. Just say the words with me, 'Our Father who art in Heaven. . .'"

Jenny stopped and after a moment repeated the words with Faith. Repeated them over and over. The three of them clung to each other and after a while the storm had passed.

"Faith," said Jenny, "Do you think we have a chance?"

"I don't know," Faith said slowly, "but I think we have to believe there is one. We have to try to stay alive."

"All right." Faith heard her take a deep breath and let it out. "In that case I'm going to eat some of this stuff and figure out a way to pee into one of the jars. I'll put the lid on and maybe Cousin Eleanor will think it's honey." She started to laugh a little wildly.

"Jenny, hush now. It's a good idea. I think the applesauce is the best bet. You take the light and find us some. I'm going to nurse Benjamin and change his diaper and clothes." For the last time, she added mentally.

While Benjamin ate, heedless of his peril, and Jenny consumed what was probably the worst applesauce ever made in New England, Faith sat and thought of Tom or rather sat and said "Tom" over and over to herself. Tom, Tom, where are you?

Tom was at the altar rail. He had left the parish hall, which looked like a kind of campaign headquarters with people streaming in and out with information, food, comfort, and offers of help. The phone rang constantly. His parents were there. Faith's were on the way. He looked at the simple cross in front of him.

Dear God, don't forsake me now, he prayed over and over. But he was beginning to doubt he would ever see them alive. They had fallen asleep again, Faith realized. She listened a moment. Yes, they were all breathing.

Faith had been trying desperately to stay awake. She was terrified that she would slip obliviously into the night. She wanted that for the children, but not for herself. She had to know when it was the end. Still, she had fallen asleep. Like someone lost in a snowstorm. Drowsiness crept up on her like a warm quilt and she had finally pulled it over her head. Yet she had awakened. This time.

She reached for the light. Where was it? She couldn't remember. Her pocket. Yes, her pocket. Why did she want it? Yes, the time. What time was it?

It was noon. The Congregational church bells were ringing. She had heard them the day Cindy died. She couldn't hear them now. But she and the children were still alive. Was it a record? She'd never know.

At twelve-one the door opened.

Faith watched it and knew she was supposed to do something.

The jars.

She picked up the jar and got unsteadily to her feet.

Benjamin was still strapped to her chest and she pitched forward.

The door opened wider.

She straightened up and threw the jar at the opening with all her might. Pickle spices and rubbery undersized cucumbers flew in all directions as the missile fell short of the target, crashing on the floor instead. Light flooded in. Light silhouetting an enormous figure clad in a Burberry raincoat now spattered with vinegar. There was a smaller figure behind him, gabbling away.

Faith swayed and fell toward the door into John Dunne's arms. He dragged her into the open air and someone darted in for Jenny.

The fog began to clear. Benjamin began to cry. Faith took a deep breath.

Of course it was John Dunne. And he was crying or at least there were tears in his eyes. But who was that holding Jenny, exclaiming in what would have been a triumphant tone of voice if it had not also been so complacent, "You see? I told you they'd be in here?"

It was like a dose of ammonia salts. It was Millicent Revere McKinley.

Millicent Revere McKinley and John Dunne. Faith had never been so happy to see two people in her life.

She turned to Jenny and they clutched each other tightly. There weren't any words now that they could safely speak.

Then Detective Dunne was guiding them up the stairs like some kind of oversized sheep dog. They got to the top just in time to see Eleanor. She was putting on her coat and hat under the close watch of two state policemen. She looked right through Jenny, Faith, and Benjamin as if they had been some particularly distasteful panes of glass. She did give an involuntary glance at John Dunne. It was hard not to. But the full force of her venom was reserved for Millicent.

"Rose never did trust you, Millicent. And to think I stood up for you all those years!"

Millicent never turned a hair; she simply gazed back steadily, and said, "I think these gentlemen are waiting for you, Eleanor, and we'd all like to get by if you don't mind."

Faith began to giggle. They might have been trying to get out of a crowded theater aisle for all the emotion Millicent put into her voice. Here she was where hours before the woman slowly putting on what Faith knew was her Sunday best coat had held a gun to her back and everyone was behaving like Emily Post. Or age before beauty. Or evil before good.

Then before she thought about it, she blurted out the question that had been nagging at her all night, "Eleanor, was the gun loaded?"

Eleanor acknowledged her presence with a look one might have given an adult asking who was buried in Grant's Tomb. "Of course the gun was loaded," she snapped, "What on earth is the use of an unloaded gun?"

Faith's legs gave way under her and she heard John Dunne say, "Get that woman out of here. What are you all waiting for?"

After that Faith knew she was in a police car and that Jenny was being taken home in another. She also knew she was pulling into the parsonage driveway, but she didn't really believe she was home until Tom flung open the front door and crushed her in his arms. Oxygen and

241

Tom. That was all anyone needed. She wouldn't have believed a few hours ago that she would ever feel this way again. Alive. Just plain alive. Then Benjamin in the Snugli, whom Faith had begun to think of as a somewhat smaller Siamese twin, was detached and taken upstairs by Pix.

Tom and Faith hugged, kissed, and cried, then hugged, kissed, and cried some more. After a while Faith found her legs, and other parts of her body seemed to be under her control again, and she said plaintively, "Tom, darling, I'm so hungry!"

He beamed. Faith was back.

Before Tom could answer, Dunne's deep voice called out from the kitchen, "I don't know how to cook any of the stuff in here, so I sent one of the guys for pizza. I told them to put everything on it and you can pick off what you don't like."

"Tom," said Faith, "that man thinks of everything."

"And so," replied Tom steering Faith through the kitchen door, "does that woman. Thank God for us."

It hadn't really occurred to Faith to wonder what Millicent was doing with John Dunne at Eleanor Whipple's house. But it did occur to her to wonder why Millicent was sitting with Dunne so chummily at Faith's kitchen table. As was most of Faith's known world. Her parents. Tom's parents. Hope. Dave Svenson. Tricia. And last but not least, Scott Phelan.

After another round of hugging and kissing and crying and hugging and kissing and crying some more, Tom returned to the point, "It was Millicent who figured out where you were, Faith."

"Millicent!" Faith was stunned. It wasn't that long ago

that she had tapped Ms. McKinley as suspect number one.

Millicent smiled wickedly. "Yes, dear, and I suppose now you're going to tell me you thought I killed Cindy and Patricia."

Really the woman was as irritating as ever, but Faith began to think she might come to like her someday. In ten or twelve years maybe.

Faith sat down next to her and Tom hovered above with his hands anchoring her shoulders, just in case.

Pix walked in and reported that Benjamin was playing happily with Samantha.

"Now," she said, "why don't I get a bottle of champagne and you can tell all."

"The telling is a great idea," agreed Faith, looking hard at Millicent, "but champagne and pizza?"

"Why not?" asked Pix. "I thought champagne went with everything."

Faith looked at her affectionately. There was a lot of work to do in this town. Maybe she'd add cooking lessons to the business.

"There's beer in the fridge, let's start with that."

Charley MacIsaac brought the pizzas, practically a carload.

"I knew half the town would be here," he said.

Finally they were all settled around the pizza-laden table either adding the virgin olive oil, grated cheese, and other things Faith had directed Tom to set out for their slices, or just methodically consuming them *au naturel* like John Dunne.

"You should try the pizza in the Bronx sometime," he told everyone reminiscently, "Now that's real pizza."

Faith was happy to sit there safe, warm, and just about

fed, but there were too many missing pieces.

"All right. Who goes first? How the hell did Millicent figure out where we were? "She knew she was swearing; she figured she had the right.

Millicent looked over at Detective Dunne. They seemed to have developed their own special brand of communication. Faith wondered what the odds at Vegas might be on Millicent's joining the force. Like some sort of Yankee Miss Marple.

"You start, John. After all, you had figured it out, too, and it was only a question of time before you would have found the closet."

John, was it!? This was worse than Faith thought.

Dunne gulped the last of his pizza, reached for another beer, and leaned back in his chair.

"I have never felt so helpless about a case before. Suspects seemed to be literally jumping out of the bushes. "He shot a friendly glance at Sam, who had come in shortly after Charley. Sam managed to return a smile still fraught with guilt.

"That damn box was taking us up one blind alley after another," he continued, "We managed to identify some of the gentlemen, but they weren't leads worth pursuing, although it was probably one of them who broke into the Moore's. Pearson didn't have much of a motive either. Nothing made sense. And if Svenson had wanted to kill her, why didn't he wait until after they were married and do it in some less obvious way? I figured he would have inherited the money, too. Of course now I know about the will, but even so he would have come away with something. The condo, car, whatever they bought together.

"And there was another thing. Her murder was planned. Dave may have hated her enough to think about murder, but if he had actually done it, I was convinced it would have been on the spur of the moment. One of the times she was goading him. He'd just reach over and choke her to death to shut her up. Plus he didn't have any medical training and the way the knife as angled, just under the fourth rib, whoever did it knew precisely where to stick it. Now Dave is mostly interested in trees or tomatoes or something, I understand. Still, we had to take him in.

"That is until Sam here very conveniently entered the ring, entered, that is, with just about every member of the Massachusetts Bar." He swung around to look at him. "Say, Sam, is it true that they were starting a defense fund for you at Lock-Ober's?"

"No, it was at the Last Hurrah," Sam retorted.

Dunne nodded. "Much more appropriate." Everybody laughed.

"Anyway, Sam had too much to lose. Not that a murderer doesn't, but somehow I didn't see this guy giving up home, job, not to mention the Porsche for the satisfaction of doing away with an adolescent, but pretty professional, blackmailer."

Sam spoke up, "I had just about decided to tell Pix, then explain as best I could to the kids. Cindy did have me rattled, but I know what happens with blackmail. I've seen enough of it. The ante keeps going up and up. I like to think I would have been able to say no."

"Of course you would have!" exclaimed Pix. "And if I hadn't been so dimwitted, I would have figured out that something terrible was bothering you and we would have taken care of her, believe me."

Sam looked at her gratefully. Faith was glad that neither one of them knew that in fact almost every teenager in town had known of Sam and Cindy's affair. They might never get ice cream at Friendly's again.

Dunne's deep voice resumed, "So that left Robert Moore. He had been in medical school before he went to law school. Bet you didn't know that, Faith. And he didn't have much of an alibi. I began to sniff around for a motive. Everyone has money troubles, so why not him? He wasn't exactly going to starve, but he had put a lot of money in the house in New Hampshire and the boats, plus the kid's college expenses. Things were a bit tight just at a slack time at work.

"I had checked with the lawyers and they said the money went to Patricia, a lot of money. Unfortunately they didn't tell me about this fool thing with the female descendants of the Captain and Persis. I had to read the books to find that out."

Faith was annoyed. So that was who had taken the books out. She might have guessed. If he had left them where they should have been, she wouldn't have had to go to Eleanor's for them. But then she might have gone anyway to ask her more about the family and how she was related, so it would have ended up the same. Maybe.

"He had the knowledge, opportunity, and it all made a lot of sense, but I didn't have any evidence. So I figured I'd let things ride for a bit and see what he did. Sam and Dave weren't exactly in the clear, but no one was hurting."

"That's what you say," Sam said. Dave nodded in vehement agreement.

Faith interrupted, "What made you change your mind?

"Something completely unscientific. A gut reaction. I just couldn't see this guy killing his wife. And I had the advantage of having Charley here, who practically knows the number of cavities every person in this town has. He told me not to waste time on Dave and Sam, then after Patricia was murdered, to forget Robert."

Charley looked a bit abashed. "I'd never want Robert to know I suspected him, but of course we had to consider everybody. My God, Faith here even thought it might be you, Millicent."

"Thanks a lot, Charley," said Faith.

Millicent just smiled and stored it all away.

Charley spoke sadly, "I knew how Robert felt about Cindy. It had been going on for years. She was almost destroying his home and family. If a man isn't driven to kill for that, I don't know what for."

"She was about to leave, true," Dunne picked up the narrative, "but he might have wanted to cast some blame elsewhere—Dave maybe. And besides the wedding was going to set him back a lot. All that made sense. Then came his wife's death. I've seen people grieve, but few like this."

He paused and they all thought of Patricia.

"Then there was the rose in Faith's mailbox. I still had him pegged at the time, in fact he was under surveillance. But the rose business. It seemed more like something a woman would do. All right, all right," he said as a sea of accusing fingers was raised, "That's sexist, but I was right, wasn't I? It was Eleanor Whipple."

"Only partly right, John," Faith was glad to supply some new information. "It was a female, but it wasn't

Eleanor and I think it was told to me in confidence, so I can't tell."

"Okay, so it wasn't Eleanor." He grinned. "It's not really hard to guess, Faith. After all, who have you been with for the last nineteen or twenty hours? Jenny—protecting her old man, right?"

Faith flushed. "You're beginning to talk like cops on TV. I thought you went to Harvard."

"Better. Columbia." He reached across the table for her hand, "So don't tell. As long as the three of you are safe, I don't care what girlish secrets you may have shared."

Faith was touched. Tom had left his post behind her and sat down in the chair by her side. He grabbed her other hand. For a moment she felt like some sort of electrical connection and a pleasant feeling of warmth came over her. Dunne let go. Tom didn't.

"No." Millicent hadn't heard her own voice for a while and must have been lonely. "Robert loved Patricia very much. I was at their wedding—I was almost a child, of course."

"Of course," everyone murmured tactfully, smiling slightly into their sleeves.

"Perhaps you were the flower girl?" queried Faith, not so tactfully.

"Not as young as all that, dear," Millicent answered tolerantly, "I do remember thinking, however, that if they looked at each other for the rest of their marriage the way they did when they exchanged their vows it would be a very happy marriage indeed. And they always did. Cindy was a terrific burden, but she never caused problems between the two of them."

She gave a regal little nod to John and he acknowledged

it with one in return and continued.

"When two people in the same family are killed, the obvious thing to do is start digging around in the past— their common past. So that's what I did. And I gather," he looked at Faith quizzically, "the same idea occurred to you, despite all our warnings and all your assurances?"

Charley looked particularly downcast. "Really, Faith, I thought you had promised. I never would have forgiven myself if something had happened to you. I mean something much worse. We figured you wouldn't get involved, not after Patricia's murder."

"But Charley, it was exactly because of what happened to Patricia that I had to—and you felt the same way. Even if it hadn't been your job, you would have tried to find out who killed your friend."

Faith found she could be comfortably adamant now that she was alive.

"And don't blame Tom. He had no idea what I was doing. And really all I did was ask to borrow a book. You can't imagine how surprised I was when she suddenly turned a gun on me."

Tom tightened his already bone-crushing grip on her hand.

Pix gasped. "Faith, I'm going to get the brownies I made yesterday morning and that champagne I mentioned. I have to have something to fortify myself and probably you'll say they don't go with champagne, but you'll just have to bite the bullet—whoops, that's not exactly appropriate, I mean you'll just have to grin and bear it this once. Now don't say a word until I get back."

"Champagne and chocolate are fine, especially your brownies," Faith reassured her. The idea of one of Pix's

249

dense, dark brownies and a glass of champagne appealed to her, even on top of pizza and beer. She was tired, euphoric, and still hungry.

They all needed a stretch and got rid of the pizza boxes and empty beer bottles. Tom took out some ice cream and by the time Pix returned with her arms full, they had resumed positions and were ready for the next round.

It was Millicent's turn.

"Of course," she said daintily, sipping at her champagne as if she never touched the stuff and had not earlier put away an entire bottle of beer, just this once for the shock. "Of course, I had no idea anyone was missing. I didn't see you or Jenny go into Eleanor's house, Faith."

Faith was astonished. Was Millicent slipping?

"I was having my hair done at the Beauty Shoppe."

Faith was relieved. There had to have been some logical explanation. Since Millicent's hair was unvarying in both its shade, white as snow, and style, Mamie Eisenhower, the Beauty Shoppe would never have suggested itself.

A thought struck her. How long does it take for a marcel wave or two? "But Millicent, if you knew where we were, why didn't you get us out sooner?" Faith knew there was bound to be some retribution for ringing the belfry bell, yet this was going a little too far, even for Millicent.

"Yes, it was unfortunate," Millicent managed to make it sound like a nasty cold, "You see, I went straight from the hairdressers to a meeting of the Historical Society in Fitchburg." She turned and addressed the room at large, so no one would miss the importance of her next remarks, "I was the featured speaker. My talk was 'The French Connection: Apollos Rivoire and Paul Revere.'" She hastened to add lest anyone think her title frivolous or worse, "I like to have a catchy opening. It gets people's attention. The Reveres originated in France you know." Everybody nodded solemnly except Scott. Millicent reminded him of his third-grade teacher—as cracked as the Liberty Bell, and was she strict! He'd spent most of the year in the cloakroom or the corner.

Since no one had offered to book Millicent for the season, even though she had paused meaningfully, she was forced to go on, "I stayed overnight with my cousin and didn't get back home until close to noon. Of course as soon as I heard the news I called the police.

"I had begun to have very strong suspicions about Eleanor and while I was away I thought I would talk them over with someone. It struck me that Detective Dunne here was an intelligent and understanding man." Millicent managed to suggest that in this he was the only one in the greater Boston area.

Dunne blushed, or maybe it was the champagne.

"So when I called the police department, I asked for him. Unfortunately, he wasn't there, because he was so busy looking for you." She looked at Faith in mild reproach for all the delay and inconvenience she had caused.

"You see, I knew about the will, but when I first thought of Eleanor, I found it hard to believe. Consider, she is a member of your church and the DAR. Then as I began to think, it seemed she was the only possibility.

"I remember when Eleanor, Rose, and their mother moved to Aleford. They were so proud and you know," she turned to Tom and Reverend Sibley for support, "pride can be a sin. They were so proud they wouldn't make friends with anyone and they made poor Patricia's

251

mother terribly unhappy. On the one hand they expected her to give them everything, then on the other they wouldn't take it. I knew right away that they were terribly jealous of the Harveys. That was Patricia's maiden name. I think it had all started even before the doctor, Eleanor and Rose's father, died. They were brought up on their mother's stories of life in the Captain's house and when they went to visit, it must have been a great contrast. Doctor Whipple could never make much of his practice because he was a very lazy man. Just liked to take a bottle and a sandwich and fish in the Concord River. It drove his wife crazy. I think she actually *was* a bit disturbed anyhow. There always was a slightly hysterical strain in the Cox-Dudley line." Millicent took a breath and preened on her own impeccable nonpeccadilloed ancestry for a moment.

"Of course, after he died, he became a saint and it was 'the doctor this,' 'the doctor that.' But we all knew and felt sorry for them. Which of course they hated. There was really just no way things could work out as they wanted. Unless of course all the females between Eleanor and the inheritance died. When I realized this, I knew she was the killer."

"But," protested Faith, "she seemed to have so many friends here and she was always so kind."

"When their mother died, Rose and Eleanor did come out of their shells, particularly Rose, who was always the more social of the two. It was a shame she never married, but her mother didn't think anyone was good enough for her. Rose got Eleanor out and active in things. Of course they had always gone to church," she assured Tom.

"After Rose died, Eleanor seemed all right, but I began

252

to notice that she was very touchy about certain things, anything to do with Rose's memory, for example."

"She said Cindy had hurt Rose's feelings once. I think in her mind that justified the murder," Faith told them.

"Cindy called them 'dried-up old maids' supposedly out of their hearing, but in a loud enough voice to be sure they did hear. Eleanor didn't particularly care, I imagine, but it must have hurt Rose bitterly, since she had had her chances and was always very pretty."

Dunne had leaned forward. "So what you're saying, Millie, is that Eleanor began to lose touch with reality after Rose died. She put her up there with the rest of the family in her shrine."

Millicent beamed. "Exactly. And Eleanor must have believed that she had been cheated out of her birthright. This was what I wanted to tell you and I thought you might want to borrow my books on the family," she added generously to one so obviously in tune.

Faith poured herself some more champagne and reached for a brownie before she thought better of it. When lightning did not strike John Dunne dead on the spot for calling Millicent "Millie," she knew for certain there were mysteries in life beyond our ken. Still, she wanted to find out more about the one to hand.

"I still don't know how you found out where we were," she told him.

"Robert Moore called us at about seven o'clock. He had come home from work at six and discovered that Jenny wasn't there. He telephoned every friend of Jenny's he knew and had them all call around. It wasn't like her not to leave a note and he was worried. We started looking and then Tom called about a half an hour later. When we realized you were all missing with no word left for anyone, we knew it had to be connected. Especially after Tom told us you hadn't given up your campaign to embarrass the police by unveiling the murderer first." He gave Faith a sidelong glance. "Which actually you did."

"Are there awards for this?" Faith wondered.

"Faith, this isn't like merit badges, you know," said Tom. "We were all frantic. I came home and assumed you were at Pix's or someplace and had lost track of the time. The car was here, so I knew you hadn't gone far. It was getting darker, though, and I began to feel uneasy. I started calling people.

"I even called Eleanor and she was very concerned .

She hadn't seen you, but could she help in any way? I was completely taken in.

"Then I phoned Charley and we all fanned out to search."

Faith shuddered as she pictured them combing the areas, afraid of what they might or might not find.

Millicent picked up the thread. "The young man at the station told me that John and Charley might be at church, so I ran over there." Faith pictured Millicent trotting across the green as fast as her Enna Jettick's would allow.

"John was coming down the front stairs of the church and . . . "

Dunne interrupted, "She grabbed me by the arm and started pulling me toward the street. All she said was, 'They must be at Eleanor's and I pray they are still alive.' I called back to Dale Warren to get Charley and come back up over there, and we took off.

"I didn't want Millie to come in, but she just said I'd never find you and she was right. Or it would have taken a whole lot longer.

"Eleanor answered the door. If you can believe this, she had been out searching with the rest of us and had even brought some pies over to the church. She must have assumed we wanted more help and invited us in. We went into some kind of living room crammed with stuff and the place was as silent as the grave, pardon the expression. Before I had a chance to do anything, Millie here walks right up to her and says, 'All right, Eleanor, where are they? We know all about Cindy and Patricia, so you might as well tell us what you've done with Faith and Benjamin and Jenny.'

"Eleanor just folded her arms across her chest and said, 'If you're so smart, Millicent Revere McKinley, you can figure it out for yourself.'

"Millie looked at her and I was about to have the guys start searching the house, when she said, It's got to be the preserves closet. The attic has windows. Follow me.' And you know the rest."

Faith felt a little foolish. Millicent was Millicent, true, but she was also a hell of a smart woman and brave. Just like her ancestors, if she was to be believed—and Faith rather suspected she was.

After that it was Faith's turn and she was duly admired for her valiant efforts to escape.

"I wondered where that pie crust table was," mused Millicent. "You must have broken it, Faith. I'm sure Eleanor was quite upset."

"She's not going to need a tea service or table where she's going," said Pix grimly. She had moved her chair close to Faith's as Faith was recounting the hours in the closet and her efforts to locate a window. She looked as

255

though she would have liked to take Faith in her lap, like one of her children or dogs, and hold her tight. Both sets of parents had been alternately losing and gaining color since Dunne had started filling them in.

"But why didn't Robert say something about Eleanor? Surely Patricia must have told him she suspected her?" Faith suddenly remembered.

Charley answered, "Apparently Patricia never mentioned anything about Eleanor to him, Faith. And we don't know for sure that Patricia herself suspected her cousin. It could be that she wanted to tell us something completely different, maybe something about some man and Cindy. This is a part of the puzzle we'll never know."

"I don't want to contradict you, Charley," Millicent interrupted. Could Faith be hearing correctly? Contradiction was the spice of life to Millicent—or Millie, as she seemed to be now. "But I am pretty certain that Patricia did suspect Eleanor. If *I* tumbled onto it, I know she must have too and probably sooner, since she knew her better. I think she must have been absolutely horrified that a member of her own family could have committed a murder. So horrified that she couldn't talk about it to anybody. Patricia was certainly not an ancestor worshipper—rather an odious trait I've always thought—" Pause while the audience sat suspended in disbelief. "Yet she was proud of them and I'm sure she found it difficult to share her fears about Eleanor, even with Robert. To be sure, it is rather a terrible thing to suspect that someone you know may be a murderer," she concluded, shooting a rapierlike glance at Faith.

Faith saw the scene on the deck in New Hampshire and heard Patricia's voice. She knew Millicent was right.

Patricia was trying to protect Eleanor. She must never have suspected the full extent of her madness. It was also possible she wasn't sure and hoped the police would prove her wrong. Faith's mind whirled.

"So it was just a coincidence that Eleanor killed her on a Friday and after Patricia left the message for you?"

"Unless Eleanor herself opens up, which is unlikely if her behavior at the house is anything to go by, that's another thing we'll never know," Charley said in a resigned tone.

Faith wasn't resigned at all. "I thought when you solved one of these things, all became clear! What about the denouement in the drawing room?"

She was still protesting an hour later, but it wasn't about crime.

"Oh, Tom, I feel so cozy, I don't want to budge, but I don't think I can stay awake any longer."

They were back on the couch, where they had immediately headed after everyone had gone and the phone had stopped ringing with calls from friends and just about every newspaper in New England. Faith agreed to a press conference together with Charley, Dunne, and Millicent the next morning and begged them to leave her alone for the rest of the night, although she realized the publicity for *Have Faith* would be worth its weight in gold.

Her parents had gone to stay with Tom's and would be back in the morning. They had seemed uneasy about letting her out of their sight even overnight. Aunt Chat was in Spain as planned and they sent a cable in case some of the news services picked it up for the *International Herald Tribune*. (They didn't, though, and a much puzzled Chat called the following day to wonder why she had received a message, "Faith fine. Don't worry.")

Faith was almost asleep and the stairs to the bedroom seemed as impossible to climb as the ones in Eleanor's basement. They had resisted the impulse to wake Benjamin to be sure he was all right and not traumatized in any way. They had talked. And now they were just holding on to each other. For dear life.

"Faith," murmured Tom when they were in bed, "I don't want you ever to do anything like this again. I can't take it. Promise?"

Faith's thoughts drifted over the events of the last few weeks. She hadn't been all that bad as a sleuth, but Tom was undoubtedly right. Besides, it was exceedingly unlikely that anything like this would happen in Aleford a second time.

"I promise, darling," she said. With her fingers crossed. Just in case.

Dear Reader:

I hope you enjoyed reading this Large Print mystery. If you are interested in reading other Beeler Large Print Mystery titles or any other Beeler Large Print titles, ask your librarian or write to me at

Thomas T. Beeler, *Publisher*
Post Office Box 659
Hampton Falls, New Hampshire 03844

You can also call me at 1-800-818-7574 and I will send you my latest catalogue.

Audrey Lesko chooses the titles I publish in Large Print. Our aim is to provide good books by outstanding authors—books we both enjoyed reading and liked well enough to want to share. We warmly welcome any suggestions for new titles and authors.

Sincerely,